Paul Scott was born in London in 1920 and educated at Winchmore Hill Collegiate School. He served in the army from 1940 to 1946, mainly in India and Malaya. After demobilization he worked for a publishing company for four years before joining a firm of literary agents. In 1960 he resigned his directorship with the agency in order to concentrate on his own writing. He reviewed books for *The Times*, the *Guardian*, the *Daily Telegraph* and *Country Life* and devoted himself to the writing of thirteen distinguished novels including his famous *The Raj Quartet*.

In 1963 Paul Scott was elected a Fellow of the Royal Society of Literature and in 1972 he was the winner of the *Yorkshire Post* Fiction Award for *The Towers of Silence*, the third novel in *The Raj Quartet*. In 1977, *Staying On* won the Booker Prize. He went to the University of Tulsa, Oklahoma, as a visiting Lecturer in 1976.

Several of his novels were adapted for radio and television, in particular *Staying On* and *The Raj Quartet*, which was turned into a highly-acclaimed television series under the title *The Jewel in the Crown*.

Paul Scott died in 1978.

By the same author

The Mark of the Warrior
The Alien Sky
A Male Child
The Chinese Love Pavilion
The Birds of Paradise
The Bender
The Corrida at San Feliu
Staying On

The Raj Quartet

The Jewel in the Crown
The Day of the Scorpion
The Towers of Silence
A Division of the Spoils

PAUL SCOTT

Johnnie Sahib

PANTHER
Granada Publishing

Panther Books
Granada Publishing Ltd
8 Grafton Street, London W1X 3LA

Published by Panther Books 1979
Reprinted 1979, 1985

First published in Great Britain by
Eyre & Spottiswoode Ltd 1952
Republished by William Heinemann Ltd 1968

ISBN 0-586-04865-0

Printed and bound in Great Britain by
Collins, Glasgow

Set in Monotype Times

For
My Wife Penny
with love

Contents

Author's Note

The characters in this novel are all imaginary.
I am indebted, and thank, Lieut. Col.
T. R. Newman for technical advice.

P.S.

PART ONE

Comitarla

1

Lieutenant-Colonel Baxter, assisted by a sweat-stained, bush-hatted airman to alight from the mail plane which had flown in from Calcutta, was under the impression that he had walked into a Turkish bath. The heat shimmering up from the tarmac seemed to envelop him in a hot, moist blanket. The smart cotton bush-shirt and drill trousers which he wore and which had looked and felt so well earlier that morning as he left the Grand Hotel and proceeded to Dum Dum airfield, were now creased and damp, and as he shielded his eyes from the glare of the midday sun that beat down upon the airfield at Comitarla he told himself that he had been a fool to come.

He alone of the passengers had not been met; the others were already greeting friends and walking towards the jeeps and lorries drawn up at the side of the apron. The Colonel felt out of place and bad tempered. Banks of sun-yellowed cloud were coming up from the south-west, and as he walked alone towards the control tower he had to avoid the wide puddles which dotted the tarmac and reflected the broad blue of the sky. 'Thank God I go back to Calcutta this afternoon,' he muttered to himself. An enormous puddle confronted him. There seemed no way round it. Turning, somewhat at a loss, he saw an army officer dressed in jungle green running towards him. The sight of the approaching figure filled Baxter with relief and annoyance; relief at finding himself being met after all; annoyance that the man was late. The officer halted a few feet away and saluted.

'Colonel Baxter, sir?'

'Yes. You from this air supply company I've come down to see?'

'Yes, sir. My name's Scott.'

Baxter stifled his annoyance, knowing it to be childish, knowing it would soon evaporate. Scott was explaining something, but the Colonel hardly listened, contented to give himself up to the care of this shabby, tall, thin officer and be led by him across the burning airfield towards a snub-nosed fifteen-hundredweight truck drawn up in the shade of some trees behind a sheltered bay.

' . . . and of course,' Scott was saying, 'we only had your message

7

about half an hour ago.'

'I'm sorry, Scott. I seem to be putting you to a lot of trouble. This your truck?'

A trio of fighter planes swooped suddenly overhead, flashing their quick shadows across the road, and Scott's reply went unheard. The cloud banks in the south-west were building up across the sky, underhung with layers of dense black. A Dakota transport was coming up the runway, its fuselage lifting. The Colonel turned his back and got into the truck through the door which Scott held open. He hated aeroplanes. He was afraid of seeing one rise and hover uncertainly, then crash and grind into the rough fields and stunted trees which seemed always to surround aerodromes. The interior of the truck, on the other hand, was familiar to him. He had driven in scores of the self-same pattern. The cabin was confined and cramped, but he felt able to expand for the first time that morning, a morning which had been full of uncertainty, strangeness and maladjustment.

'You chaps are only half in the army, aren't you? The other half's in the air force.'

'We have to liaise pretty closely, sir.'

'When I first heard there were units in the R.I.A.S.C. called air supply companies I thought they were something to do with the old mineral water sections, Scott.'

Scott laughed.

'There aren't a lot of companies. Just a few.'

'The less companies the more work, eh?'

'We've been quite busy, sir.'

'I know. That's why I came down.' He paused. A bit of flattery might not, in the circumstances, come amiss. He said, 'You air supply chaps've put yourselves on the map recently.'

'Have we, sir?'

'Of course the Japs were mad to invade Assam. It nearly came off, mind you, but they were mad.' He looked at Scott. 'They forgot that lines of communication can't be stretched too far.' Scott nodded but made no reply. Baxter watched the road. The scenery was strange to him. He hated to feel out of place, to feel, too, that practice had disproved the theories of a lifetime and of a career. An army advanced as far as it could be supplied through ground communication. Or did it? There had been that chap Wingate.

'Did you supply Wingate?'

'Some of the time, sir.'

Wingate; the Arakan; and now the siege of Kohima and Imphal; armies moving from place to place by air transport;

8

armies penetrating deeply into jungle; and armies being fed and supplied by aircraft based as far back as places like Comitarla in Bengal. He turned again to Scott. 'What's on now?'

'Things have slacked off a bit, sir. We're not quite sure what comes next.'

'Drive the Japs back into Burma and then out of Burma.'

'Yes, sir.'

Baxter paused, then added, 'And I suppose you think however far we advance you'll be flying your stuff in by air.'

'I hope we shall.'

'Um.'

He saw that they were approaching the outskirts of the town, and as they turned off the road which circled the airfield into the main road of Comitarla the sun was obscured and ahead of them lay the grey houses and beaten-down gardens that had once belonged to rich merchants, departed now for the comforts of a more peaceful India.

Situated as it was on the Bengal Assam railway, Comitarla had become, like Comilla further to the south, a mildly prosperous trading centre in peace-time. Of that Baxter knew nothing, but he guessed that war had also brought its reward to local contractors, for everywhere amid the green fecundity of grass and glistening leaves, jostling against the stone houses and temples, and lined along the banks of the water tanks were the locally constructed bamboo huts known as *bashas*, and in these as well as in the requisitioned houses were signs that the army had taken over and established itself with an air of ownership, erecting signboards, festooning telephone cables through the trees which lined the metalled road. The soldiers he saw walking in the town were predominantly Indian, but here and there were British and African and occasionally, as a reminder that war is transitory, a dhoti-clad, cycle-riding civilian.

Baxter breathed out. The place had suddenly become real for him. It bore the hall marks of an active service area and relighted almost forgotten memories of other places, other times.

'So this is where you work?'

'Yes, sir. We've got used to it by now. Been here over a year.'

'Have you, begad?'

'There's a club *and* a cinema.'

'Luxury!'

'Luxury is always comparative.'

'I suppose it is.' He chuckled. He was glad of his roving commission in Delhi. No doubt about it, coming at short notice to places like Comitarla gave an edge to life, a spice, a tang. He tried to picture for himself the place as it must have been during the last few months ever since, in April, the Japs had crossed the border between Burma and India and threatened Kohima, held Imphal to siege. This town he knew had played its part in what had become known as the Imphal Flap. There must have been nights before the rains came when the roads here had been choked with lorries moving blindly in their own dust; moving backwards and forwards to the airfield. Even now, in June, with the wet monsoon covering the sky with grey blankets of cloud, the town still shook to the vibration of aircraft. The focal point of the war had become the airfields of Bengal, and Baxter felt himself moved suddenly to excitement; for what sort of a soldier would one be, he asked himself, if one did not embrace new techniques enthusiastically? 1944 was the year of confidence; 1942 the year of dismay. Connecting the years there must have been the enthusiasm of men of vision to whom the skylanes were now clearly marked as those on maps. One had heard of these men and perhaps had smiled slightly; new techniques could be dangerous in many ways. Baxter cleared his throat. He would soon see.

Scott moved off the metalled road and into a rough dust track which, with the rains, had become a long ribbon of red mud and deep puddles. On either side there were bamboo shelters and road-side stalls displaying bottles of violently coloured soft drinks. Nondescript buildings lay well back from the pathway, and here and there were clusters of military bashas. Gradually the track widened. Scott pointed to a signpost twenty yards ahead.

'That's our company headquarters, sir. We'll drop in and see if the C.O. is back from his conference. If not, perhaps you'd like to go on to the mess. It's nearly lunch time.'

Baxter nodded but said nothing. 'This place smells of the army,' he told himself. 'The army's my life, and this is where I ought to be.'

When the Major returned from the conference his good humour was immediately dispelled by the message his chief clerk gave him.

'Sir, there is message from Captain Scott.'

'What's he want, Prabhu?'

'He tells me I must say he has gone to airfield to meet Colonel Baxter, sir.'

'Meet who?'

'Colonel Baxter. This is the name of the officer coming from Delhi.'

The Major stared uncomprehendingly at Prabhu, who smiled sadly and shook his head from side to side as if to say, 'All this is without meaning.'

'Who the hell is Colonel Baxter?'

'This I am not knowing, sir.'

'Then what is Colonel Baxter coming for?'

'This I am not knowing either, sir.'

'This you are not knowing either!'

'No, sir. We just had message to meet him at airfield.'

Prabhu wilted under the Major's steady gaze. 'Sir, is possible for inspection of air supply company. In Delhi they have not seen. Now flap is over they come to see.'

'Is probably right, Prabhu. Not,' the Major added, 'that there is anything for him to see now. Three weeks ago, even last week, yes. But not now.' The Major sighed.

'Did Captain Scott warn the sections?'

'Yes, sir.'

'What are they going to do?'

'Squads will be packing parachutes. Other squads will be packing compo rations for dropping. Etcetera.'

'Probably mostly etcetera.'

Prabhu grinned.

'All right, Prabhu. I'll cope now.'

Alone, the Major sat at the trestle table in the bare room. Square, thickset and middle-aged, he suffered the tortures of prickly heat and longed to take off his jacket and sit sweating and half-naked, dozing comfortably to the sound of the clerks' typewriters in the next room; to doze for a while and then stroll quietly up the lane round to Johnnie's section lines where they had their mess in the two-storey house. The Major blinked. This man from Delhi would have to go to the mess too, would be for the space of an hour right on top of Johnnie Brown's section. He called out to Prabhu.

'Has Captain Brown been warned about the inspection?'

Prabhu appeared in the doorway. 'He is not at his section, sir, but Jemadar Moti Ram Sahib knows and is doing parachute packing.'

The Major nodded, and Prabhu went back to his typewriter. Taking a bent, damp cigarette from his pocket the Major lighted up and inhaled deeply. It was typical, he thought, that Johnnie should not be there. No doubt he was at the hospital or the club, with Nina or with Brad. Was Johnnie becoming a problem? For a moment he shut his mind to the thoughts forming there. Perhaps there was no problem. Perhaps if there were it would turn out to be of little consequence, easily dismissed, as would this annoying visit from the unknown Colonel. He sighed. He resented Baxter even before he had met him. He felt that every man in the company deserved the rest they were having after weeks of working night and day. It was the first break they had had since they came to Comitarla a year ago, and so he had taken the opportunity of sending men off on leave. In the lull one could take stock.

The men were all right. They had been magnificent. The officers, too: Bill Parrish, bluff and hearty and, no doubt, enjoying the amenities of Darjeeling where he had gone for his leave while his second-in-command, little Johns the Anglo-Indian, looked after his section; Scottie, a bit humdrum, 'service-corps minded' perhaps, but pleasant and kind enough as he had proved when at the depot in India he had accepted as second-in-command the Indian officer, Ghosh, whom nobody else had wanted. Ghosh was on leave too, in Bangalore with his wife and uncountable children.

One and Two Sections could always be relied upon, just as, the Major admitted, could Three Section; but in a different way, for Three Section was not so much a part of the company as an independent unit. Three Section belonged to Johnnie Brown, and if the other sections worked well, Three Section had worked with what the Major could only call style, for that was part of Johnnie's influence upon it. They were different, and with operations temporarily suspended the difference could be seen anew by looking at the section lines. They would make a man who was a stickler for cleanliness and order wince. The Major smiled. Was it important? In all other ways, in ways which in the long run mattered most, Johnnie could not be criticised. It had been Johnnie who first improvised new methods for dropping stores. Johnnie who laid the foundations for friendly cooperation with the air force by his habit of bringing back to the mess men of the aircrews with whom the company worked. One of them, Brad, was always around. It was Johnnie, too, who looked after what little they had of social life, who organised parties with the nurses from the General Hospital. He knew that Johnnie could not be shaped into a pattern for the sake of pattern; and they had all worked together for a year. It wasn't possible that things could change. He stubbed out his cigarette in the lid of a tobacco tin. The sections were linked together by experience. It was his job to see that the links held.

Even as he told himself that one should not criticise Johnnie too strongly for the state of his lines because he had for several weeks been single handed, with no second-in-command, he recognised that there was always an excuse for him. He picked up the field-telephone and rang through to Three Section, reaching on his desk at the same time for the signal that had arrived seven days ago from the Training Depot in Marapore:

Lieut. Taylor J., despatched by air ex Marapore via Delhi Calcutta Comitarla. Will report for duty Three Air supply section.

If Taylor were anything like Johnnie's previous man, Bates, he wouldn't last long. Johnnie would never stand for him. Taylor was late, and until he arrived, Johnnie, who needed leave badly, would have to stay put. A voice at the other end answered.

'Moti Ram Sahib?'

'Yes, sir?'

'You're prepared for this inspection, I suppose?'

'We are ready, sir.'

'And the lines?'

'All is ready, sir.'

'Where is Captain Brown?' There was a pause and the Major could not help grinning when Moti Ram replied, 'He is gone to Field Supply Depot, I am thinking, sir.'

'Right, Sahib.' He put down the receiver. Three Section were loyal to a man. At Marapore, where the sections were formed, he had watched a parade of volunteers lined up, with Johnnie moving slowly along the ranks. Every now and then he stopped and placed a hand on a particular man's shoulder. From where the Major stood he had been aware of the undercurrent of tension and the recognition by the sepoys that here was a man they would love if given the chance to serve him. There had been something a little theatrical in it; more, far more than Scottie and Bill had put into their own selection parades. But if the other two had resented it they had not shown it.

He heard the sound of Scottie's truck.

'This, I suppose, is Baxter.' He rose, adjusted his tunic and went out to meet him.

There was no exact British equivalent of the Indian Army rank of Viceroy's Commissioned Officer. The men who held such commissions guarded their traditions and privileges jealously. Johnnie's V.C.O. Jemadar Moti Ram Sahib, was no exception.

When the Major had rung off, Moti Ram left the clerk's office, where Nimuji should have been sitting, and stood in the porch of the house from which five stone steps led down into the muddy courtyard.

'Ai! Nimuji!'

The courtyard was large, and among the stunted banana trees three big bashas had been erected to hold stores. The section area had been extended into the field beyond where there was a small water-tank, and there more bashas could be seen, and beyond those, at the end of the rough, rutted driveway the section transport of ten three-ton lorries was harboured beneath tall trees.

Nimu appeared from one of the bashas and began walking towards the house.

'A babu, not a soldier,' thought Moti Ram. Then he shouted again and Nimu broke into a slow jog-trot, hop skipping to avoid the puddles of red water. From behind him, in the basha he had left and in which an 'exhibition' squad was packing parachutes, Havildar Dass shouted, 'Double, Nimuji!'

Nimu grinned, good-naturedly, and as he drew near he raised his thin voice. 'You called to me, Sahib?' he asked in English.

'Why aren't you on duty in the office? Major Sahib has been ringing.'

'I had to make water, Sahib.'

'In the parachute packing store?'

Nimu laughed.

'Be at your desk. The Burra Sahib from Delhi is coming.'

'This I am knowing. But a man must make water once in a while.' Nimu climbed the steps and brushed past Moti Ram, then went into his office and lighted a cigarette.

Moti Ram shrugged his shoulders and went out into the courtyard. The feud between himself and Nimu had lasted for a year, but it was not serious; it was a testing of the wits, a battle in the use of the English idiom; most enjoyed when Johnnie Sahib was there to hear. As he walked round the lines he smiled at the thought of Johnnie Sahib and where he had gone. Early that morning he had discovered the orderly, Jan Mohammed, squatting disconsolately in the office, talking to Nimu.

'What is this, Jan Mohammed? A cookhouse, that you squat?'

The little man, whose hair was tinged with grey above the temples, had risen sheepishly, for there had been a time when the Jemadar had beaten him with his fists.

'He is worried for Captain Sahib,' Nimu explained.

'Why so?'

14

'Tell Jemadar Sahib.'

Jan Mohammed said, 'The Memsahib is going today.'

'He means the Anglo-Indian nurse, Jemadar Sahib.'

'Who told you this, Jan Mohammed?'

'Captain Sahib himself.'

Nimu said, 'In war-time, all is saying goodbye.'

The news had spread quickly, and men were watching from the windows and doorways of the bashas when, at eleven o'clock, Johnnie Sahib had driven off to the hospital with Mohammed Din. The gentle routine of the day had been upset, and before midday had come the order to pack parachutes for the benefit of the Burra Sahib from Delhi.

Havildar Dass stood to attention as Moti Ram went in through the doorway of the basha where eight men were squatting in a row, shaking out the rigging lines of the white canopies.

'Colonel Sahib is coming, Dass.'

'See, we are doing.'

Moti Ram nodded. Then he turned and walked off in the direction of the transport harbour. Dass stood in the doorway. The sky was overcast. Soon it would rain, and when the Burra Sahib had gone the men could go to their bashas and stretch out on their charpoys.

'Captain Sahib is not back, Havildarji?'

'No.'

Captain Sahib was still at the hospital. Dass watched as the men began folding the panels of the parachutes. For a year they had worked hard. Recently there had been no sleep for sometimes two or three days at a stretch. But now the big battle was over. Johnnie Sahib had said so. The relief of Imphal in far-off Manipur was imminent (that had been Nimu's expression, and Dass only half-understood its meaning); now the air supply company at Comitarla could rest, and go on leave, and do all the things which were good and comfortable just as – Dass smiled to himself – Johnnie Sahib was probably doing this very morning. But then, he always gave the lead.

Johnnie was a man who looked at you out of strange, clear blue eyes in such a way that you could never tell the lie you had rehearsed. A quick substitute had to be found, but he saw through it immediately. You had first known that frank and overpowering stare months and months ago at the Depot during the parade of volunteers for Three Section which was destined to go with the company eastwards into Bengal.

He had come along the ranks, and as he approached you were

afraid he would pass you by, and that, in a way, would be a matter for shame. Then he had stood in front of you and you could feel how he measured you as a man and made his five foot eight seem inches taller than your own five foot nine. His hand, with its short, thick fingers, had reached out and grasped you firmly by the shoulder.

'Nam?'

'Dass, Sahib.'

'Mera Section. Thik hai?'

'Thik hai, Sahib.'

Then he had gone to the next man, and past him, and past several more until you had heard, further away, the clipped English voice say, with what you had later heard called a 'cockerney' accent, 'Nam?'

Afterwards you, with the others chosen by Johnnie Sahib, had paraded in front of the Depot Office, and he had told you about what you would be doing in Bengal.

To fly, high over the green ridges of Burma in the large steel birds and heave at the pile of bales, and watch them tumble out into the great empty space until they drifted suddenly beneath the white flowering of the parachutes; clusters, poised above the jungle; that was the life he promised you, the life he rehearsed with you, beside you, stripped to the waist, sweating and dirty in the training plane that made you feel sick and dizzy.

And if the life he had promised had turned our differently, if, instead of flying, you worked more like a coolie, at least the spirit of the promise was still alive, because Johnnie made it stay alive with his look of caring about you, with the comradeship that was never too familiar, but familiar in the right way, at the right time, so that your own integrity and stature remained. It was Johnnie's talking and leading, his standing up for you against the least threat of outside interference that made the back-breaking routine sparkle somehow, that made Bengal bearable, that made you unhappy this morning because you knew someone Johnnie liked was going away.

Dass turned as the sound of a truck drawing up at the house broke his day-dream. The Major was climbing out, and at the other side the tall figure of the Burra Sahib eased itself from the cabin. Dass shaded his eyes, and after a while he spoke to the men behind him.

'The Burra Sahib is only a Lieutenant-Colonel, after all.'

The packing squad paused.

Then they relaxed.

The Major had hoped that by bringing the Colonel direct to the mess and consequently the Three Section area first, he would not notice the look of neglect the lines bore. But Baxter did notice, and when he pointed it out, politely, the Major found himself sticking up for Johnnie with far greater heat than the occasion demanded.

'Brown may be a bit unconventional, but he's a damned good section commander. The best I've got.'

'Quite, quite. But these lines are rather shocking, aren't they?'

'They've been working night and day, sir. And Brown's had no second-in-command.'

'My point is, Major, that units engaged in new techniques are apt to forget things like everyday administration. It's just the fact that interests me. That's all. God knows it's nothing to do with me except in a general sort of way, as a senior officer in the corps. What I'm afraid of is that although you chaps are in the corps, the unconventional work you're doing might convince you you're quite separate from it.'

The Major pursed his lips and Baxter dropped the subject. They went upstairs into the mess. Scottie had rounded up Johns, the Anglo-Indian, and they came over to join Baxter and the Major at lunch.

Baxter, surprised at the small number of officers at the table, turned to the Major. 'You're getting leave in?'

'It's our best chance, sir. Scott here has Two Section. His two i.c. is on leave. So is Parrish, who commands One Section. Johns here works for him.'

'And Brown?'

'Brown's out on a job for me, sir.'

The Major cursed under his breath because he was lying for Johnnie, and lunch proceeded in a series of long silences which Baxter, angry with himself for having got on the wrong side of the Major, did his best to fill in. They listened respectfully, but, he considered, without enthusiasm.

After lunch they all climbed into the Major's truck and visited the other two sections. Baxter, noticing the comparative order and cleanliness of the other areas, said nothing further about Brown. But the words he would have spoken were there to be felt just the same.

On edge and feeling an increasing bitterness towards the absent Johnnie, the Major swept the Colonel through basha after basha, from demonstration squad to demonstration squad, across ditches, through puddles, talking almost without pause; careful,

17

too, to use as many technical terms as he could.

At three o'clock the Colonel called a halt.

'My plane goes back at four, Major. I'd better think about getting back to the aerodrome.'

'Will you have tea first?'

Baxter paused.

'I should like that.'

Back at Three Section he purposely avoided glancing around the courtyard. He followed the Major up to the mess and, there, he took out his cigarettes.

'Smoke?'

'Thank you, sir.'

'I'm afraid my matches are too damp to light.'

'I'll go and get some.' The Major went out, and the Colonel, alone, looked round at the room they called a 'mess'. A large table took up most of the space, and chairs, roughly knocked together, were placed in position around it. Two small windows, one at each side of the wooden doors opening on to the small verandah, were unglazed, barred and shuttered. Baxter stepped out on to the verandah and saw that it was beginning to rain. He shuddered, imagining the abominable plane trip he had to make, bad for him at any time, infinitely worse in this sort of weather. For an instant he hoped the plane would be grounded and that he would have to spend the night here, in the sort of atmosphere he had very nearly forgotten existed. He went back into the room. Against a wall there was a long trestle table, piled high with an assortment of magazines, gramophone records and papers. A pressure lamp, which he guessed did not work, stood on a pile of books. The Major came back with a new box of matches and they lit up. They chatted for a while about the war, and then the mess waiter, Kaisa Ram, came in with tea.

While they drank in silence, Baxter studied his host. He liked him. He recognised the latent qualities of a good leader that the Major's job was bringing out in him. He liked the unit the Major commanded, and the job the unit was doing. But if air supply were to be accepted as a major, important technique, it would need organising. When he got back to Delhi, Baxter decided, he would put out a few feelers to find out what was in the wind.

He sipped his tea. The rain was beginning to drum on the banana leaves and on the thatched roofs of the bashas; on the flat roof above them.

Whatever was in store in the way of reorganisation, he knew that men like the Major here, men who had worked the thing in its early, tentative stages, would resent what they would feel to be interference from above, a cashing in on their spade-work. Baxter, thinking of his own youth, sighed. There had been disappointments. Many of his contemporaries had gone far ahead of him in the race for promotion. Thoughts such as these hurt him.

'Well, Major. I'd better be getting along.'

'I'll drive you to the strip.'

'Thanks.'

They put down their cups, rose and went downstairs. The tall Hindu clerk was standing in the porch. The Major said, 'I'll bring the truck closer to the steps. You'll get drenched.'

'Don't bother.' Baxter ran out and opened the door of the truck and climbed in. With a smile of good fellowship he looked round at the Major, who was still standing with Nimu in the porch. For an instant their eyes met and the expression on the Major's face brought Baxter up sharply.

'I've been a fool,' he told himself. 'The chap has problems I know nothing of.' He faced to the front. The windscreen was streaming, obliterating from his view the sad mess of the section lines.

The Major turned to Nimu.

'When Captain Brown gets back, Nimu, tell him I want to see him.'

'Yes, sir. I will tell him.'

The Major ran out.

2

It was because Nina was going away early that afternoon that Johnnie had gone out in the morning to collect her at the hospital.

With Nina crouched in the back of the truck away from the view of inquisitive military police, he drove out of the hospital lines, leaving the grinning driver to wait outside the reception basha; and then, with Comitarla behind them, he continued out into the countryside until he found the spot he was looking for: a place where the truck could be turned off into a screen of trees on the edge of a patch of scrub jungle. Johnnie got out and climbed into the back, where he spread a greatcoat and blankets on the floor of the truck for her to lie on. Then they made love, swiftly, in a businesslike way.

Afterwards, as they stubbed their cigarettes and made ready to go, the sight of her adjusting her uniform over her dark breasts and smoothing her slacks round her trim waist fired Johnnie to a renewed desire of her, so that he caught her round the shoulders and pressed her downwards again.

She laughed and said, over and over, 'Johnnie! Johnnie!' until her voice grew husky and loving. This time their full passion seemed spent, and they lay exhausted together, her scent mixing with the fumes of petrol that came from the woodwork of the vehicle.

At last Johnnie took his weight from her and she stretched her cramped limbs and watched him dress. His back was glistening with sweat and she thought, 'I shan't see him again.' He vaulted from the truck and went round to the driving seat, where he sat and twisted around so that he could see her through the small cabin window combing her hair, a cigarette in her mouth. If it hadn't been for the soreness he could have taken her again, then and there. He handled the controls of the truck violently, grinding the gears until they shrieked. He backed out of their hiding place and she clung on with both hands as they pitched and rolled over the uneven surface of the track that led back to the main road. He heard her faint protest; 'Johnnie, be careful!' He winked at her. Then he was on the road, shifting from reverse, pressing hard on the stiff accelerator; taking Nina back to Comitarla; speeding her on her way out of his life.

Nina's other name was Mackenzie, the surname of her Scottish father, who had planted tea in Assam and gone down into Burma one year where he had met the Indian girl who was her mother. Nina had never seen him. Her skin was toned with a dark, purplish shade that was accentuated on her lips, beneath her armpits and in the shadows of her breasts and belly.

When the Japanese came to Burma she and an old schoolfriend had made their way to Calcutta and there she had been whisked by American troops, promiscuous and gum-chewing, into the night-life of Chowringhee; dancing at the Grand Hotel in skirts absurdly short, the powder on her face and arms too white for the pigment of her skin. She had been taken on white-sheeted beds beneath whirling fans that feathered the hair of her lovers; uncomfortably in the back of Sikh-driven taxis that scorched along the wide roads at midnight; in soldiers' billets, breathless and adventurously; in the backs of trucks; and once in the company of another man and woman in a four-seater

20

berth on the Frontier Mail.

Exhilarated, she looked for further fields, and on the advice of a colleague she joined the Auxiliary Nursing Service. At the British General Hospital in Comitarla she had met Johnnie, and perhaps because in this new life he was the first, she had fallen in love with him. Tomorrow, she was going back, towards Burma.

She recognised the turn in the road that led up to the Hospital. There was, she thought, an end to it now. There was nothing further except the sight of suffering, of which she was afraid, and the sound of guns that had scared her once before; and Johnnie would not be there to lift her in his arms, to love her fear away.

The rows of bashas, the wards, flicked past the back of the truck, whose canopy made for her the shape of a motion-picture screen. Then the truck pulled up with a jerk and she saw Johnnie's driver rise from where he had been sitting beneath a tree, smoking, waiting for them to return. The truck door slammed and Johnnie appeared and let the tailboard down. She walked forward and his arms came to clasp her and lift her lightly to the ground, where she stood for an instant close to him, feeling the warmth of intimacy that contact still generated in their bodies.

When she looked at Mohammed Din, he smiled, and she smiled back at him. She felt, in a way, proud that the driver knew she and his Sahib had been together. She had seen that all Johnnie's men worshipped him. She had seen the love and understood she could have no part of it except by being a part of Johnnie. She needed love more than anything else.

Mohammed Din closed up the tailboard and Johnnie told him to wait while he led her back to her quarters.

'He's a good type.' That was Johnnie's voice. She had come to know that if Johnnie liked somebody he called them 'good types'. If he liked them very much then he called them 'damned poor types', meaning they were irresponsible: irresponsible and admirable. It was the European way, a way foreign to her in spite of her Scottish name; the European way of twisting things round to mean something else, in the same way that they twisted hearts. She was crying silently.

Johnnie had seen the tears, but he said nothing. That was his way too, but she knew that Johnnie could be moved, and that when he was moved he grew silent, as if remembering. But, she told herself, Johnnie is a man and his silence therefore unfathomable, unlike a woman's silence which is a clear well.

At the door of the hut she stopped.

Let me come in,' he said.

She managed to whisper, 'No.'

He kissed her and pressed his groin hard into her belly and, embarrassed suddenly, a core of resistance turned into a tight knot of pain inside her so that she twisted away from him, catching the look of bewilderment that came into his eyes.

She said, 'There has to be an end. It's now, Johnnie. It's now,' and then she turned and ran into the room where all her things were packed and waiting. She leaned against the door and heard him moving on the verandah outside. Then his footsteps died away and she let the tears fall.

He had seen the tears before, and there had to be an end. But for men there was never an end because they never recognised the beginning. But he had seen the tears. She stood there and opened her eyes wide, not understanding why her things were packed; understanding only that in the distance she heard the familiar truck cough into life and moved away; understanding only that Johnnie had gone.

Perhaps it was wrong to let a man see tears. Giving pain, they never recognised the pain for what it was. The evidence of pain, tears, was twisted in their minds. In the end tears were an accusation.

His face grim with the hurt of Nina's sudden reaction away from him, he ordered Mohammed Din to drive him to the Comitarla club and leave him there, and Din, seeing that Johnnie Sahib was upset, silently obeyed.

Johnnie thought: 'Poor little bitch. She took it to heart.' He felt uneasy because he knew he had grown to need the comfort of Nina and depend upon her affection and love without realising it until it was too late. It was always the same with women; with men, he told himself, you knew where you stood, because you could recognise in men your own weaknesses or your own strength. If there was nothing recognisable in a man, then you avoided him. But all women were unrecognisable. Not one of them liked you for the same reason; they loved you in totally different ways.

At the club he went to look for Brad. He looked first in the small bar at the far end of the low club building. Behind the tiny, semi-circular counter stood the airman who served there and whose name, by common consent, had become 'Squiffie'.

'Morning, sir.'

'Hello, Squiffie. Seen my mucker?'

22

'Which one is that, sir?'

'The Canadian air force type. Flight-Lieutenant Bradley.'

'No, sir. Not yet.'

'If he turns up, tell him I'm having tiffin.'

'O.K., sir.'

Johnnie hated eating alone. He thought: 'Better alone though than go back to the mess and listen to 'em taking shop.' He walked down the verandah, which was covered by the over-hanging roof of thatch supported by bamboo poles. At the end of the club building was a dining-basha with a concrete floor on which were set out small tables covered with dirty white cloths. There was nobody else in the room except a couple of whispering bearers.

Eating alone, there in the empty room with the greyness of the day framed in the open doorway, his tough little body crouched over the table, Johnnie tried to shut his mind against his loneliness. With every mouthful of the curry he looked up to see if Brad were in sight. The bearer took his plate away and brought two slices of fresh pineapple; then there was coffee, sweetened with *ghur*; and afterwards only the long hours of the angry afternoon. The thought, unformed, produced a scowl. He shot a swift glance at the bearers who watched him and caught them grinning. He grinned back, rose and went out to the verandah, where wicker chairs were set out round low tables.

He sat down, and the bearer brought more coffee, shouting to his colleague to begin removing the chairs, as the wind that would bring the rain bent the thin palms in the small, scuffed garden. Johnnie watched them as they piled the wicker chairs and pushed them against the wall. Solitary, he sat and drank his coffee and let the wind blow into his grimed face.

At three o'clock it began to rain, and there was no sign of Brad. With the rain the temperature dropped, and he shivered in his thin cotton uniform. A pale streak in the sky where the clouds were broken brought a strangeness into the daylight, and in that light Johnnie's eyes were stubborn. Little muscles twitched across his cheeks, and his short, thick hands were clenched into fists upon the arms of the chair.

In half an hour the rain diminished. The change in its rhythm, the lifting of the dead sound of the torrent, brought relief. There were men shouting and dogs barking and the tinkle of bicycle bells as Comitarla came out from shelter. Johnnie got up and dashed out from the shelter of the verandah, across the beaten-down grass of the garden to the gravel path leading to the gate.

23

Four bicycle tongas were grouped there, and choosing the nearest he climbed into the canopied seat.

He ran from the tonga, which had drawn up at the gateway of Three Section lines, and the sepoy on sentry-go grinned a welcome. Johnnie, his head bent against the rain, raised a hand in greeting and splashed through the slimy mud of the courtyard, up the stone steps and arrived, dripping wet, in the office, where Nimu jumped to his feet.

'Sir, Flight-Lieutenant Bradley is upstairs in your room.'

'Christ! Thanks, Nimu.'

He ran up the stairs, calling, 'That you, Brad?'

The familiar voice was raised: 'Johnnie?'

Going into his bedroom he found Brad stretched out on the charpoy, a magazine open on his belly, one arm cradling the back of his head.

'Christ, you're a clot, Brad!'

'Why so, Johnnie?'

'I've been stuck up there at the club waiting for you.'

Brad scratched his head and yawned.

'Was that the arrangement?'

'You always lunch at the club, you wingless bloody wonder, you. Christ! I don't know. You choose the one day in a thousand to be clueless.'

'You'll get a cold in those wet things.'

'I know.' Johnnie over at the open, barred window, began to take off his tunic.

Brad watched him.

'I was only being tactful.'

'Tactful?'

'I thought you'd be lunching with Nina.'

'She had to parade with kit at half-past one. I thought you'd be at the club, and I wanted to get bloody pissed.'

'Did you?'

'By myself?'

Johnnie went to the doorway and called for Jan Mohammed. Below, Nimu echoed the call. Through the windows of the bedroom the orderly's answer drifted from one of the bashas. Johnnie came back into the room and Brad threw him a cigarette. Smoking, Johnnie rubbed his back and shoulders with a green-dyed towel. Then the humidity of the room drew the sweat out of his pores, and limply he sat down in his camp chair.

'Nina was all right,' said Brad.

The use of the past tense was like the shutting of a door. For a second their eyes met through the cigarette smoke, and then Brad said, 'I'm being posted myself, Johnnie.'

Jan Mohammed, slippers on his feet, appeared at the doorway. 'Sahib?'

'Char, jeldi.'

'Thik hai, Sahib.'

Brad scratched his stomach fiercely. 'This charpoy's got bugs.'

'Where you going, Brad?'

'Training Squadron attached to your depot in India.'

'Jesus! When?'

'Soon. Not sure. I'm grounded.'

'About bloody time you were.'

They smiled, and Johnnie got up from his chair to look for records to play on the portable. With his back to Brad he was able to say, 'First of all my girl goes. Now you're going. I'll have a hell of a good time from now on.'

Brad sat up, shifted round on the bed and dangled his feet backwards and forwards.

'You can take over Ethel.'

'Not my type.'

'They don't come in types where it matters.'

'The air force's made you coarse. Tch, tch!'

Brad, watching Johnnie's back, smiled.

'What about your leave, Johnnie?'

'Leave?' Johnnie wound the portable.

'You're due for leave.'

'Major says I can't go till my new two i.c. gets here.'

The record, playing, was scratchy. The tune, for them both, nostalgic. Brad was silent. Finally he said, 'I thought we could go together. Can't you work that? Won't the Major do that?'

'I don't know. He might.'

'Ask him.'

'I'm his bad boy.'

'You've done all right by him.'

'I could join you later, anyway. My new side-kick'll be here soon.'

'Then you can come straight away. Directly he gets here, I mean.'

'I don't know.' Johnnie paused, listening to the music. 'I ought to give him a few days' training. It's my section he'll be in after all.'

'You and your section!'

25

'Piss off!'

'Let Scottie take him in hand.'

'No bloody fear! Scottie'd push his nose in well enough without being asked.'

'Scottie's a good type.'

'He's all right. So's Bill Parrish. So's the Major. But *I* run my section, and any bloke coming in it helps to run it the way I want it run.'

The record ran out, and for a while they let it revolve with the sound-arm jerking up and down monotonously.

'Still the same old Johnnie.'

Johnnie reached out and stopped the table of the portable.

'When you going on leave anyway?' he asked.

'I just have to wait until my posting comes through, then off I go and kiss Comitarla on the arse.'

'You're welcome to that part.'

'I may be sorry.'

'I'd not be surprised.'

'To go, I mean. You get used to a place. Even a stinking hole like this.'

'What about Ethel?'

'You got first refusal; but there's a waiting list.'

'They can have her.'

'She was all right.'

'You never did have any taste, Brad.'

'You don't need taste. Just feel.'

Jan Mohammed came in with the tea, and while Brad helped the orderly clear a place on the small table at the side of the charpoy Johnnie thought: 'Nina said there has to be an end. There has to be an end, Johnnie, and this is it.' The dining-room at the club flashed in photographic clearness across his mind. Was that how the end was? Himself alone, and the past slipping out of his grip, the future hidden? He stared at the tea-tray. In Benares, on the way to Bengal, the little orderly had bought a teapot. It stood there now with a thin wisp of steam coming from the tiny hole in the lid. An outlet. Jan Mohammed went quickly out of the room.

It always came back to this: that there was the section; that outside were the men he had chosen, in a moment of startling clarity, back in India. He remembered, as Brad poured the tea, the electric shock of recognition that passed through his own body as his hand clapped a shoulder so that it seemed that another reached out and touched his own. On that hot, parched afternoon

26

there had been no uncertainty, no half-felt fears for the future or regret for the past, only the direct communication between himself and the men he picked. Whenever he was with them, even now, the communication remained. It was always there, solid and dependable; there for the asking; there, comforting in the background, even without the asking.

'Here's your char.' Brad held out the cup.

'Thanks.'

He sat 'on the edge of the bed and stirred with his spoon. Looking out of the window he saw that the rain had stopped and the grey sky was streaked with wide bars of yellow where the sun filtered. From the airfield a noise, of aero-engines testing, vibrated. Suddenly, from behind a fast cloud, the sun shone, sucking up the steam from the sodden earth and glistening on the thick banana leaves. He said, 'I'll tackle the Major anyway. Christ, he owes me leave.'

'That's the boy. I could get a couple of girls, maybe.'

'I'd bloody well hope so. Not Ethel, though.'

'She has a friend.'

'Who cares? I leave it to you, though.' He paused. 'We'll have a good time.'

He went to the table for his cigarette tin and offered it to Brad. Lighting up, he handed his cup. 'Here, pour me another.'

The hot tea drew the perspiration from his cheeks and from his upper lip. The salty tang of it was comfortable. He let the sweat drip to his lips and licked it with his tongue. Things would work themselves out. The future spread out again, wide, infinitely promising. Things would work themselves out. He would talk to the Major. He knew how to do that; knew how far he could go with the old boy. His new side-kick – what was his name? What had the signal said, Taylor? – Taylor would arrive, perhaps tonight; perhaps tomorrow. In the future he would need Taylor, so long as the chap wasn't a clot like Bates had been. He would need Taylor with Brad gone, with Nina gone, and with the taste of being out of step with Scottie and Parrish in his mouth. The Major, God bless him, never saw things like that; never saw that Scottie and Bill had shown signs of resentment because *his* section had somehow gone that step or two ahead of theirs. And men were always rivals; rivals for women, for honour, or reputation; and if deprived of these, then they were rivals for whatever was left over. In Comitarla there was precious little.

A truck was turning into the section area. Johnnie walked to the window. Even, he told himself, even if things went wrong, there was always the section, the men who were part of him and belonged to him in a way nothing in his life had ever belonged.

He looked out of the window and saw that the Major had arrived. He was jumping down from the truck and climbing out of the opposite side was another man whose style of uniform struck a sudden note in Johnnie's memory.

It could only be Taylor. A new man in khaki instead of jungle green, with a revolver holster fixed to his webbing belt. Johnnie watched as Taylor straightened his body and turned slightly from side to side, a look of anxiety mixed with eagerness on the thin face that was partly shaded by a brand new bush hat.

The plane which flew in from Calcutta with Jim Taylor on board was the one in which Lieutenant-Colonel Baxter had reserved a seat for his return journey. It had been, the Major explained, a case of killing two birds with one stone.

The three of them stood in Nimu's office. Outside, a couple of sepoys were dragging Taylor's kit from the back of the truck and piling it up just inside the porch. While the Major described his meeting with Taylor and the departure of Baxter – 'More of Baxter later, Johnnie, by the way,' – Johnnie watched the face of his new second-in-command.

At last he said, 'I've no idea who Baxter is, but you might introduce me to my new side-kick, sir.'

'You'll be hearing all about Baxter, me lad. Well, this is Johnnie Brown who commands Three Section. You'll be working with him. This is Taylor.'

Taylor held out his hand.

'I'm sorry I'm late. It's a bad start.'

Johnnie took the proffered hand in his own, for an instant at a loss. Then, because the right words came to him, he knew that Taylor was going to be all right.

'Don't worry about that. Starting's always bad anyway.' With a sideways look at the Major, he added, 'I've been sweating on leave, though.'

'I didn't know. I'm sorry. I was outranked at Delhi by a Brigadier and lost my seat on the plane.'

'That's always happening.' The Major smiled as he said it.

Johnnie walked to the porch. 'This all your stuff?'

'Yes, there's not much.'

'I'll get it sent upstairs. By the way, what about a charpoy for him, Major?'

Taylor broke in, 'My camp-bed's in the bedding roll.'

28

'Christ! you don't want to sleep on one of those. I'll get a spare one from one of my men.' Johnnie walked out into the courtyard and shouted for Moti Ram.

The Major, staring after him, turned suddenly to Taylor.

'In a way, Taylor, you're lucky to be with Johnnie.'

Then Johnnie came back as the call for Moti Ram Sahib was taken up by voices of men standing in the doorways of the bashas. The section area had suddenly come alive. It was an effect that Johnnie had, and Taylor noticed it.

'Would you like to take Taylor upstairs, Major? Brad's up there. Then I'll get another charpoy and all this kit sent up.'

The Major said, 'Fair enough, Johnnie. I'll lead the way, shall I, Taylor?' Johnnie watched them go, then turned back to see Moti Ram doubling across the courtyard.

'Hello, Sahib.'

'Good evening, sir. Everything is all right, sir?'

'Everything's fine. Look.' He pointed at the kit.

'The new Sahib is come, isn't it, sir? I heard just now.'

'Get a couple of blokes to cart it upstairs, together with a spare charpoy.'

'Spare charpoy, sir? I don't think. . . '

'You'll find a spare one for me, won't you, Sahib?'

'I will find, sir.'

As Johnnie walked back into the office the Major came down from the room above and said, 'I want a word with you. Let's go into your office.'

'What's this, Major? You going to tear me off a strip?'

'I just want a word with you.'

'O.K.' Johnnie went through the doorway leading from Nimu's office to his own. There was a curious deserted air about it. He said, over his shoulder, 'Anyway, I want to talk to you too, Major. About my leave.'

'We'll come to that.'

'Cigarette?'

'Thanks, Johnnie. Look, can't you get it into your thick head that it's no good letting ordinary unit discipline and administration drift the way you do?'

'You choose a funny time to start all that, Major.'

'I choose the best time. Apart from it being the only time today I've been able to get hold of you. Where were you by the way?'

'At the hospital. Then at the club. Nina's been posted.'

'We had an inspection.'

29

'I didn't know. This chap Baxter you were talking about?'

'Yes.'

'Who was he, anyway?'

'Someone from Delhi.'

Johnnie smiled. 'I missed a lot.'

'That's not the point. The point is, Johnnie, that you can't let your section wander around all day like a lot of dopes. Half-baked dopes.'

'First time I've heard 'em called that. I thought they did pretty well.'

'Oh, we all know about how good your blokes are. The blue-eyed boys of the Training Depot.'

'So they damned well were. Just as good, if not better than a bunch that rushes around sweeping and polishing in their spare moments. When they need to work, they work.'

'I'm not arguing about that, Johnnie. Three Section is – well – it's Three Section. But God-dammit – look – come over here!'

The Major went to the window and Johnnie followed. The Major pointed. 'Look at the mess over there by that corner basha! And look at that! Is that supposed to be a fire-point? And that ammunition just lying around in the open. Christ! It's two weeks since you had the ammunition programme.'

'It'll be needed again.'

'But you can't just let it stay there.'

'The store is jammed tight.'

The Major ignored the excuse. 'Look at that! Is that supposed to be a fire-point?'

'I don't know.'

The Major twisted round and stared at him. It was going wrong. The anger of the morning was returning and yet, when he had started this talk he had not been angry. The anger, such as it had been, had evaporated when Taylor had put in his appearance. The Major had been genuinely glad, partly for Johnnie's sake, because it meant that Johnnie could get off on leave, and partly because with Johnnie away he would be able to set Taylor on the proper lines, gently, almost imperceptibly, but firmly. Knowing his Johnnie, the Major guessed that Taylor would either be out on his ear, or Johnnie's closest friend. It was the only way it could work. And yet, perversely, he wanted it to work in whatever way it must. Dimly he knew that the future held changes. Baxter's visit had been a warning of change, a change that would come when some higher authority stepped in and took over. As he stared at Johnnie he saw in his mind, ranged with him, the

30

other two, Scottie and Bill, and the paler figures of Johns and Ghosh. These were his officers. Together they had set out a year ago, bringing with them a conviction that the work they were doing was worth-while; and bringing with them the special feeling that always accompanies men who create out of nothing; improvise with little. It had been, in spite of frustration and fatigue, infinitely worth-while; perhaps the most worth-while thing in his life. The reins were still in his hands, but they seemed to be tautening, multiplying. In the end, he was afraid, they might be too many; for it was men he drove, and men, after a period of contentment in harness, sometimes begin to pull in different directions.

He had said nothing for so long that Johnnie turned away. Regretting it, even as he said it, the Major remarked to Johnnie's back, 'It'd do you good to run your section the way Bill runs his, or Scottie, for that matter.'

Johnnie spun round.

'D'you want me to chuck in?'

'Good Lord, can't you take criticism?'

'You pick a fine time to make it.'

The Major thought: 'I forgot about Nina.'

He said, 'I don't want any of my officers to chuck in, as you call it. As far as I'm concerned, we're the best air supply company operating.'

'You think that way about your company. I think the same way about my section.' Johnnie paused. 'You see that, don't you?'

'Yes, I see that. But that's ... that's different. Besides,' he rested against the edge of the desk, 'I don't stick out my chest and say I've got the best company and then let a pile of refuse go stinking stale in the middle of my lines.'

'I know. But when it's a question of worth-while work, we work.'

'Oh, be your age, Johnnie.'

He paused, and then said more quietly, 'Anyway, how old are you? Twenty-four? Twenty-five?'

'Twenty-five.' Johnnie stubbed out his cigarette and reached for another. The Major held out his own stub as a light.

'Twenty-five. I was peddling vacuum-cleaners at your age.'

Johnnie glanced up, his head bent.

The Major said, 'Nineteen-thirty. That dates me, doesn't it? There was a widow down in Slough. Know Slough?'

Johnnie shook his head.

'You haven't missed much. I used to work Slough the first week of every month.'

They were silent as they sat smoking.

After a while the Major said, 'We'd better think about getting you off on leave.'

'It's an idea.'

The Major nodded. 'Now that Taylor's here you can go almost straight away.'

'That's what I thought.' Johnnie paused. The Major's words were still rankling. He would have preferred silence; an indication of his resentment. But, he thought, the old boy's a decent enough bloke and you can't help liking him. He blurted out, 'Brad's going to be posted. We thought of getting off on leave together.'

'Not your lucky day, is it?'

'I'm not complaining.'

'You lose your girl and your best pal and get Taylor and a bawling out from me instead.' The Major smiled. 'That's life.'

'Taylor looks all right.' He wanted to add – 'and perhaps I deserved the bawling out.' But there was pride stopping the words, and they went unsaid.

'Don't spoil him, Johnnie. That might be said to be a weakness of yours.'

'It couldn't be one of yours too, could it, Major?' Johnnie's lips curved into a smile, but above the smile the eyes were steady enough and the Major knew that Johnnie's meaning was twofold. It implied, 'Don't interfere with Taylor,' as well as, 'I always get what I want even from you.' The Major found himself staring back. But before a challenge could take shape Johnnie had moved. He went towards the door, then turned.

'Come and have a drink.'

'What, before my tea?'

'Tea's late. The sun's going down, anyway.'

'All right.'

'We can fix up about me and Brad at the same time.'

The Major rose from the edge of the table and Johnnie went on ahead. Going again to the window he saw two men, with a charpoy raised high above their heads, coming towards the house. There were men lounging in doorways, squatting just outside the huts, smoking and talking.

He looked up. The clouds had been miraculously washed away and the sky was empty. The sun, low, was a glare behind a network of leaves and branches, and the roofs of the bashas, golden now, were striped black where the thatch was rotten and gathered water. Washed, the earth seemed to shine and reflect colour. As the sun sank the sky would turn turquoise and then a deeper green; the green of the banana leaves would darken, and all at once the whole land would be dark with the sky gentle and luminous above it.

3

The following morning, at midday precisely, the short rest the company had been enjoying ended abruptly, and although at first it seemed there would be little else involved beyond a few occasional supply drops to scattered patrol units, as the hours passed that first impression had to be put aside. There was, it appeared, something quite big brewing.

Johnnie and Taylor, however, remained unaware of what might be in store until they returned to Three Section lines at four o'clock. They were met by the sight of great activity, presided over by Moti Ram Sahib, and going upstairs, weary and dirty, they found the Major waiting for them, and he told them the news.

'Where the hell,' he asked first, 'have you two been?'

Johnnie explained. 'We went on that supply drop.'

'Together?'

'It was a good chance for Taylor.'

'Section officers aren't supposed to fly together. You know that. Supposing you'd both gone for a burton?'

'I know. But it's turned out all right.' Johnnie, grinning at Taylor, flung himself on his bed which was now pushed further towards the window to make room for Taylor's.

Taylor said. 'Jemadar Sahib told us there's something on.'

'You came just in time, Taylor.' The Major paused. He looked across at Johnnie. 'I may get an order to cancel all leave, you know.'

But Johnnie was not to be baited. The afternoon had been too good to spoil by beginning to worry. 'Something tells me, Major, that you won't get that order until I've gone. It's my lucky day.' Still grinning, he reached for a cigarette and threw one to Taylor.

The Major waited. 'Don't I get one too?'

'If I get my leave. Here, catch.'

The Major caught.

Then he turned to Taylor. 'Well, Taylor, how did it go?'

Four hours before, the field telephone had rung, and Johnnie, sitting in his office with Taylor, answered it.

'Johnnie?'

'That you, Major?'

'Yes. I've got a job for you.'

'Christ! What's happened? Is there a war on somewhere?'

'Didn't I tell you? No, no kidding. There's a drop for you.'

'When for?'

'As soon as you can make it.'

'Jesus! We do sweet fanny for a couple of weeks, then they start off all over again in a hurry.'

'It's only one plane load. Straight compo ration.'

'Indian or British?'

'Indian.'

'Got the plane number?'

The Major called the number over, then said, 'The plane can take off as soon as you can get down. You've got enough compo packed for dropping I take it?'

'Sure.'

'Get cracking then. By the way, how's Taylor shaping?'

Johnnie winked at Taylor, who sat nearby.

'O.K! I've just been showing him the layout. Now we're having a natter and a well-earned cup of char.'

'Right. Get that demand tied up.'

Johnnie hung up. He said, 'We're operating,' then he shouted for Nimu. Nimu looked into the office.

'Tell Dass to load up one planeload of I.T. Compo for dropping.'

'Now, sir?'

'Yes, now. Go on. I'll expect the lorry loaded in twenty minutes.'

Nimu nodded, and from where they sat they heard his high voice shouting from the porch for Dass.

'We may as well watch this,' Johnnie said, and they both got up from the canvas stools and went out to where Nimu was standing. 'O.K., Nimu, you go and type the dropping note. I'll get hold of Dass.'

'Only one planeload, isn't it, sir?'

'Only one.'

Following Nimu's call for Dass there had been no sign of movement anywhere in the lines. Now Johnnie raised his voice, standing with his hands low on his hips, and men appeared in doorways. Dass came running.

Johnnie dropped his voice. 'Dass is this short-arsed little bugger.' He paused, glancing at Taylor. 'Same as me.'

Five minutes after Dass had turned about and run off to the

Transport Harbour one of the three-tonners came lurching along the muddy track, and a group of half-dressed sepoys was already gathered at one of the store bashas, directing the lorry, tailboard down, towards the dark entrance. Their eyes on Johnnie, they shouted and laughed as they carried out the heavy canvas containers from where they were stacked in readiness for such an occasion. Johnnie, stopping one of the sepoys, smacked the container the man carried on his back and said to Jim, 'You've seen one of these of course?'

Taylor nodded, but fingered the closed flaps at the end which covered the folded parachute. He said, 'But they look different somehow,' and smiled. Johnnie tapped the container and said to the man, 'Thik hai, Nada,' and Nada stumbled to the lorry.

'Beats me how you know their names, just like that.'

'I've had 'em over a year.'

Johnnie went up to the lorry and watched the containers stacked. When the loading was finished he looked at his watch. 'Twenty-two minutes. Not bad, seeing they were either asleep or having konna.'

Suddenly he twisted round and faced the men, who were wiping their foreheads. 'Ejection wallahs?' He made a motion to indicate pushing out. Only one man hung back. Johnnie beckoned to him. It was Nada. 'Push out karo?' Nada swallowed. 'Thik hai, Sahib. Push out karo.'

Taylor said, 'Can I go?'

'We're both going. But we'll take Nada with us.' The rest of the men dispersed after Johnnie had selected from them a squad to go with the lorry and load the plane. Nada with them, they climbed into the back and looked shyly at Taylor.

'Let's go over to the office and get the dropping note.' Johnnie paused. 'By the way, what's your first name? I can't go on calling you "you".'

'Jim.'

'Come on then, Jim.'

As they walked Johnnie said, 'Last side-kick I had was a chap called Bates.'

'Bates? I think he gave us a lecture at the Depot.'

'That would be him.' Johnnie paused. 'I didn't like Bates.'

The turbulence was rocking the Dakota, and for a moment Jim thought he was going to be sick. Little Nada had long since succumbed to the effects of the plane's flying into air pockets and being tossed, spasmodically, up and down like a football played on heads. The sepoy lay hunched and miserable, curled up on the floor of the plane by the lavatory door.

The removable door of the plane lay in the jumble of ropes, boxes and tools in the tail, and Jim stood near the open exit looking down through the white puff clouds to the swollen green jungle beneath. Johnnie, leaving Nada to his air-sick misery, came and stood at the opposite side of the open doorway and looked down too.

Up here there was safety – a measure of safety. It seemed impossible that below, hidden by that dense green and undulating forest, were men, dressed as they were; men who from above seemed not to have identity of any sort; and yet men who came from places they themselves knew and were familiar with. Now these other men were merged into the jungle, and invisible in it. The covering trees might hide a handful, or a battalion – a division.

The door of the pilot's cabin opened, and one of the crew slid and climbed over the waist-high pile of containers.

'Better stack up,' he said, and began untying the ropes which lashed the load firmly on the floor of the craft. Johnnie and Jim dragged containers to the doorway. The dust rose and stung the eyes.

Two abreast, three high at the open door. They uncoiled the static lines from beneath the flaps and began tying them to the rope which joined the strong-points above their heads. The first stack ready, they placed another close by it.

The member of the crew who was helping pointed at Nada.

'We need him.'

Johnnie went over to Nada. 'Thik hai?' Nada opened his eyes. Then he rose to his feet and caught on to Johnnie's arm. Jim saw the sepoy's lips move, and Johnnie nodded. He led him to the rear of the stack and motioned him to sit on the floor again with his back to the fuselage, his feet in contact with the containers.

The land beneath began to heave up as the Dakota turned, and for a split second Jim caught sight of an open space cut from out of the jungle. There was a white strip of cloth, and smoke rose from a fire. Then the wing was even again and there was sky instead of earth; and in a moment a bell rang abruptly.

He stood on one side, and Johnnie on the other. There was another ring, and he saw the green light flick on and Johnnie yelled, 'Heave!'

His feet shuffling to keep their grip, Jim pushed outwards at the stack with his arms, and Johnnie's face was close, closed up with effort. Suddenly the weight was gone, the static lines still fixed above, stretched now diagonally across the open space of the doorway, flipping their ends in the slipstream. Nada, pushing with his feet at the base of the stack, lay hunched on the floor, the nails in his boots scraping the metal ridges as he slithered forward.

They grabbed at the next pile and stacked the containers up as before, checking the knots in the static lines while the airman shoved more containers forward. The bell; the light; and the weight going again with the dust rising, settling on faces now wet with perspiration.

Third circuit. The bell; the light. These was a rhythm now, and Johnnie tore off his shirt, yelling. 'You get soaked, and it's cold going back.' Fourth circuit. Fifth. Jim saw that the airman was stumbling, pushing almost blindly at the diminishing load, with Johnnie, the muscles on his shoulders and arms trembling, pulling them towards the door. The bell; the light; sixth circuit.

The load tore at the finger-nails and left the palms of the hands scraped and raw. Each time it cost more in effort to raise and pile high and heave, and kick the stubborn bale that threatened to block the exit, and turn to haul forward the few that were left.

Seventh; the weight tumbling into space. The eighth and last, with an extra container precarious on the top of the other six; the last, waiting for the bell and the light, leaning against the load, swallowing and gulping air that was dust.

Johnnie yelled, 'Push the bastard!' and it tumbled, and the containers fell with the canopies developing in white, streaming ribbons until suddenly, as if with relief, they filled, paused, and swayed downwards like white petals.

Johnnie pulled Jim by the arm, 'Come up front!' he shouted the words hoarsely and they lurched towards the cabin. The pilot turned and smiled and they went behind his shoulder and followed with their eyes his pointing finger.

Low, the plane flew swiftly above trees, and suddenly in front was the clearing, now dotted with blobs of whiteness where the canopies had died.

And running into the open from the surrounding trees, a man, waving.

When they went back, Nada was being sick.

Johnnie shivered in the cold and put on his shirt again. They lay down on a pile of sacks, and the steady drum of the engines was a background to weariness. Taylor shut his eyes and heard

Johnnie say, 'Poor bastard!' and knew that he meant the man who had run, waving, from the jungle. He opened his eyes and looked at Johnnie and thought of what the Major had said. 'In a way you're lucky to be with Johnnie.' Johnnie was saying, 'Sometimes I stick some books or mags in the containers. Best of all, newspapers from England if you can get hold of any.' Dirt and sweat channelled his face and his tongue kept reaching out and licking his parched lips. Suddenly he said. 'What were you doing before, Jim?'

What had he been doing? There had been nothing until now, nothing really to remember except boredom and an infinite stretch of meaningless days spent in the scorching sun of India. Lahore; Ambala; high, cool messes with silent bearers grouped round a morose Colonel for whom the war could only mean the remorseless shelf of neglect; a dying-on-the-feet, out of date and limited by tradition and experience. The war had never reached the cantonments, and to be set down in one, by reason of war, had had its own irony, its own hopelessness.

He answered, 'Nothing.'

And added, 'I mean nothing any good.'

Johnnie nodded, understandingly. After a while Jim got to his feet and walked unsteadily to the open doorway Once again he leaned against its side. Far below, for they were flying high, the green of the land was dark and grey and patched, and the vapour of clouds kept obscuring vision like sudden, intimate fogs. His hands, resting on the cold metal, were still trembling and sore and he stood with his knees slightly bent to ease the ache in them.

It had been little enough he had done; but it had been better than nothing, and he needed, after so long, to feel that what he was doing was not an end in itself. He shivered.

Cold and tired he went back to the pile of sacks and sat there hunched into himself for warmth.

Johnnie and Nada seemed to be . . . sleeping.

Jim answered the Major, 'It was harder work than the training drops we did in India, sir.'

'I expect it was. By the way, Jim, just call me "Major". All the other disrespectful dopes do.'

Johnnie called from the bed, 'Now you know what we are, disrespectful dopes.' Stretching, he breathed out tobacco smoke.

'Moti Ram said we're collecting ammunition from the dump.'

'That's right, Johnnie. We had the wire this afternoon. As I said before, Jim, you came at the right time.'

'And I'm *going* at the right time, aren't I?' Johnnie narrowed his eyes a little as the Major seemed to hesitate.

'I might have to cancel leave.'

'But not before I've gone.'

'Depends when you intend to go.'

'I could go tonight,' said Johnnie, sitting up suddenly. 'I could go tonight and wait for Brad in Cal.' Then he looked at Jim and added, 'But I can't, can I? I've got to see old Jim here's O.K.' He lay back again. 'Tell us about the ammunition.'

'It's simple enough,' the Major explained. 'The order was we should be prepared to operate an unspecified number of ammunition landings into Imphal.'

'Big battle, Major? Flap on again?'

'No Johnnie. The flap's over. Stocking up, I suppose, for an advance of some sort. Scottie's going to supervise bods.'

Jim looked puzzled. 'What does that mean?'

'Bods? You know, men. Reinforcements.'

'Do we fly those as well?'

'We fly everything. Well, almost everything. Parrish's section'll be standing by for any dropping commitments.' The Major rose from the edge of the table where he had been sitting and wandered over to the window. From below came the noise of men shouting and Moti Ram's sharp, high voice raised in protest.

'It's the beginning of the steady old plod again, boys. Every now and then it'll flare up into a major or minor flap. But from now on there'll be the plod.'

Johnnie winked at Jim behind the Major's back.

'You sound browned off. What about some leave for you?'

'It'll fit in somehow.' He turned. 'Christ, Johnnie, we can't all go on leave!' He came back and flopped down in one of the canvas chairs. He watched Jim for a moment and then spoke to him. 'Can you cope if Johnnie goes?'

'I think so, Major. I'd better, hadn't I?'

'He'll cope.' Johnnie's voice was matter of fact.

'Suppose he will.'

Then they fell silent and Jim felt they were considering how he would shape, so that he grew embarrassed and concentrated on the sound of the lorries which were now droning through the lines in convoy, off, no doubt, to the ammunition dump. For a moment he felt detached; particularly from these two men who had been down here a year and to whom all this was familiar.

The Major said, 'If you have to cope you'll find you will. It's always the same for a new chap. One minute he's nowhere, the next he's just dropped into place. Easy as falling off a house.'

Johnnie sat upright again, then got off the bed.

'I'm going to see how my blokes are getting on.' At the doorway he halted. 'Coming, Jim?'

'I want to talk to him, Johnnie. You leave him alone for a bit. You've shown him the section.'

'O.K.! But don't brass him off with one of those hygiene lectures of yours.' Johnnie went.

Jim reached into his pocket and found his cigarette packet was bent and damp. 'Have one, Major? They're not very good, I'm afraid.'

'They'll do. Thanks.'

They lit from the stubs of the others.

'Johnnie's a good type, Jim.'

'I know. He's liked a lot by his men, isn't he?'

'He hand-picked them. Hasn't he told you that yet?'

'He did mention it.' He added, 'How long d'you think we'll be here? In Comitarla, I mean?'

'Don't know. Been here a year. Might be here another. On the other hand, in a week's time we might be miles away.' Involuntarily they both looked round the room that bore the stamp of Johnnie's personality.

It was the Major who spoke first.

'You know what I'm thinking?'

'No.'

'Something very much like Johnnie'll stay behind in this room when we've gone.'

'I know what you mean.'

'It worries me sometimes.'

'How d'you mean?'

'Johnnie goes along in one straight line. It's fine. It shows style. Flair. But it worries me.'

'Don't worry about Johnnie.' Jim paused. 'It's funny I should say that. I hardly know him. But it's what I feel.'

'I like to feel it too. Not only about him, but all of us. He just happens to be the shining example of someone with his neck stuck in the sand. We all do it though. I do it all the time. So will you. But Johnnie . . . you notice him doing it. Johnnie's what I call larger than life. Or perhaps we're all smaller than life. I don't know.' His voice dropped. 'It all boils down to this, Jim. Johnnie's Johnnie, and you are you. And somehow you're going to have to work together and still remain that way. With Johnnie it's going to be difficult.'

Outside it was beginning to rain, and they heard Johnnie pounding up the stairs. When he came into the bedroom he said, 'Christ, it's pissing down!' Then he yelled for Jan Mohammed. 'What about some char?'

'Suits me, Johnnie.'

'He been shooting a line, Jim?'

'No.'

'I don't believe it. And don't you believe anything he tells you.'

'Pity, Johnnie. I've told him what a bloody good chap you are.'

Johnnie smiled. 'You'd better leave him to find out for himself what sort of a chap I am. Don't want him to start under a false impression.' He winked at Jim as he said it, as if to imply that already they were allies. And Jim was surprised to realise that this was so; surprised, he supposed, because he and Johnnie were so unlike. But during the flight Johnnie's unspoken thoughts had found echoes in his own; the same spark of feeling had been struck; its glow remained.

He felt suddenly completely at ease. 'It's always the same for a new chap,' the Major had said; 'one minute he's nowhere, the next he's just dropped into place.' It was true, and he was grateful as he had been that afternoon when he had felt what he was doing had some purpose. He looked at Johnnie, and for the first time since his arrival he thought of another friend, Geoff Smith, whom he had left in Marapore, and he found cause to wonder that two such different men should seem to help him to deaden a sense of emptiness.

He looked away. The emptiness was always there, like an abyss. The abyss was not bridged by a loose comradeship supposedly brought to life by war. That was a half-truth, the result of groping round the edges of thought. The need for companionship was always there; and the abyss was always there to be bridged. War only stripped the camouflage so that, in the holocaust, a man could see all that was worth keeping, all that was worth saving from destruction.

At the rear of the house a verandah jutted from the first floor, and where Johnnie's bedroom gave on to the verandah a screen of tarpaulins had been erected, and within the screened-off portion canvas bath equipment was set out.

The Major had stayed to have tea, and at five o'clock, when the rain stopped, Scottie and Johns came round from their sections and forgathered in Johnnie's bedroom to discuss the new operations.

41

Jim, at Johnnie's suggestion, had gone outside to have a bath. The air was cooler after the rain, and this evening the sun remained partly obscured by grey clouds. He shivered as he stripped and sat down in the low, canvas hip-bath. The parapet of the verandah was waist high and from where he sat he could see only the clouds and the thin palms bending gently against them. A Dakota, homing, flew low across the house, drowning, for a minute, the buzz of talk and laughter in the adjoining room.

Gradually the ammunition-laden lorries began to crawl back into the lines, and so Jim did not distinguish the sound of the truck which brought with it Brad, who now came running up the stone steps, yelling to Johnnie.

A loud shout of derision greeted Brad as he went into the bedroom, and in the short silence that followed it Jim heard Johnnie say, 'Well, Brad?'

'Tomorrow, Johnnie. The order came through half an hour ago, and the C.O. says I can go on leave from tomorrow.'

'You're a lucky bastard.' That was the Major speaking,

'Hi, Major! Don't you wish you was me?' Brad's Canadian drawl was eccentuated when he was in high spirits.

'And Johnnie comes with me? That's right isn't it? I'm fixing up comforts for both of us.'

'What about us?'

'You don't need comforts, Major. You got your little company and little operation to keep you happy.'

'Sarcy bugger!'

'Well, Major?' Jim heard the faint note of worry in Johnnie's voice, but then the Major must have smiled, or nodded, or in some way indicated his assent, because suddenly Johnnie's voice was close, just outside the tarpaulin, and he shouted for Jan Mohammed. Then the tarpaulin was pulled aside and he looked in.

'I'm going tomorrow, Jim.' He paused. 'Is that O.K. with you?'

'Of course. Good luck to you.' Jim rose up from the hip-bath and began to dry himself.

Johnnie dropped his voice. 'I'll get rid of these blokes soon and then we'll have another natter.'

'Fine.'

Then Johnnie was gone and somebody inside began singing.

Before it grew quite dark Johnnie took him round the airfield to explain its intricacies to him. They went in Johnnie's truck and Johnnie drove.

As they came on to the circuit the last tip of the sun was red, and dying behind the control tower which stood a sentinel in the strangely silent field, and before the tour was finished the swift darkness of the East had settled and the moon made the road white in front of them. Nestling in angles were sheltered bays: some empty, some occupied by the dead bulk of silent Dakotas.

At the north point of the airfield there were signs of further building. The rubble foundations of a taxi-lane led into a clearing. Here Johnnie stopped the truck, and through the open window of the cabin came the smell of petrol and rubber.

'Smoke, Jim?'

'Thanks.'

The silence was broken by the sound of a Dakota coming in to land. The shape of it was hardly discernible in the sky, but it flew on its riding lights as if held together by them. The room at the top of the control tower was illuminated brightly. They watched as the plane landed, smoothly, with a sudden complaint of rubber on tarmac. At the end of the runway it turned and taxied back down the apron and then off to a southern corner of the field. The silence fell again.

Johnnie said suddenly. 'You'll look after my section for me, won't you?'

'Of course, Johnnie.'

'That's what I thought.' Johnnie breathed out smoke and took a swift, sideways look at him. 'I'd like to think you were looking after 'em properly.'

'I'll do my best.'

'Don't let the Major, or anyone else for that matter, run you around either. If you're run around you'll find yourself taking it out on the men. They won't like that and then they won't like you and you'll be piling up grief for yourself.'

'I expect the Major'll keep an eye on me.'

'Just let it be an eye. See what I mean.?'

'I do.'

'The Major's all right. He's a good type. So's Scottie. And you'll like Bill Parrish when he gets back off leave. He doesn't give a damn.' In the growing darkness Johnnie's smile was only half seen. 'Christ, he's a bastard with women, too.' He turned confidentially. 'I've just lost my girl. She was a nurse up at the hospital.'

'Posted?'

'Yes, gone forward, poor kid. She was bloody good to me.'

'What was her name?'

'Nina Mackenzie. Chi-chi, of course.' He blew out smoke and the red tip of his cigarette glowed as he sucked in more. 'What you want to do, Jim, is get yourself comfy with one of the nurses. You'll meet 'em all at the club, one way or the other.'

Jim said, 'It's a surprise to find there's a club.'

'Comitarla's all right. At least, it's better than some places. There's a place called Prulli a few miles north. Christ, that's a piss-hole if ever there was one!'

Jim laughed. 'They dressed me up for the jungle back in Marapore.'

Johnnie laughed too. 'Marapore!' Then he said, 'I'm going up that way on leave. I may look in on the depot.'

'The depot?'

'Yes. Want me to give any fond messages anywhere?'

'Not the sort you mean.'

'A bloke?'

'Chap called Geoff Smith.'

'A pal of yours?'

'We came out from England together.'

'He's at the depot now?'

'Yes. We were on the same course there.'

'I'll tell him you're O.K., shall I?'

'Yes, tell him that.'

Johnnie shifted in his seat. He leaned forward with his chin resting on hands clasping the top of the steering wheel. 'I don't know anyone there now,' he said. 'It's a year since I was there.' He hesitated. Then he said, 'We'll have to get together when I come back.'

Jim nodded as Johnnie turned his head round to look at him. It was funny how Johnnie with his toughness and his resilience could suddenly appear so vulnerable to the hurt of loneliness. Pathetic, too, because a man like Johnnie would not understand that these moments of isolation were known to everyone; he would only be aware of the bleakness and the need for reaching out; angry at himself for reaching out because doing so shook the foundations of his self-reliance.

But when Johnnie came back, he and Jim would get together. It was a pact which stemmed from childhood days and strange taboos and initiations under summer suns with the hot smell of grass remembered long after the pact itself had died.

He sat there in the truck beside Johnnie and for a while they talked of the past, of home, delving by questioning deep into each other's background. But time and distance had merged the separate parts into an indistinct whole, fostering the idea of alliance and things in common. And when, as if satisfied that as much as needed to be told had been told, Johnnie sat back, Jim thought: 'It's a new beginning; it's the end of stagnation and futility.'

Twin beams of yellow light stabbed suddenly into the darkness as Johnnie, without speaking, switched on the headlamps. In a few moments the truck was moving along the road and then, as it turned and headed for Comitarla, the sound of its engine was carried away by the night wind that blew over the desolate airfield.

PART TWO
Prulli

4

Prulli was thirty miles north of Comitarla and was connected to it by rail. The station, such as it was, was made up of a few small huts and a neglected siding. One of the huts served as a restaurant where travellers, constantly held up at this point by the in- efficiency of the station staff, could sweat and fume away their irritation while they ate whatever food could be scraped together and drank quantities of locally distilled whisky and gin.

Three days after Johnnie had gone on leave with Brad the com- pany was ordered to Prulli without notice.

The ammunition that weighed down Three Section lorries had hastily to be returned to the dump in Comitarla. For some reason the airfield had suddenly been closed to air supply opera- tions. In Prulli or rather five miles east of the station, there was a neglected all-weather strip, and from there the Major was to fly out his commitments. What those commitments were to be he had no idea, and looking round the area allotted to him for quartering his company, an area which was a mile from the air- field and which he inspected with Scottie, he could only pray they would not be large.

They stood looking at the dilapidated bashas, half-hidden in the profusion of trees and rough grass through which a mud road snaked and curved.

'What,' he asked of Scottie, who stood pushing his lips in and out nervously as he mentally tried to fit his section into the jumble of huts, 'what in Heaven's name have we done to deserve this?'

'For once, Major, I've got no explanation.'

'Jesus! What a bloody abortion of a place it is.'

Then the rain swished down and disconsolately they ran splashing through the red mud to find shelter in the small basha they had decided should be the mess. Inside there was a smell of musty decay. The Major narrowed his eyes. The rain increased the smell of desolation. The supporting poles of the hut looked damp and rotten.

'They say,' he reflected, 'that Calcutta is the arse-hole of India. They made a mistake. This is.'

Scottie nodded. Then he had a thought.

'Just wait till Johnnie gets back and sees this.'

'I'll hate to.'

'And poor old Bill Parrish too. He's due soon. Can you imagine what he'll say when he arrives in Comitarla to find we've come here?'

'I can.'

The Major took out his cigarettes. They were drenched. His dismay and annoyance found an outlet in a fierce scratching of his prickly heat. He whipped off his tunic and went outside, standing in the rain and letting it beat down on his pricked, raw skin.

Then he shivered and came back inside the basha. 'They say it's good for it.'

'What's good for what?'

'Rain for prickly heat, you dope. I wasn't having a bath.'

'I don't follow.'

'Don't bother.'

Together they watched the rain. They could feel the sweat gathering on neck, in armpits and in crutch. It tickled the skin as it flowed freely beneath their clothes.

'Perhaps,' the Major began, 'perhaps . . .'

'What?'

'I'm a dope. I was thinking perhaps there are some women.'

He made a vague gesture in front of him that dismissed the possibility. In Prulli there was nothing.

When the news of the move had first come through and the Major told Jim to return the ammunition to the dump, Jim had called for Moti Ram.

So far, the men in Three Section had hardly emerged for him as individuals. They were Johnnie's men, and as such he felt he knew quite a lot about them. Moti Ram, for instance. The Jemadar came in smiling. He saluted, and Jim offered him a cigarette.

'Thank you, sir.'

Nimu, in the background, came forward and struck a match.

'Thanks, Nimu. Look, Sahib. We're moving.'

'Where to, sir?'

'A place called Prulli.'

Moti Ram grimaced. 'This is a bad place.'

'Yes. Captain Brown said as much the other night.'

'He knew about this move, sir?'

47

'No. He just mentioned Prulli. The point is, Sahib, we've got to send all the ammunition back to the dump.'

'When, sir?'

'Right away. We're to move first thing tomorrow morning. Some extra transport'll be allotted from one of the Transport Companies here.'

'There is no rear party, sir? No handing over?'

'Not as far as I know, Sahib. Major Sahib told me all of us go, lock, stock, and barrel.' Moti Ram looked puzzled and Nimu said, 'Lock, stock, and barrel, Sahib? You are not knowing what is the meaning of this?'

Moti Ram pursed his lips. If Johnnie had been there he would have spread his hands and shrugged his shoulders. But, he thought, it was not part of the game for Nimu to make fun of him in front of the new officer.

He said, 'I am knowing what is the meaning. You had better be off to pack your things, Nimuji. Even the babu must be in step with the section.' Nimu went back to his own office. The Jemadar, pleased, sat down on the camp-stool next to Jim.

'Sir, there is one thing.'

'What is that, Sahib?'

'You say there is no rear party. Is there not an advance party?'

'The Major Sahib is flying to Prulli to recce.'

'Ah! That is what I was thinking, sir. It will be good for us if you go with him.'

'I don't think . . .'

'Sir. Prulli is poor and there will be no good place for us to live. If you are going with Major Sahib to do this recce, then you will get best quarters for Three Section. This is what Captain Sahib would have been doing, isn't it, sir?'

'I'm afraid it's too late, Sahib. Captain Scott is going with him.'

'Captain Scott? Then his section will be getting the best places.'

'I suppose so.'

'It cannot be changed, sir?'

'Not very well.'

'That is a pity.' Moti Ram looked round the room. 'Here when we came Captain Sahib straight away said, "This is for Three Section, Major Sahib. It is best area and best area is for best section." And Major Sahib gives this to Three Section and at once all officers mess here because it is a good house and good lines and near to aerodrome.'

'If I went away on an advance party the section would be looked after by Captain Scott or Lieutenant Johns. I don't think

Captain Brown would like that.'

'Is only for one day and I would be here, sir.'

Somehow the Jemadar was working him round to an apology.

'Well, I'm sorry, Sahib, but there it is. We all go up to Prulli tomorrow and make the best of it.'

'This we must do. Make the best of it.' Moti Ram got up and Jim remembered that he was Johnnie's V.C.O. and had slogged down here for a year, and that he was perfectly right about the section area. Scottie would grab the best, and when Johnnie came back Johnnie would think the same as Moti Ram was thinking: that he had not been on his toes, and had let somebody else slip in and put one over on him.

'I will be sending the ammunition back, sir.' Moti Ram saluted and went out. He said a few words to Nimu and then left the house. Directly he had gone Jim rang through on the field telephone to the Major. The Major's voice was faint, and behind it Jim could hear the noises of the confusion that had settled on Headquarters office.

'Taylor here, Major.'

'What is it, Jim? I'm standing on my head. Don't tell me you want some help over there!'

'Can I fly with you to Prulli?'

'Scottie's going. Didn't I tell you that?'

'Scottie?'

'Yes. Anyway what do you want to come for?'

'It struck me Moti Ram can cope this end. I'd be more use deciding on the layout for the section up there.'

'We'll do all that for you.'

Jim paused. 'You'll give me a decent set of quarters?'

'Decent? In Prulli? You ever been to Prulli?'

'No, Major.'

'There's no decent quarters in Prulli. Johnnie and I went up there about six months ago when there was a rumour we were moving to the bloody place. Well, now we are. That all?'

'Sure I can't come with you?'

'Christ, Taylor! I'm climbing up the wall as it is without carting you along.' There was a pause. Then the Major, understanding, shouted, 'You're as bad as Johnnie! God, I see it now! You want to go up there and pinch the best section area. If that's not bloody cheek coming from you! You get that ammunition back to the dump and come up by road tomorrow. Johns'll be in charge of the convoy by the way.'

With the telephone dead, Jim put down the receiver. He

caught himself thinking: What would Johnnie do now? Then he pulled himself together. He wasn't Johnnie.

For the rest of the day Moti Ram seemed to avoid him. It struck him, too, that the ammunition took about twice as long to return to the dump as it had to collect it, but he said nothing. He was aware now that the section was beginning to show him its own personality. Hitherto he had combined it in his thoughts with Johnnie; with Johnnie gone the section came into focus.

He did not see Johns until, at six o'clock, the little Anglo-Indian arrived in his truck. He strutted importantly into Jim's office, and although Jim had looked on him as shy and retiring, he was now voluble.

'It's a crazy show, isn't it, Taylor?'

'I suppose it is.'

'You're coping all right?'

'Yes, I'm coping.'

'Convoy starts at 0800 hours, y'know.'

'Yes, I know. I'll be all set.'

'Good show! See you upstairs?'

'Yes, I'll be along.'

When Johns first joined the company, so Johnnie had told him, he had been full of himself, pretending to a childhood in Buckinghamshire. He had never been further west than Bombay, but from books and from talking to others Johns had formed for himself a vision of England and at the last convinced himself he had been there; for it was a confession of mixed blood not to have been 'home'. But the coming of Bill Parrish, who knew Buckinghamshire like the back of his hand, had put a stop to it. At first, afraid of discovery, Johns had given battle. It was Bill who quietly dropped the subject after the first few days; Bill who had said, 'Poor little bastard. I'm sorry for him. Let's not make anything of it, chaps.' And from then onward they gave no hint that they knew he had lied and that the lie proved his descent. And Johns had gradually closed up into himself, working for Bill, working well, grateful for what was not said.

After a while he went upstairs and found Johns sitting at the head of the table waiting for his dinner. Jim sat in his usual place and Johns began to talk.

Suddenly he said, 'Know Buckinghamshire?'

Jim said, 'No.'

'A fine county. Very fine county indeed. Though, of course, Sussex has its points.' Jim agreed that this was so.

'Where d'you come from Taylor?'

'London.'

'Ah, yes. Nothing quite like London either. What part of the city d'you live in?'

There was a pathetic eagerness in Johns' face as he waited for Jim to talk to him about London; talk that he could remember for other occasions; talk by which he could transport himself and make himself believe.

Jim said, 'I don't like to talk about London.' He smiled; 'It makes me nostalgic.'

Johns looked at him. Then he said, 'Yes. It does. It does make us nostalgic,' and Jim could have sworn he saw tears flood into the dark brown eyes.

They ate their dinner in silence. Somewhere in the lines a sepoy began to play an accordion. A high voice was raised. In the voice there was the heart of India, and suddenly Johns banged down his coffee cup and blurted out, 'That rotten music! That bloody din!' He got up. He stared at Taylor. '*You* don't like it, do you?'

'I don't understand it and it gets monotonous. But I like it, yes.'

Johns' eyes were unbelieving.

'Well, see you tomorrow. You'll be at the tail of the convoy, won't you? Pick up any breakdowns.'

'Yes. I'll be at the tail.'

'Goodnight, old chap.'

'Goodnight.'

Johns went.

Jim walked to the open window and listened to the music. Johns would be walking down the dark road towards his own lines. Thinking of Johns helped him to shake off some of the depression that had settled on him during the day. In a way Johns' sudden change in manner explained things to him. With certain influences at work a man remained on an even keel; take those influences away and the man, momentarily lost, stumbled off in some direction of his own. Without the influence of the others in the mess Johns had reverted to a former absurdity.

And with Johnnie gone, Three Section had changed as well.

That was all. There was nothing more to it than that. Jim smiled. The voice of the sepoy broke suddenly, as if with emotion, and then resumed. For a moment he was tempted to go down and talk to these men; stand there in the dark shadows inside the basha looking towards the small pool of light where the music was contained. He took up his lantern and went out, walking quietly down the stairs. As he turned into the clerk's

51

office he found Nimu there, hunched over his table, and by his side, little Jan Mohammed.

They looked up, surprised, and Jim saw that the orderly was being taught to read. A child's coloured story book was open in front of them. Quickly Nimu made to cover it up, but then, smiling, he relaxed and stood up.

'Don't get up, Nimu. Is he learning well?'

'Yes, sir. He is learning very well.'

Jan Mohammed mumbled something in Urdu and looked sheepishly down at the table, but with a sly grin on his lips.

'What did he say?'

'He said, sir, soon he will be babu-log. Like me, sir.'

'Tell him, then he will get more money. A lot of money.'

'I tell him, sir.' Nimu spoke swiftly and Jan Mohammed rolled his eyes and wagged his head from side to side. But turning to Jim, Nimu added, in English, 'This of course is not true at all, sir.' He sat down. 'We are paid very badly.'

'Don't worry, Nimu. You'll save a lot in Prulli.'

'All except soul, sir.'

Jim laughed. 'Well,' he said at last, 'I'm off to bed. It's an early start, don't forget.'

'There will be a lot of time to sleep, sir, in the truck. I am thinking if Lieutenant Johns Sahib is leading convoy then we wake up in Dimapur, isn't it, sir?'

Somewhat taken aback by such frank criticism of Johns, Jim found nothing to say.

'Only leg-pulling, sir. Afraid we shall arrive Prulli all too soon.'

'I'm afraid so. Goodnight, Nimu.'

'Goodnight, sir.'

Jim returned upstairs. The lantern he carried threw distorted shadows upon the bare wall of the verandah that led to his bedroom; Johnnie's bedroom. The bedroom itself was dark. He set the lantern by the side of the charpoy around which the mosquito net had been let down. Then he undressed and climbed in beneath the net. He lay naked and perspiring. Tomorrow, the room would be empty.

At last he fell asleep.

They should have been in Prulli at midday.

By then Jim's suspicions that Johns had taken the wrong road were confirmed. He told Mohammed Din to halt the truck in which he was driving at the tail of the convoy and got out, and with Din's help, removed the motor-cycle from the back. The road was scarcely more than a track, and to thread his way to the head of the convoy in the truck itself would waste precious minutes. It began to rain.

Cursing, any sympathy he had felt for Johns now gone, he rode on the spluttering bike, splashed and jolted, and at last came abreast the leading truck, in which Johns sat in state. The bike stalled and he yelled, 'You're on the wrong road, Johns.' Johns pulled up; his face was drawn and it was obvious he too had realised the mistake he had made but had driven on hoping for a miracle. They consulted Johns' map.

'Anywhere near Prulli,' Jim thought, 'there are no miracles.' He said to Johns, 'We'll have to turn back.'

'On *this* road?'

'Halt the convoy here and I'll go ahead and find a place we can turn.'

He didn't wait for Johns to reply but kicked the bike into life and churned ahead, upright on the footrests to negotiate the deep ruts and pot-holes in the road. In half a mile he had discovered a place where the lorries could turn and head back along the road. He was soaked from head to foot, and all up his trouser legs was caked the raw mud from the puddles. As he lit a cigarette his hands were trembling with anger and the stress put upon his arms by the effort of riding.

The jungle on either side was thick. Even now, as it rained, steam was rising from the fat, incredible leaves of plant and tree. Sweat streamed from his hair and forehead and soaked the cigarette where he held it between clenched lips. He rode back to meet Johns.

'Half-a-mile ahead there's a place you can turn. You'd better get cracking.'

Without a word Johns motioned the driver to start. The convoy was closed up bonnet to tail. Jim waved them on from where he stood. The lorry in which Moti Ram was riding slowed as it went by and the Jemadar called, 'We are on the wrong road, sir?'

'Yes, we're on the wrong road.'

Moti Ram smiled and Jim felt the smile was one of smugness; an indication that he, Jim, was in some peculiar way to blame. Then he rode back to the turning point to make sure Johns kept the lorries parked close in to the side of the road to allow the returning ones to pass. The turning point was chaotic; with Johns he again consulted the map.

'You took the wrong fork. There. When you get back you take what would have been the left fork. Now it'll appear as a sharp turn to the right. O.K.?'

'I'm sure there would have been a way if we'd kept on, Taylor.'

'Not according to the map.'

'Well, we'll have to go back.'

'That's obvious.'

Johns paused. 'You'll bring up the rear again, Taylor?'

'I'll bring up the rear.'

Johns relaxed. 'Good show, old boy! Good show!' Happy again, he waved a hand and the truck started with a jerk.

With his bike propped up under a tree Jim directed the vehicles to turn. They lurched off, and in the back of them sepoys stood, holding on to the superstructure above them. To them it was a huge joke, and gradually the sight of their grinning faces softened Jim's annoyance until, when Mohammed Din reversed into the track and drove out ready to take Jim on board, he was able to smile.

'Bahut taklif, Sahib.'

'You're telling me.'

Mohammed Din opened the door and made as if to get out and help Jim put the motor-bike on board again. Jim shook his head. He said to himself, 'I've bloody well had it now.'

In another minute he was jolting back along the road, soaked, tired.

And so, they came to Prulli.

When he arrived, half an hour after the head of the convoy, leading a lame truck which had broken down, Moti Ram was waiting for him.

'Sir, we have worst billets of all. Lieutenant Johns Sahib had the choice of the two that were left. He has taken the best. Now we have the worst.'

For a few moments Jim, still astride the bike, his shoulders and arms aching, his clothes saturated, mud and oil on his hands and face and the taste of petrol in his mouth, stared at Moti Ram.

Then he said, 'That's just too bloody bad, isn't it Sahib?' He twisted the throttle and let in the clutch and the bike shot forward, spraying the Jemadar's trousers up to the knees in mud. He rode to where he could see the Major, standing in the entrance of a small basha, stripped to the waist and rubbing his chest and arms with the rain water.

'It's good for my prickly heat,' he shouted, as Jim approached.

❋   ❋   ❋

54

Before Jim went in to supper that night, Moti Ram came to make his peace. He stopped in the entrance and peered into the room where Jim, a towel round his middle, was waiting for Jan Mohammed to boil his bath water in the old kerosene tin he kept for that purpose.

The officers' basha was long and low, divided by bamboo walls into separate rooms. It was strange how quickly even the humblest basha could be made comfortable. They carried few things with them and once these few things were in place, the camp-bed, the tin trunk covered with red cloth, the folding table already stacked with a few books and magazines, a room would have an appearance of home.

Jim sat in his camp-chair, smoking a cigarette.

'May I come in, sir?'

'Yes, Sahib. Come along.' He rose and offered a stool for the Jemadar to sit on. Moti Ram stood, uncertainly.

'We are sorry you have so much trouble on the convoy, sir.'

'These things happen, Sahib.'

In the adjacent room Jim knew that Johns could hear. He smiled, realising that Moti Ram knew it too. That accounted for the unnecessarily loud pitch of the voice.

'If it had not been for you, sir, we should now be asleep in the jungle somewhere.'

It was flattery, and Jim knew it. He asked, 'Are the men all right?'

'They are all right.'

'And you, Sahib?'

'I am always at home, anywhere, sir.'

'Good.' He paused. 'I'm afraid I can't offer you a drink, Sahib.'

'I can send you some rum, tonight.'

'No, thanks all the same.'

Moti Ram looked vaguely round the room. He said, 'Captain Brown Sahib will not like Prulli.'

'No, he won't.'

But somehow even the mention of Johnnie's name did not bring him tangibly into his room in which he had never been. It was growing dark and his hurricane lantern was on the table, turned low. He looked at Moti Ram and thought; 'He senses it too; that Johnnie isn't here.'

Why had he come, anyway? To conclude a pact? But what sort of pact? A pact between them to carry on as Johnnie would desire, or a pact which excluded Johnnie, relegated him to the past, as old friends are relegated; discarded because they are

55

absent and their personality and affection have no longer the power to dictate? He frowned. At once he saw his frown had been misinterpreted by Moti Ram. 'Now he thinks I dislike Johnnie.' Jim got up and Moti Ram lingered a moment.

'I must go now, sir.'

'Right, Sahib. I'll see you in the morning.'

'Goodnight, sir.'

'Goodnight, Sahib.'

They were left with the taste of formality in their mouths.

The mess was tiny and unbearably hot; hotter too with the warmth from the hurricane lanterns which attracted insects around them. After a while conversation died.

The Major, at the head of the table, looked at his officers, Scottie, Johns and Taylor. The rest, absent, were shadows in empty chairs.

'It's changing,' he thought. 'This is the beginning of change.'

Scottie asked, 'When do we start work?'

'Don't know, Scottie. There's supposed to be a squadron moving in soon. Until then we just enjoy the amenities of Prulli, God help us.'

He rose. 'There's a joint army-air conference tomorrow. You come with me, Scottie.'

'Right.'

On his way out, carrying his lantern, he stopped and turned to Jim.

'Sorry you've got such rotten lines, Jim. We'll do something about them. Get hold of a contractor, I suggest, and fix those bashas up a bit.'

'They'll be O.K.'

'That's the stuff.'

He said goodnight and went out, walking across the open space to the officers' quarters. 'Taylor's all right,' he thought. It was a relief. Taylor was not unlike Scottie. But he recognised the greater fund of imagination that Jim had in comparison. That could, in this sort of life, be a liability. Taylor was the sort of chap who because he felt his own individuality had to admit that other people had a right to theirs. That sort of chap – the Major paused for a moment, standing in the middle of the field with his lamp – that sort of chap gets put upon. For Taylor's sake he would need to keep an eye on him. He sighed and continued walking. 'Like a bloody nursemaid. Who'd have thought that grown men need nursing?'

At the door of his room he stopped again, and looked out into the night. After Comitarla it was like being in a wilderness. It was a wilderness. Hot, humid and savage; Prulli was scrabbled out of the festering jungle. Even the darkness was raw.

He and Scottie drove back from the conference at top speed. As the truck jerked into the empty space that fronted Company Headquarters he saw Taylor and Johns standing at the office door. He jumped out and shouted at them, 'Flap on! Flap on!'

'What, before we've even settled in?'

'Johns, you've been long enough in this company to know we thrive on flaps. Come on. Into the office with you both.' He turned at the entrance and yelled to Scottie, 'Come on Scottie!'

In the office he called for tea. It was half-past eleven in the morning and so far the rain had kept off. The sun was scorching. When the Major removed his tunic Jim saw the enormous rash of prickly-heat that tortured him. The Major scratched. Then as Scottie came in he said, 'Scottie, you'll do the reinforcements, and Johns' section'll do the collection of ammunition.'

'Right.'

'You'll also fall for any supply drops we get.'

'Right.'

'In which case,' he turned to Jim, 'you and Johns'll have to sort out who collects the ammunition from dump and who loads it on to planes.'

Scottie interrupted. 'Start from the beginning, Major. They aren't in the picture.'

'You're too bloody logical by half. All they need to know is they have to collect ammo and load it. The rest comes easy.'

But he paused. 'You tell 'em.'

He went round to the back to sort out the clerks, and make them hurry the tea, and Scottie sat down and in his quiet, controlled voice said, 'It's like this chaps – ' and then he lit a cigarette.

'The strip at Comitarla has been reserved for fighter and bomber operations. Don't ask me why. Prulli's more suitable for that as far as I can see.'

'If Prulli's suitable for anything,' Jim suggested.

'Quite. Anyway, we operate from Prulli. First and foremost there's going to be a landing programme of ammunition into Imphal. Jim, Three Section has always done ammunition so it's mainly your job. As you know, all sections are below strength with chaps going on leave, so Johns, I want you to help Jim's section.'

Unconsciously, Scottie had assumed the role of commander.

The Major, coming back into the office with a steaming cup of tea in his hand, stood in the background and listened. He thought: Scottie ought to have a company. He's better at this detailed work than I am. Not so good with his men.

Scottie continued. 'Johns, you concentrate on collecting from the ammo dump and supplying Taylor on the strip. There's another point. It's not Dakotas you'll be loading. Yankee Mitchell bombers.'

'Lord!'

'That's what's called improvisation,' the Major added from where he stood.

'Apparently the bomb-bays have been converted to carry ammo boxes. They won't take much weight because of the restricted space. I'd guess about a thousand pounds, or less.' Scottie looked at some notes he had made at the conference. 'According to the cubic capacity of the bomb-bays, I reckon they'll be filled by about a dozen boxes at eighty-pounds each.'

The Major smiled to himself: Scottie and his statistics!

Scottie went on: 'It's not a lot of weight to send out per plane load. I honestly can't think why they won't give us Dakotas.' He paused. 'My reinforcements, of course, will go in Dakotas. An English squadron.'

Jim asked, 'When do we start?'

The Major sat down at his desk. 'Straight away, Jim.'

'Right.'

'It'll be simple enough, and while Scottie does his bods and odd supply drops I'll help you out on this crazy Mitchell business.' He looked at Johns. 'And don't you bloody well get lost on the way to the ammo dump.'

Scottie broke in, embarrassed by Johns' embarrassment.

'You'll have to send a convoy off this afternoon. Those Mitchells are due tomorrow morning and they want to start their sorties straight away.'

'And Johns,' the Major said. 'See that Jim's kept fully supplied with full lorries. You'll have to operate a shuttle service on the lorries while he does a shuttle service with the bombers. There's no fixed programme. Just full planes flying directly they're full. Empty lorries returning to dump directly they're empty. It is,' he smiled, 'a piece of cake.'

After Johns and Taylor had gone the Major said, 'I like Taylor, you know. But he got on my tits yesterday about wanting to come on that recce.'

'That was the day before, Major.'

'So it was. Anyway, Taylor's all right. I hope Johnnie doesn't spoil him.'

'Shall we go through my notes, Major, and see if we've forgotten anything?'

'Good idea.' They sat together, and Scottie began sorting his papers. There was, with Scottie, a feeling of satisfaction that there was a job to do; a confidence that it would be done well. And when they were working again the Major told himself that he would not be worried about the company, or the men, or the officers individually. Perhaps a resting period was a time to sum up the past and assess the future; a breathing space in which to re-group energy; a time granted to a man to help him see pitfalls. He breathed out; then took the cigarette Scottie was offering him. He was filled with a super-abundant goodwill; a driving energy; an urgent wish to fulfil whatever task came his way.

He thought: 'This is what makes us stick together. Work. Without it we could be lost.'

5

In the evening Scottie and the Major watched the men arriving from reinforcement camps. They came in convoy, and after climbing out of the lorries they stood in groups, waiting to be directed to the rows of empty bashas beyond the loading apron where they would sleep and wait; wait perhaps all the next day, even two days; more; an infinite capacity for waiting seemed even that evening to have settled on their shoulders. It was Scottie's job, in liaison with the temporary camp staff, to get the men on to the planes which might come tomorrow; or the day after; to continue loading them until the convoys had ceased to deposit more at the field and the bashas were empty again.

The conducting of a reinforcement lift was an unpopular job in the company. Scottie with his tact, his lack, too, of imagination was the most successful at it, for the sight of these men gazing into the sky as if praying it to remain empty could be depressing; as depressing as lining them up on the apron by the planes which landed with stretcher borne wounded.

When the last group of men had been allotted quarters the Major turned to Scottie. 'Well, that's your little job ready. All we need now is the Mitchells for the ammo.'

And on the following day twenty-four Mitchell bombers, marked with the white American star, flew in like a swarm of angry hornets; their strangely shaped wings making them look arrogant, aggressive.

'The Americans,' thought the Major as he stood watching them with Jim beside him, 'do things with style – like Johnnie.' The lumbering Dakotas of the English and Canadian Squadrons would come in well spaced, at decent invervals; but now the sky was loud and heavy with bombers circling the field, one touching down almost before the one it followed had decently taxied to the end of the runway and off on to the loading apron. Drawn up at the side of the road were the first half-dozen lorries that carried ammunition loads. The Mitchells bunched and grouped close together and opened their bomb-bays with an air of grotesque hunger.

The Major saw that Jim would have his work cut out. 'These Yanks,' he said, 'need watching. They're so keen to get into the air and bump up their flying hours you'll have difficulty keeping 'em on the ground long enough to get loaded up.'

And so it was. The bombers, perversely, were based at Comitarla, so one of the lounging crew told the Major. They would fly in from there every morning to get their loads. The trip to Imphal would take an hour; no more; they'd get in two trips a day, and return to Comitarla at night.

The pilot who explained this looked around at the airfield.

'Christ! Major. There's piss-all in this dump.'

'Only us.' The Major peered into the open bomb-bay, and the pilot, chewing, watched him amusedly.

'We oughta be bombed up. Your army's crazy.'

The Major, looking at the pathetic improvised shelving inside the bays, was inclined to agree. 'It doesn't seem worth it, I grant you.'

'I should worry, though. I still clock up my hours an' get my tour filled in.' The pilot went away to talk to his crew. The Major, turning, found Jim behind him.

'It's a sod, Jim. You'll have to manhandle the ammo quite a distance. You can't back up lorries to these bastards.'

They whistled the first lorry up and watched as the bomb-bay was gradually filled with boxes of .303.

'Scottie's right.' The Major grimaced. 'Twelve boxes. Nine hundred and sixty pounds. A Dakota takes seven thousand. O.K., Jim, do your best on those lines.'

As soon as the loading was finished the crew climbed back in, and in a moment or two the bomb-doors swung back into position.

Before more than two or three planes had been filled the first was streaking across the runway. And in an hour, the end of the runway was thick with jockeying Mitchells swinging their tails, shaking their flaps, hunching themselves to hurtle forward and throw themselves into the air; one; two; three; four. Two craft taking the strip at once. It wove itself into an ear-splitting, audible pattern. And when the last had gone – late, shamefaced almost, rising with an air of angry frustration, the first Dakota was seen circling Prulli, and Scottie, watching from his tiny hut turned to the infantry officer who sat reading and said, 'First one.'

The officer looked up, surprised. Then without a word he rose and went into the blinding sunlight to call his men.

All day the Major was on the strip; and on the following day and each successive day for a week. He strode up and down between the jostling Mitchells, shouting for lorries, exchanging jokes with the American pilots who, when he turned his back, raised eyebrows and shrugged shoulders as if to say, so what? for to them the job was a boring one; a job that consisted of flying between Comitarla and Imphal, stopping at Prulli, Godforsaken Prulli where there was not even a canteen, to have a crowd of Indians getting under their feet in such a way that their tempers soon shortened. They did not see that to the Major the Mitchell operation was something else: a problem and a problem solved; a new improvisation in a campaign of improvisation.

But as the Major grew more voluble the men in Three Section became silent and morose. To the Major their silence indicated that they were tired. More exhortation was needed, and he gave it. His energy was astounding; his eagerness and obvious enjoyment of the routine transparent.

On the seventh day Jim noticed Moti Ram no longer came to the loading apron but kept behind where the lorries were parked. He sought him out.

'Why do you stay here, Sahib? There's work to do at the loading point.'

'Sir, we are too many officers here.'

'What do you mean, Sahib?'

'Major Sahib and yourself. I would be in the way.'

'What nonsense is this?'

'Not nonsense, sir. These sepoys are running hither and thither. If I go to loading point then is only for chivvying them on. And this is being done already.'

Moti Ram's attitude was no surprise to him. He had been

expecting something of this sort for days. He had remembered clearly, that first day with the Mitchells when he realised the Major intended to stay, what Johnnie had said.

'Don't let the Major or anyone else for that matter run you around. If you're run around you'll find yourself taking it out on the men. They won't like that and then they won't like you and you'll be piling up grief for yourself.'

Now it was happening.

Jim left Moti Ram with the lorries and wandered back towards the Mitchells. In the distance he heard the Major's voice, commanding, calling. It was true he was being run around. How could he avoid it? The Major was entitled to stay, and he set an example of keenness and efficiency into the bargain. That was the C.O's job. But – explain it to Moti Ram? To the men? Above all, explain it in time to Johnnie?

When he arrived back on the loading apron he stood still for a moment and watched. Then he made a decision. He would have to speak to the Major. The Major would understand, and tomorrow it would be all right. Moti Ram would have no cause to complain.

That evening the Major was in good form. He talked long in the mess. He talked of Marapore and of what he did before he went to Marapore. He talked of the early days, then with a snort he waved his hands, indicating the open doorway of the basha.

'We come to this! God, we come to this! But we'll make something out of Prulli yet. When we're gone Prullie won't be recognisable.'

Scottie, aching for bed, yawned.

'When we're gone, you say. Something tells me we're here forever.'

'We always say that! Look at Comitarla! A whole year we were there. Now we're here. Tomorrow? Next week? Who knows? Imphal maybe.' He paused. 'I'd like to go to Imphal. We've flown stuff into it long enough.' He sat back and looked at Scottie, Johns and Taylor. 'Imphal is the next logical step for us.'

Scottie seized his chance.

'My next logical step is bed.' He rose. 'Goodnight, Major. You don't mind, do you? That reinforcement business is a bore.'

The Major grinned.

'What we want is some women.'

Johns rose too. The Major looked dismayed. 'Christ! What is this? Bedtime for the nursery? Jim, you'll stay, won't you? I couldn't go to bed yet.'

'Yes, I'll stay.' It was the chance he had been waiting for.

The others said goodnight and when they were alone the Major leaned forward.

'Tell you what, Jim, at Prulli station there's a place we can get a drink.'

'Suits me.'

The Major's face lighted up.

'Thank God somebody can keep awake. Come on then.'

'I'll get my truck.'

'O.K., Jim. Let me just go and pump ship.'

Outside in the darkness the Major made water under a tree and Jim walked off towards his transport harbour. He found his truck drawn up by the track opposite Moti Ram's quarters. As he got in and slammed the door Moti Ram's silhouetted figure appeared in the doorway.

'Kaun hai?'

'Only me, Sahib.'

Then the Jemadar came across. 'You are going out, sir?'

'I'm taking Major Sahib for a drink in Prulli.'

Moti Ram was silent, and his expression could not be seen in the darkness. Jim thought: 'He thinks I'm crawling.' Aloud he said, feeling he must explain, 'I hope to get Major Sahib to agree not to come to the strip tomorrow.'

'Sir?!' It was half question, half exclamation.

Moti Ram smiled, then, and Jim could see the whiteness of his teeth.

'This is good, sir. Tomorrow we work as section. We work well and I put dynamite under sepoys, sir?'

Jim laughed, pleased. 'I only said I hope to make Major Sahib agree.'

'This you will be doing, sir.' The Jemadar chuckled and stepped away from the truck with a gesture that seemed to imply 'Godspeed.'

West of Prulli station was the river and the stench from it rose and mixed with the stench of Prulli. The Major held his nose as they got out and walked through the mud to the squat building from which a naked electric lamp sent a bright glare into the mosquito loud night.

'Supposing,' he ventured, 'supposing they haven't any booze.'

But they had. The restaurant was empty. They sat at one of the two long tables which were covered with dirty white cloths and after five minutes of shouting a bearer came in, his eyes popping. There was no train at this hour and customers were unexpected, but he brightened on seeing they were English officers. They might get drunk and then there would be the opportunity of selling them a bottle and keeping the money for himself.

Above their heads was a punkah, but the ropes by which it was pulled backwards and forwards were looped and unused. As Jim and the Major sat there the mosquitoes swarmed. The Major's prickly heat began its tormenting and when the bearer came he demanded that the bottle of gin should be left on the table with glasses and soda water, and the sticky bottle of lime juice.

Then they began to drink.

The Major said, 'You're making a good job of the ammo, Jim.'

'Thanks. It's a bit chaotic, isn't it?'

'We thrive on chaos. Thrive.' The Major was pouring.

Now was the moment to say, in well chosen words, something that would mean, 'Let me have my head, the men don't like your interference.' It was easy to say; better to say it now before the drink took effect and the Major could later believe Jim had taken advantage of their intimacy. And yet he shied from saying it; shied, not because he suddenly lacked courage, but because in this squalid room the spirit of the pact, the spirit from which his suggestion would spring, the spirit in which with Johnnie he had formed an alliance, faded; in the shoddiness of the room the shoddiness of the emotion took shape and form. Here was the effect; one of the effects; and the cause no longer had the power to move him.

Despising himself, a kind of stubbornness drove him all the same to say what he had set out to. Without touching his drink, afraid of the label Dutch Courage, he said to the Major, 'Can I handle the Mitchell business myself?'

The Major seemed surprised.

'What d'you mean, Jim.'

'You may not have noticed but Johnnie's men take it rather to heart that I have to be looked after by you. It's silly, but there it is.'

'Christ, I'm not looking after you.'

'I know. But they don't. They think because you're on the strip all the time that you don't trust me. And that reflects on me in their eyes.' He paused, smiling slightly. 'They miss Johnnie of course.'

The Major banged his glass down; already he had drunk two stiff gins. 'Johnnie's a bloody fool.'

Jim felt constrained to say, 'Not really you know.'

64

'Why? Why don't you think he's a fool?'

'He's got his section. He makes them work. If his way of doing it seems to us a bit far-fetched, perhaps that's our loss. I don't know.' He took a gulp from his drink.

Now that he had begun talking he was aware of Johnnie. The shoddiness receded into the background. The pact was still there. He clung to it because the Major's eyes were suddenly hostile.

'I don't want Johnnie to spoil you, Jim. Remember what I told you. You are you and Johnnie is Johnnie. Somehow you've got to work together without being trodden down by him. If I didn't actually say so before, that's what I meant. Trodden down.' He drank. 'Don't be trodden down. That business about the recce, remember?'

'Yes.'

'That wasn't you talking. That was Johnnie and his section talking.'

'Let's say it was the section talking. I was speaking for it.'

'Are you a bolshie?'

'No, sir.'

The 'sir' relieved the tension that had come. The Major grinned; then he poured more gin into their glasses.

'There's only room for one Johnnie,' he said, thickly. 'I'm not going to have you acting like him as well.'

'I'm sorry.'

The Major watched him. He thought: He brings back the problems; brings back the worries. I won't be worried.

There was a line to take; the line of least resistance perhaps, but a valid line nonetheless; one had to appreciate a situation; perhaps gain time as well.

'All right, Jim. You can carry on by yourself tomorrow.'

Jim nodded and drank up; but there was no taste of victory; no taste of victory at all. Perhaps one thrived on opposition and no difficulties; just as the Major had said the company thrived on places like Prulli which were a challenge to body and soul. They talked of other things. At one point the Major, as if recalling something to mind, broke in on what Jim was saying.

'Mind you,' he said. 'If you slip up at all either tomorrow or any other time, I *will* be after you.'

This sort of thing was never a success, the Major told himself; this singling out of a man to talk things over with. He had outgrown the need, perhaps, for such confidences. His individuality had gone; he was but a reflection of six other men; and a reflection of himself. His every action was dictated by majority will. He saw that now. And here in this squalid little room on Prulli station he was suddenly afraid because he felt there was no loneliness equal to that which comes when a man realises he no longer exists separately as a man; that to rule demands sacrifices, the greatest of all sacrifices; that he has ruled; that he has sacrificed; and is now nothing.

He grew silent and Jim saw that he had drunk too much.

'Shall we go now, Major?'

The Major nodded and stood up; as suddenly paused.

Taylor had said, 'shall we go?' and he had agreed. Had it really come to this? He mumbled, trying to say to Jim, 'God blast you, Taylor! God blast you!' He stumbled out of the restaurant into the hot night air. He wavered there, calling to Jim who was settling the bill. He turned and looked back towards the sordid building and the stench of the river quivered in his nose, and ran down to heave in his stomach. Panic took him. 'I mustn't be sick! Not in front of a subaltern! Not in front of a subaltern who has drunk glass for glass and remained sober – and paid the bill.'

There are sacrifices and there are duties and, as Taylor came out and took his arm firmly, he thought – there are friendships too; affections to be snatched out of whatever milled around in the darkness; above all, there are reasons for everything; even for the flash of the headlamps that is traversed by a bright stream as water is made by their light; reasons for men and for life and for death; and reasons for being in Prulli; and reasons such as this last were greater than the whole individual will; the whole absurdity of cause and effect; the whole stupidity of mankind destroying itself; greater than all these trivial moments that made one smile and yet find pride somewhere and nod with satisfaction that a job was done and a job was waiting to be done; tomorrow.

Meanwhile, tonight, there was sleep.

6

There had been a dream of home, a strange home bearing some resemblance to Comitarla, so vague now was the home of the past; and when the Major woke the vision remained until his orderly pattered soft-footed across the rush-mat flooring and placed a cup of tea on the tin trunk that served as a bed-side table.

'Major Sahib?'

The Major opened his eyes to early sunlight, the figure of his orderly dark in silhouette and blurred by the mosquito net.

Then he knew it was Prulli. There was something else, too, but for the moment the nature of it escaped him.

'Sir, Prabhu is outside with message.'

'Prabhu?' W'a's want?'

The thin voice of Prabhu floated in. 'Good morning, sir.'

'What's it, Prabhu?'

He lay back, gazing through the net and Prabhu came to the bed and stood to attention before relaxing into an informal attitude.

'You are to go to Comitarla, sir.'

'Comitarla?' The Major jerked himself up and a sledge-hammer inside his head struck each temple.

Prabhu cleared his throat. 'All air supply company commanders, sir. There is conference in Comitarla at twelve hundred hours.'

'What's the time now?'

'Half-past seven, sir.'

'Get on to Squadron at once and see if there's a plane.'

'Captain Scott already has fixed. There is plane at ten hundred hours, sir.'

'Thank you, Prabhu.'

'Right, sir.' Prabhu rose slightly on his toes, turned and went out self-consciously. The Major sank back on his bed.

After a while he fumbled with the net and eased his feet out to grope for slippers. The sun where it slanted through the window was warm on the bare flesh of his legs. He walked slowly towards the doorway and stood there for a minute, looking out into the greenness which hurt his eyes. He turned back into the room and drank his now tepid tea. Then he called for his orderly and began preparations for the day.

The first Mitchell flew over as he was driven to the airfield at half-past nine and it was only then that he remembered the previous night and what Taylor had said. His mouth was still raw with gin and cigarette smoke. The scene in the restaurant was suddenly vivid; but only up to a point, then it was blurred and indistinct. All that came out of it now, driving to Prulli airstrip, was the sense of being alone. He had never felt so alone before.

And going back to Comitarla, if only for a few hours, was almost unbearable, for in Comitarla he had not been alone or felt alone, and Comitarla would be mocking, and enviable. The house in the old Three Section lines past which he knew he must go would, at best, be empty and desolate, at worse, stripped of all memory by the advent of other people.

As they came on to the field he could see Three Section men loading the Mitchells and he turned to the driver and said, 'Take me to Captain Scott's hut.' The driver nodded and headed towards the loading apron. As the truck drew abreast with the men it slowed and the Major saw them turn suddenly towards him and he saw, too, the expressions of relief when they realised he was not going to stop.

Scottie was sitting alone in the hut from which he directed the flow of reinforcements.

'Morning, Major. Your plane's all laid on.'

'I know. Thanks.'

'Rather sudden this conference, isn't it?'

'I suppose so.'

'What d'you think it means?'

The Major shrugged. 'Your guess is as good as mine.'

They walked to the door and Scottie shaded his eyes and looked towards the Mitchells. He said, 'Perhaps we're on the move again.' He waited, then added, 'It'd be good to get out of Prulli, wouldn't it?'

The Major said nothing. Scottie turned and glanced at him.

'It'd be good, wouldn't it, Major? To get out of Prulli?'

At last he replied, 'One place is as good as another.'

Then, with a wave, he walked back to the truck and in a moment was speeding off towards the control tower.

There, the Major waited for his plane to go. He stood on the verandah of a small hut adjacent to the tower and shaded his eyes from the white glare from the strip. He was surprised to find Taylor at his elbow.

'Good morning, Major.'

'Morning.'

'I'm feeling pretty bloody. I don't envy you going to Comitarla for a conference.'

'How d'you know I'm going to Comitarla?'

'Scottie told me. I went along there when I saw you'd gone in to see him.'

'Something wrong?'

'No.'

Jim hesitated. Then, 'I didn't mean to speak out of turn last night,' he said.

The Major stared at him. 'You'd better go back and get on with that loading. Remember, I don't want anything to go wrong. Nothing's to go wrong.'

'Right, Major.' Jim touched the peak of his cap and walked away and the Major watched him walking and thought, 'That's not what either of us meant. He didn't mean to toady up but that's what it looked like and that's how I chose to take it; and I didn't mean to say what I did.'

Then the corporal who worked in the control office came along to tell him the plane was going. The Major followed him into the sunlight.

And Jim, looking back over his shoulder saw the two of them come out from the verandah of the hut. There was still, about the Major, the touching, isolated look there had been when he had driven past the Mitchells. There had been the need for speaking to him; and there had been the rebuff. When Jim came back on the apron the men were working with a will. The pact with Johnnie had been sealed and the things it meant had been fought for. It was a victory, he supposed. But it was very small and the sun sucked most of it away.

Because the Major was absent the men of Three Section worked with a sudden flare up of good-humour and by the afternoon Jim felt himself carried along on its tide. The Mitchells were loaded quickly with a minimum of fuss and bother. He felt he was seeing the men for the first time. There was Dass, the senior Havidar; taciturn; with a sudden unexpected turn of dry wit. Little Nada was like an old friend met again. New names impressed themselves on his memory; Mohan, Krishan Lal, Ram Sarup who was lithe and tall, and the big man they all called Jai; Jai who could lift three times the weight the others could; Jai who sweated and tied a brightly coloured handkerchief round his forehead to stop the drops from blinding him.

The ball of enthusiasm rolled and grew larger; and at last it was out of control. Before Jim realised exactly what was happening one of the pilots was clutching him round the arm.

'Say, bud!'

'Yes?'

'I gotta take off and I ain't loaded up.'

Jim peered into the open bay. Three boxes were piled on the shelving.

'I'll get it finished right away.'

'It'd better be right away, too. I gotta get off. The weather's closing in.'

It was true. The sunlight had died, and in the sky great banks of rain clouds piled up.

The unloaded Mitchell was isolated at the end of the apron.

Jim ran to where he could see Moti Ram resting against the bonnet of a lorry. Moti Ram called as he approached, 'All is now finished, Sahib. Now there will be no more flying and we go home.'

'There's that plane up there.' Jim pointed at the waiting Mitchell.

'That one is loaded, sir. I did it myself.'

'But there are only three boxes on it.'

Moti Ram began to walk off towards it.

'I've seen for myself, Sahib. Get this lorry over there.'

'This lorry is empty, sir.'

'Where are the others, then?' Jim looked round. A quarter of a mile down the apron he saw them, returning to the lines, for with the exception of the one solitary plane the other bombers had all gone, or were preparing for take off at the end of the runway.

'Get after them, Sahib.'

But before the lorry could turn the rest had gone out of sight. From behind the pilot called, 'Hey! Hey, you!'

Then, with a shrug of his shoulders he turned back to his craft and hoisted himself through the opening in the bottom of the fuselage, and a few seconds later the bomb bays closed and the airscrews twisted against the grey sky.

Jim, alone now on the apron, began walking down it. Ahead of him Moti Ram's empty three tonner was hurtling off. At the end of the apron he stood and lit a cigarette. In a moment or two a full lorry came up with Moti Ram standing on the footrest.

'You're too late, Sahib.'

'He has gone, sir?'

Jim nodded.

'But if he is not loaded, sir . . .?'

'Loaded or not, he's flying.'

'These Yanks, sir. They are all time in a hurry.'

'We've made a bloomer, Sahib.'

'Bloomer?'

'Mistake.'

'This I am sorry for, sir. But if the pilot would not wait.'

'Three boxes, two hundred and forty pounds.' Jim smiled.

'That'll look nice on the detailed return we make to Major Sahib, won't it?'

Moti Ram said nothing.

The grey skies were full of lightning and now its bright streaks were above them and all the leaves on the trees were lifted upwards by the suck of the air; then the rain began to fall. As they drove back Jim forgot about the empty Mitchell. The day that had been bright with sun had been, for the most part, a day of success; of revelation. Now, with the rain falling and the red mud spattering the bonnet of the lorry, Jim felt a comfortable tiredness. Back in the lines he would sit in the office and listen to the rain dripping through the holes in the thatch while he drank hot tea that Nimu brought; tea that brought the sweat staring from his pores to trickle down his bare chest and back and collect in the folds of cloth above his belt. These discomforts were yet part of a routine; discomforts that were comfortable because they were familiar and brought a continuity into life.

And when, at five o'clock, he sat checking the typed statement of the day's achievements he found he had signed it without recalling that one of the planes had flown underweight. He checked back along the figures, looking for the numbers 240. They were not there. What had been the number of the plane? U.43. He slipped his pencil along the column and found it. On the opposite side of the page was typed the figure 960. He called for Nimu.

Nimu appeared and behind him was Moti Ram, smiling widely.

'Nimu, there's a mistake on this statement.'

Nimu, his mouth pursed with suppressed humour said, 'Mistake sir? I am not making any mistake.'

'Plane U.43. I see you've shown it as taking a full load.'

'Yes, sir.'

'It didn't.'

Nimu burst out laughing and Moti Ram came forward.

'Sir, we all are knowing that the babuji does not make typing mistakes. But this once, sir, then I think a mistake is necessary.'

'You mean we don't disclose that U.43 took only 240 pounds?'

Nimu broke in, explaining to Moti Ram, 'Disclose, Sahib. To show up, or admit.'

Moti Ram laughed, 'No, sir. We should not disclose this.'

'It's a nice thought, Sahib, but I'm afraid we've got to.'

'You want the statement to show 240 pounds, sir?' The Jemadar was incredulous.

'Afraid so, Sahib.' He handed the statement back to Nimu.

'Here, Nimu, take it away and bring it back when you've altered it.'

Nimu stepped forward and took the statement. He hesitated.

'Go on.'

Then he went and Moti Ram stood close to the desk.

'This will cause trouble, sir. Mistake on airfield was bad. Will not happen again. We got too happy, sir. Too happy because for the first time here we work as section and Major Sahib is not running us hither and thither because you speak to him and say, "Three Section is Captain Brown's Section and I am his deputy. I am enough." '

Moti Ram paused. 'We get too happy and something goes wrong. Tomorrow we shall still be happy. We shall work all the time as today and as in old days. But we do not again make mistake.'

'That's right, Sahib.'

'And so, sir, this is good. But what a little thing is needed to stop trouble coming. Babuji knocks wrong keys and all is happy. No one is knowing, sir. Query from Imphal long time coming, if at all coming. These planes just fly into blue, sir, and where ammunition is going, this is not known.'

'You make a very convincing case, Sahib.' Jim leaned back and smiled at him.

'Then you are seeing, sir? If Major Sahib hears of the error then all time he will be on strip again. All time he will be running and we shall be running also. Then this is no good, sir. He will think Three Section is no good.' Moti Ram paused again. 'This is but a little for much.'

For a moment they watched each other. Jim was surprised and annoyed. Surprised that Moti Ram should suggest the deliberate cover up; annoyed that he should recognise the truth of what he was saying. He shook his head, and the sudden anger that flashed into the Jemadar's eyes challenged and drew his own anger. He was being controlled, directed, used. Used as one is used by others and blackmailed into a lie with continued, grudging favour as the lie's reward.

Was that it? That the favour, if given, was given grudgingly? And would he find, too, on investigation, that even Johnnie's star shone less brightly in places? That his own was reflected brightly where Johnnie's was dull? That, if he wished, he could divide and by dividing rule with Johnnie?

But these were thoughts which gave birth to intrigue. He said, 'You are probably right, Sahib, and if you were in command you would be right to do as you feel. As it is, I am in command and

72

my way is to send the statement in correctly, however foolish you may consider it.'

'You should be asking, sir, what would Captain Sahib do in the circumstances?'

'Perhaps, Sahib, the circumstances would not have arisen if Captain Sahib had been here.'

Nimu came in and stopped on the threshold.

'Come on, Nimu.'

'Here it is, sir.'

Jim reached for his pen and dipped it in the dirty bottle of ink. Then he initialled the correction.

Moti Ram said softly, 'Truth is a happy thing, sir. Sometimes to sacrifice it gives happiness also.' Then, saluting, he walked out of the office.

He went slowly towards his own quarters. Taylor Sahib was mad. Only a madman would do what Taylor Sahib had done. And tomorrow he and the men would suffer for Taylor Sahib's stupidity. Tomorrow and the next day and all the days that would have to pass before Johnnie Sahib came back. It was the first time Johnnie Sahib had been away, and without him something more than friendliness lacked. He had seen the absence of this other thing in the faces of the men. What was it? Unity? Unity and co-ordination and comradeship; the things Johnnie Sahib inspired? That was it. Without a doubt these things had gone and the reins were stretched; the reins that he and Johnnie controlled were, without him, beginning to twist and tangle. If only for his own esteem he longed for Johnnie Sahib's return.

He shook his head and went to have his tea.

The conference was over at half-past two and the Major went straight back to the airfield at Comitarla, turning his head away from the old Three Section lines as the borrowed truck raced past them.

A storm was brewing and he thought again of Prulli, of Prulli beaten by rain, surprised to feel that Prulli was home and Comitarla strange and alien. In some imperceptible way even the airfield had changed, and when outside a hut were passengers waited he saw Bill Parrish and Ghosh sitting on their hand-luggage, he ran towards them calling, relieved that friends should be there.

Parrish was big and beefy with a large moustache curling upwards from his red lips. His mouth dropped open when he heard, then saw the Major, and Ghosh, small boned and light-skinned, leapt up and said, 'My God! What luck!'

Bill Parrish's voice boomed, 'Hello, Major! Hello!'

As they shook hands Ghosh said, 'We nearly went on to a place called Prulli. They told us you'd moved.'

'But you're here after all,' Parrish shouted. Why, thought the Major, does Parrish always shout?

'We're in Prulli all right. I've just been here for a conference, that's all.'

'Big stuff, eh Major?' Bill winked at Ghosh.

Ghosh coo-ed, 'Don't let's talk of things like that. My God! Leave was very fine.'

'All right for you, Ghoshey,' said Parrish. He turned to the Major. 'Know what?' he asked. 'First couple of weeks I thought the old machine'd run down. There was a ravishing WAC (I) and even me moustache wouldn't curl at the sight of her.' He looked at Ghosh. 'All right for Ghoshey here. All laid on at home in Bangalore. But me? I have to snoop around and as soon as I'm fixed up and the machine gets in trim leave's over.'

Then he said, 'How's Prulli?'

And added, 'For the goods, I mean.'

The Major looked from one to the other. They were a month out of date. They were echoes of Marapore and echoes of Comitarla. He said, 'There's nothing in Prulli but us.'

'Christ.'

Ghosh piped up. 'Who's on leave now?'

'Apart from about half of the men, only Johnnie.'

'Who's looking after the Blue Eyed section?'

'Here it comes,' the Major told himself; 'the small dig that in Comitarla meant nothing; in Prullie everything. Time and place change even the meaning of words.'

'Chap called Taylor. He's Johnnie's new side-kick.'

'Good luck to 'im.'

Bill added, 'Hope for his sake he's not like Bates.'

The Major hesitated. 'He's a bit like Johnnie,' he replied.

'Christ!' But Bill laughed as he said it.

It's absurd, the Major thought, absurd to make something out of this. Now, in retrospect, he knew all this had been said before in different ways. But things had changed. They were going to change even more. He remembered the conference.

He said, abruptly, 'What time's there a plane? Found out yet?'

'About four, the bloke said.'

'Not sooner than that?'

'No, Major. Don't say you're anxious to go.'

Only in Prullie could he think clearly; or stop himself thinking.

More likely that. Comitarla was a vacuum and thoughts were shapeless and confused. Only impressions remained and the impressions were uncomfortable.

They ran suddenly into the hut because it began to rain, Parrish and Ghosh grabbing their leave kit, cursing.

'Don't let the plane be grounded.' The Major blinked. He was praying. Stupid to pray; to pray on Comitarla airstrip was utmost folly. But he prayed and the plane was not grounded. At ten minutes past four Comitarla was spread below them and Ghosh was suddenly sick. Poor Ghosh. His air sickness came violently and unexpectedly. For several flights there would be nothing. Then he would succumb.

For a while Parrish shouted at the Major above the sound of the engines, pumping him about Prulli, about the conference. The Major shook his head and raised his voice. 'If I tell you now I'll have to go all over it again this evening for the others. Wait till then. We'll have a session in my room.' He paused, then yelled, 'Got any gin with you?' Bill shouted back, 'What do *you* think?' He patted the canvas hold-all by his side and zipped the top to show the necks of the green bottles. The Major turned away, reminded of the previous night at Prulli station. He shut his eyes and said to himself, 'I'm like a tracing that won't fit over a map. I'm losing my grip. I mustn't lose my grip!'

At Prulli, Scottie was waiting with transport. They clambered into the back and the Major sat in the driving cabin, isolated with the driver while Scottie demanded news of their leave from Bill and Ghosh. The Major knew by heart what would be said, behind, out of his hearing. Leave and the broken machine. Ghosh with jam on it in Bangalore. And by a process of elimination, Johnnie. Then Taylor.

He told the driver to go direct to the officers' basha and there, the truck parked in the teeming rain, Parrish leapt from the back shouting derisively. Ghosh and Scottie followed and as they all three dashed under cover of the overhanging roof Johns and Taylor came out of their rooms.

The Major stopped. For the first time for so long he had, with one exception, all his officers together. It could have been pleasant. In a way it was.

He introduced Taylor to Parrish and Ghosh, then he said, 'Right boys, we'll skip tea. Bill's got some gin. We'll have a session in my room.' He led the way.

A bottle was opened and they scoured the room for suitable mugs and glasses. It was stifling. The Major sat on the edge of his bed watching them, listening to their talk. He watched them very closely because he was seeing them in the old way; as they had been, with the exception of the new man Taylor, at Marapore. There had been an evening like this, then; the night before they entrained for Comitarla. Two faces were missing; Johnnie's and that of Johnnie's very first second-in-command whose name he had already forgotten, so far back in the past it was now one.

He wanted very badly to have Johnnie there; to be able to spirit him from wherever he was in India; not for Johnnie himself, but to complete the picture, the picture that was his company and the picture that in a few moments he would have to dispel. He tried, too, to fit into that picture. He failed.

There was a lull in the conversation, so he said, 'I've got something to tell you.'

As he lit a cigarette he knew he was exaggerating the importance of what he had to tell them. He, and other commanders in the field had often submitted plans to increase efficiency; any plans, put into action by higher authority, should be welcomed. But one clings to what one creates. Now one must learn to relinquish; to grow.

They were waiting for him to begin, and knowing he must adopt a lighter note, he felt half-angry and irritated because the only way he could do it was not his way, not his personal, friendly way. And so, he thought, I change already; I become the automaton delivering the pep-talk to sugar the pill that should, in reason, not be bitter; that nevertheless, because one has possessed and possesses no longer, is.

He began, 'There's a thing called evolution.'

The others looked uncomfortable and his anger grew because he had never seen his officers look like men in a lecture hall, except perhaps that very first time when, so many months ago, he had assumed command of them.

'Like all new things,' he went on, 'once they're proved successful, once they've paid their way and proved worthy of their salt . . .' he stopped and looked away from Parrish whose eyes, usually clear, were puzzled.

He plunged on. 'What it boils down to is this. For a year or more we, and the companies like us, have run our own show. We made it that way and we liked it that way, and the way worked. We've proved that an army can move with the air as its only line of communication.'

Parrish nodded and Scottie shifted his position. The old school. They rally round. He looked at them gratefully.

76

'Well,' he was suddenly hoarse and cleared his throat. 'What comes now is to prove that what we've done isn't just a flash in the pan. That it can be harnessed. That if need be we can supply men by air right the way from Imphal to Rangoon. If we don't I can't see how we'll hope to get home for another five years.' He stopped, and reached for his handkerchief to wipe the sweat from his neck and forehead.

Parrish said, 'What's up, Major? Don't hang back on us.'

Scottie said, 'We're going back to train other chaps?'

'No we don't go back.'

'What's up then, Major?' Bill repeated.

'This is what's up.' The Major drew in smoke, then blew it in a long jet upwards. When he looked down again he knew how to say it.

'What has been comparatively small is going to be big. Bigger I suppose than we've ever imagined, although if we'd stopped twice to think we'd have realised it would be.'

They were all chaining cigarettes, stamping the old ones into the rush floor.

'Well, to make it big, we've got to lose a certain amount of our freedom. We'll find,' he went on, trying to convince himself, 'that it'll work to our advantage. We'll have more time to do the sort of things we should, more time to fly, more time to . . . well . . . everything. There'll be less paper work. No more sitting down at three in the morning to work out sums to see how many plane loads are wanted to drop an emergency demand. In short, we're going to be subordinated to a staff organisation. Things like Deputy Assistant Directors of Supplies and Transport and Staff Captains.' He grinned. 'Some of us might even get promotion, you never know.'

The others were silent, but he thought Johns looked interested. The Major couldn't blame him.

He went on. 'Getting promotion'd mean leaving the company of course. On the other hand, staying in the company means more time to be with the men, less time in the office.'

Suddenly he felt closed in. He wanted to get up and go out because even as he said these things he knew they were not true; he knew that a staff organisation would mean more paper work; more returns; less individuality; less proximity to the things that had been good to be close to.

'That's really all there is to it. Sorry if I made you feel something big was happening.'

They were silent.

'Let's drink up, shall we?'

Parrish moved. In the silence he said, 'It doesn't make sense to me,' and then they were all talking at once. The Major sat back, leaning on his elbows, watching them. They went on talking together. He remained as he was, without speaking. They seemed to have forgotten that he was there.

7

It was quite dark.

When the others had gone back to their own rooms the Major did not stir from where he lay, stretched upon the bed. The smell of tobacco smoke and gin lay heavily on the air and no breeze came from outside to disperse it. He could hear the shouts to orderlies who pattered, answering, along the caked-mud pathway behind the long basha, bringing with them the kerosene tins filled with hot water for the nightly bathe. He knew he ought to wash and change himself and observe those evening rites which helped one to self-discipline. He got up, and with his lantern in his hand went out of the basha, pausing on the verandah.

There were no stars visible and the moon, if it had risen, was obscured by a blanket of cloud. There was nothing in the night except the unhealthy warmth that brought sweat with the least movement of the body. Slowly, the lantern held stiffly in his clammy hand, he made his way across the rough grass which soaked the bottoms of his trousers, heading for the light which shone from his headquarters office. There was the sound of splashing and singing and he recognised the rich, fruity tones of Bill Parrish that broke off and then started with renewed vigour each time he doused a can of water over his head.

The office was empty, but the lantern on the Major's desk was a reminder of Prabhu's thoughtfulness. Upon the desk, stacked neatly, were papers; copies of the day's returns, copies of orders. He reached out and took a large foolscap sheet that was placed under a tobacco tin. It bore his own signature. It was a copy of an order dictated days ago, at a time, he remembered, when he had been full of high spirits, full of enthusiasm. He read it through. It was brief, clear and to the point. He placed it back where it had been, beneath the tin.

'I'm a fool,' he told himself. He said it aloud. 'I ought to've gone on leave, I'm a bloody dope. What does it matter who runs the thing or who gives the orders? What matters is that someone's got to do it.'

He began to look through the pile of papers and returns which Prabhu had left there for him. The job continued. That was the only thing that had continuity. The actions and the thoughts of men hadn't. The simile, of the reins he held, was all wrong. He didn't drive men. He was at the front leading them.

'I was getting weak. We stayed too long in Comitarla and got soft. What happened in Comitarla today can put us back on our feet.' He reached for a cigarette. As always it proved to be damp and he dragged the reluctant smoke down into his lungs until its tip burned to a fiery point.

It was good to be thinking clearly again. He had said in the mess, 'We'll make something out of Prulli yet.' Well, they would. Not only Prulli but whatever place they went to.

'Make a new start now,' he promised himself. He flicked through the pages of the returns. First there was Scottie's statement of reinforcements flown out. All present and correct, and signed in Scottie's neat, almost finicky script. He smiled. Jim Taylor's ammunition statement was next. Here again was the formal correctness that showed the division between a man and his work. He looked swiftly down the figures and at first he did not notice the isolated number, '240'. He was about to put the statement in the 'out' tray where the other papers were, when a reflex jerked his mind back. He looked again. 'Some bloody-fool typing error of that tall bloke Nimu.' But against the '240' was the betraying narrative. 'Three boxes of ammo. 303.'

Still holding the statement in his hand he grabbed the hurricane lantern with his other and walked out of the office, cursing the wetness of the grass. Ahead of him the long basha was divided into oblongs and squares of light where the windows and doors were open. As he approached, he called.

'Jim!'

The grey-haired orderly met him at Jim's doorway. 'Sahib coming,' he said and Jim came in from the rear entrance his hair streaming wet and a towel tucked round his waist.

He saw the statement.

'Is this a mistake on your ammo list, Jim?'

'The two-forty pounds, Major? I'm afraid not.'

'But . . .' the Major waved the paper. 'But you couldn't have sent one of those Mitchells off to Imphal with only that weight on board.'

'I know it's absurd, but . . .'

'Absurd! I should say it is. It's no damn good!'

'I tried to make the pilot wait, but the weather was closing in and he wanted to get off.'

'I warned you about that, the very first day,'

'I know. I'm sorry.'

'You had more than three boxes of ammo on the strip surely, for Christ's sake?'

'There was a mix-up with the lorries.'

'Mix up? Mix up? What mix up?'

Jim saw that it was no use arguing. 'I can't make excuses, Major. It was just one of those things.'

The Major flushed. 'I won't have "just one of those things" in this comany!' He threw the statement on to the table and banged his hand on it. The lantern still dangled by his side. 'What d'you think I'm going to say when Army asks me if I think it worth risking a plane and the crew's necks and the petrol they burn just for two hundred and forty pounds of miserable ammunition?'

'It won't happen again, sir.'

'You've only got two things to think of. Ammunition and empty planes. And every plane must fly with a full load.'

'It's the first balls-up I've made.' Jim knew that the others were listening from their own rooms. His anger mounted. The Major was saying, 'What d'you think we're here for? Why d'you think we sweat our guts out? To see how nice it looks when a plane takes off? Don't you know the air is the only line of communication this damned country has?'

Taylor did not reply.

The Major stared at him. An hour ago the look on Taylor's face would have worried him. Now he mustn't let it. Taylor had made a mess. There mustn't be any messes. Messes were dangerous.

He shouted, 'This is the sort of thing that makes it look as if we haven't a clue about supplying an army or a clue about the war being anything but a sort of schoolboy's outing! The sort of thing that . . . that produces a Staff to see we behave ourselves! From now on, Taylor, I'll be on that strip until you're sick of the sight of me! God! !' He wheeled out of the room, swinging the lantern violently.

He walked past the other rooms and was aware of the silence in them. He had never let off steam like that. They would be telling themselves he'd taken his own bad temper out on young Taylor who, after all, was new and inexperienced. He turned in at his own doorway and shouted for his orderly.

Well; it would do them good. No new broom was going to sweep his company clean. He was the man to do that. The old broom was good enough. He stripped off his sodden uniform and stood naked by the bed. His waist sagging and the muscles on his chest had softened. He thought: Self indulgence does that; self indulgence and weakness of mind. There had to be an end to that and the end was now. He grabbed a towel and tied it tightly round his middle, pulling in his abdominal wall to flatten his belly as his orderly came in.

Outside, at the rear, his bath equipment was screened by tarpaulins stretched from the supporting poles of the overhanging roof. He lowered himself with a grunt into the shallow canvas hip-bath.

The water that he scooped in a jug and poured over his head ran down his back, trickled over his shoulders and made the rash of his prickly heat smart and irritate.

Last night he had thought, 'Now I am nothing,' and he had been afraid. But if he were nothing then Scottie, Parrish, Taylor, Ghosh and Johns were nothing also. The staff officers who were to control them fell into the same category. The job they had to do did not.

He stood up and dried himself vigorously with the towel put ready to hand. He slipped his wet feet into the canvas sandals by the side of the bath; then he walked back to his room and dressed himself, with care.

He thought suddenly of Johnnie and stopped mid-way in the action of buckling his belt round his newly pressed tunic. He shrugged. Then, as he walked out, making for the mess, he called out, 'Bill? Scottie? Come on all of you. Dinner-time.'

He led the way across to the mess along the narrow, beaten-down track and knew that the others followed, in single-file, carrying their lanterns.

The mess-waiter saw the line of jogging lights. He went quickly into the smoky cookhouse and collected the first plates of luke-warm soup.

Johnnie came to Prulli twelve days later on the plane which left Comitarla at four o'clock.

Stepping out of the plane and looking round for a known face he felt again the quick stab of bewilderment that had thrown him off-balance earlier on in the day when he had come face to face with a bored sentry from the British Ack-Ack unit which had now taken over the house in the old Three Section lines.

Apart from a few airmen he was the only passenger in the plane and he dumped his leave-kit on the tarmac of Prulli airstrip with the same sort of rebellious gesture of possession he had made back in Comitarla, marching past the sentry, throwing his kit on to the familiar steps of the house and demanding to see the commanding officer.

Here, as then, his annoyance and puzzlement set the muscles twitching across his cheeks. At the other side of the strip on the wide apron he saw six or seven American bombing planes. One of the airmen went by and Johnnie nodded his head at the Mitchells and said, 'What are they?'

'Mitchell bombers. They're doing an ammo lift into Imphal.' The airmen saw the air supply flash on the sleeve of Johnnie's uniform. He paused, half turning back. 'You just joining the Air Supply company?'

Johnnie scowled.

'Don't you say "sir" when you're talking to an officer?'

They glared at each other, until the airman saw that Johnnie was not the sort he cared to trifle with. He lowered his eyes and mumbled, 'Sorry, sir. Just trying to be helpful.'

'Where is the company?'

The airman scratched his head and called for someone he named 'Bert'. Bert joined them and the airman repeated Johnnie's question, adding, 'This officer is just joining them.'

'I'm not joining them. I'm looking for 'em. I've just been on leave, that's all.'

Bert looked wise and stared at the packet of cigarettes Johnnie was fishing from his pocket.

'There's usually one of them on the strip, sir, over there where they collect the bods.' He pointed towards the low bashas beyond the loading apron and with his other hand took a cigarette from the packet which Johnnie shoved forward.

'Thanks.'

'Got any transport?'

'I'll see if there's a truck going round that way, sir.'

'Thanks. I'll wait here then.'

Johnnie sat down on his holdall. There was a flat, dead greyness about Bengal that struck him anew, a greyness which seemed to seep into the green of leaf and tree. It had been raining hard most of the day from the look of the place. Now no sun came to brighten the monotony.

The two airmen went away. Johnnie smiled to himself, humourlessly. 'What a bloody welcome home.' With nothing better to do he felt in his breast pocket, took out what was inside and began to sort through the collection of grubby papers. First, there was a postcard with two addresses in Rawalpindi scrawled in his own hand-writing across it, and against each the name of a girl; then an unused railway-warrant, and tucked inside the warrant was the letter Jim Taylor's friend, Geoff Smith, had given him in Marapore. Another sheet of paper had some rough calculations in rupees scribbled all over it. He pushed them all back into his pocket and stood up, grinding the stub of his cigarette into the ground with his heel. There was no sign of the two airmen or of the lorry. Cursing under his breath he humped up the holdall and marched across to the edge of the runway. On the other side was the loading apron and beyond that the bashas where he might find someone from the company. Knowing he was not supposed to cross the runway he took a perverse delight in doing so.

Safely on the other side he walked over to the Mitchells. He stood close up to one of them. 'Ugly bloody bastards,' he said to himself. Then he looked up and down. It was, he thought, as silent as the grave. A place of the dead.

He continued towards the bashas. There, too, was the same air of desolation. Then he saw that by the side of the smallest basha was a fifteen hundredweight truck and coming out of the basha was Scottie. He yelled, 'Scottie!' and ran towards him.

Scottie waited for Johnnie to come up. He looked thinner and taller even than Johnnie had remembered, but the familar nervous push and pull of lips brought a smile to Johnnie's.

'Christ, Scottie, it's good to see someone in this dump.'

Scott held out his hand. 'Hello, Johnnie. Have a good leave?'

'I'll say.'

Scottie indicated the truck. 'Coming back?'

Johnnie laughed. That was typical of Scottie. What else would he be doing but 'coming back'?

'I don't particularly want to stay here. God! It's more dead-alive than even I remember it. I came up here recceing with the Major once, about six months ago.'

'It's rather dreary. Jump in, I'll drive you back.'

Johnnie went round to the back and swung in his holdall. Then he got in at the front next to Scottie who was writing a few notes in his neat little pad. Johnnie watched him with amusement.

'How long've we been here, Scottie?'

'Oh . . .' Scottie drew a line, then put the pad away. 'Oh! about a month. That's it. Just after you'd gone on leave.'

'What's cooking?'

'Nothing much. I've been doing some reinforcements. Last batch went this morning. Least, they said it was the last batch.'

He started the engine and backed carefully across the rough ground until they were on the road.

Johnnie gestured towards the Mitchells.

'And those?'

'They've been taking ammo into Imphal. Damned waste of time if you ask me, too. The bomb-bays've been rigged up with shelving.

'Who's taking care of that?'

'Bill Parrish.'

'He's back then?'

'Some time now.'

They were driving at Scottie's careful pace along the road and Johnnie lighted a cigarette.

'But ammo is a Three Section job, isn't it?'

'Yes, but you're collecting it from the dump now.'

'What d'you mean, *now*?'

'Well, Three Section did a turn at this end, loading it, then when Bill Parrish came back he sent Johns off on leave and took over here. Johns'd been collecting, now Jim Taylor's doing it instead.'

Johnnie was silent. Scottie turned to look at him.

'Taylor did all right on the strip, by the way.'

'Then why's he doing the coolie job at the dump?'

Scottie shrugged. 'Don't really know. Suppose the Major thought it'd be as well for him to see both ends of it.'

'Or perhaps Bill muscled in?'

'I don't know, Johnnie. I've been stuck at this damned rein-forcement business.'

'No dropping programme yet?'

'One in the offing.'

'Thank God for that.' Johnnie looked at the road ahead. 'What a dump. What sort of lines we got, Scottie?'

'Pretty awful.'

'They must be if you think so.' Johnnie laughed shortly. Scottie always got on his nerves with his level, flat voice and lack of feeling. He grumbled, 'Someone might've sent me a wire about the move. The Major had my leave address.'

'Security.'

'Security, my arse.'

Scottie drove on and did not reply and Johnnie knew it was useless trying to take it out of him. But he added, 'Coming back off leave's always a bind, but coming back to this is just about the bottom.'

'You went to Comitarla first, I suppose?'

'Yeah. I went to Comitarla.'

'Who's got the old lines?'

'Some bloody ack-ack regiment.'

'Did you call in at the depot?'

'Yes. Brad's staying up there you know, with the training squadron.'

'Does he like that?'

'I suppose so. He seemed happy enough.'

'What's the depot like now?'

'Same as usual. Nobody there I knew.'

Scottie smiled. 'Glad to be back, eh?'

Was it true, he wondered? 'I don't know. I'm just bloody browned off.' He paused. 'I suppose I *am* glad I'm not stuck back in Marapore. I don't envy Brad that.'

'But if he likes it?'

Johnnie moved impatiently and Scottie said, 'After all we don't all of us like the same sort of things.' Then he turned and gave Johnnie a sympathetic look. 'There's one or two things *you're* not going to like.'

Johnnie grimaced. 'Well, Prulli's one of 'em for a start. What are the others?'

Scottie made a vague gesture.

'There are changes in the offing. I thought perhaps you'd have heard at the depot.'

'I didn't. What sort of changes?'

'The Major'll explain.'

'Can't you?'

'No.' Scottie pursed his lips. That, he decided, was as far as he could go with Johnnie; leave it at a bare mention or indication of change; and he realised he left it at that because he hadn't really thought about it until now, with Johnnie's presence acting as a whip to his imagination. Johnnie was the past, and the past had gone almost without Scottie noticing it. He had woken up one morning and been aware of change and as the days went by he saw that it was attributable to no one thing and no one person. It was a phenomenon he had seen earlier on in his life; a phenomenon that, not understanding, he had come to disregard so that he could plod on with the certainty that above him and below him was another stronger life that had no continuity and because of that could be a threat to his own peace of mind. It was in his old level voice that he said, 'Here we are, Johnnie. This is us.'

They drove across the rough wheel-made track that led to the officers' basha and he heard Johnnie say, 'Christ.' He slowed down and then stopped. 'Shall I show you your room?'

Johnnie grinned. Scottie was a card. No doubt about that. 'Shall I show you your room?' he said, like a landlady in a boarding house.

'Please do,' he answered, and saw that Scottie was unaware of the sarcasm. He pointed at the long basha. 'There's the Major's room, here at the end. Then mine. Then Bill's then yours. After that we have Ghosh, Johns and Taylor. Lucky it was divided into seven.'

'Jolly good show.'

'You're fourth one down, then.'

'Thanks. It looks snug.'

Scottie raised his eyebrows. 'Queer idea, Johnnie. I'd never thought that.'

'I was only pulling your leg.'

'Sorry. I'm a bit dense this evening.'

Johnnie walked away and heard Scottie follow him towards the fourth door. He went in and saw that there was a charpoy ready, but not made up. The rest of his kit was placed out neatly. He thought, 'Good old Jan Mohammed.' He threw his holdall down on the bed and turned to grin at Scottie who stood in the doorway.

'Thanks, Scottie. It's O.K.'

Scottie nodded. 'I'll tell the Major you're back. The office is way over there under that bunch of trees.' He pointed, and Johnnie, at the doorway with him, nodded.

'All flying to Imphal stopped at half-past two, so everyone's back in the lines.'

Johnnie glanced up and down the empty basha.

'Keen types then. All working still. What's this, make and mend period?'

'Something like that I suppose. Well, I'll be seeing you.'

'Yes, and thanks for the lift.'

Scottie began to leave. Johnnie called out, 'Where's my section?'

'Straight down that track. It's the last lot of bashas.'

Scottie raised a hand and went across to the Major's office. Johnnie turned in again and looked round the little room. He went to the table which was set against the wall. It was unbearably hot and sticky and he pulled off his jacket and then went through all the pockets to empty them before throwing it on the floor for Jan Mohammed to give the dhobie wallah. As he flicked through the pile of loose change, trunk keys and papers he found the letter Smith had given him in Marapore to deliver to Jim.

He picked it up and went out and down to the last room in the basha which Scottie had said was Taylor's. Inside, he left the envelope on Jim's table, clearing a space so that it should be noticeable. Then he went back to his own room.

He wandered to the rear of the basha. None of the orderlies was there. He looked at his watch. It was nearly half-past five. In an hour it would be dark and in the old days, before he went on leave, this had been one of the best parts of the day, a period which, however chaotic the rest of the day and night, had somehow found them all assembled; relaxed; if only briefly.

He raised his head, listening for the sound of the others returning, but there was nothing. It brought back to him memories of skipping the day's final lecture back in India and coming alone to his room with a feeling of guilt. He caught himself thinking, If Brad were here, if Nina were here . . . A short run on the motor-bike to a familiar place. Then he stopped himself short. He grabbed his cap and clapped it on his head, jerking the brim downwards on one side. Then he went outside and strode off to the Major's office.

Ten minutes later Jim led a small convoy of four lorries into the lines. For his duties at the dump he found the motor-bike, while unpleasant, more effective, and he straddled it now, and let the lorries wheel past him. Then he carried on alone to the Section office, signed the few papers Nimu brought for him, and rode the bike to the Transport harbour from where he walked to his room, tired and wet.

When he got inside he saw the envelope on his table. As he ripped it open, recognising Geoff Smith's handwriting, he did not notice the absence of post-marks. He read, 'Dear Jim, I'm sending this by Johnnie Brown who called in to give me your message.'

He stopped reading and looked at the envelope. He put down the letter and went out and up to Johnnie's room. Looking in he saw that it was empty still. But on the charpoy was the canvas holdall he had last seen in the bedroom at Comitarla. As he stood in the doorway he heard feet in gym slippers pattering along the trodden earth pathway. It was Jan Mohammed and Jim could see that the orderly had heard Johnnie was back. He carried two lanterns.

'Captain Sahib wapas, Jan Mohammed.'

'Han Sahib.'

'Kidher hai, abhi?'

'Major Sahib ka daftar.' Jan Mohammed pointed across and Jim noticed that the lanterns in the Major's office were already lit. He remembered. It was time for what Bill Parrish had begun to call 'prayers'; the name he gave to the Major's new evening conference. There was usually little to discuss at prayers, but he knew the Major felt it to be a 'good thing'; little to discuss but the day's routine; tomorrow's routine; a new regulation about the mess; not drinking in their rooms.

He returned for his cap then walked across. As he approached he heard the almost forgotten voice of Johnnie. It was raised in protest.

'And isn't that just like Delhi,' Johnnie was saying. 'For years they turn up their noses at the whole idea of supply by air and then when they see it's the thing of the future they invent it up all over again and pretend nobody's ever thought about it but themselves. Then they stick in a staff organisation over our heads – over our heads mark you – and we're supposed to be told how to run air supply by a set of half-baked bloody staff officers. It makes me bloody sick.'

Scottie, Bill and Ghosh were sitting in chairs drawn up in a rough-circle at one side of the Major's desk. Johnnie was seated by himself on a small stool. The others nodded as Jim walked in and Johnnie swung round.

'Hello, Johnnie.'

For an instant it seemed to Jim that Johnnie didn't recognise him and he could see, too, that Johnnie was in a flaming temper. Then, almost instantaneously, recognition came. He stood up stright and reached out his hand.

'Hello, Jim.' They shook hands and the Major said, 'Have a seat, Jim. Johnnie's blowing his top.'

Johnnie said, 'Don't tell me I'm the first one.' He sat down again on his stool, leaning forward with his hands clenched and his elbows resting on his spread knees. 'Or does everyone take kindly to the idea of a staff running us?' He looked across at Jim and winked.

The Major sighed.

'Look, Johnnie, we know you've just got back off leave and we appreciate that that's bad enough without having to come to Prulli as well. But let's have a bit of sense. All you've done so far is shoot your mouth off.'

'All right, Major. Let's hear more about this so-called staff.' He grinned. 'At least we'll have a few bum-boys knocking about the place if anyone gets the fancy for it.' He looked round at the circle of faces and Parrish said, 'In Prulli we'd all be after 'em.'

'Don't tell me there aren't any women either?'

'No, Johnnie. You'll have to forget all that. Admire the scenery instead.' The Major laughed at his own joke. He was kicking himself for telling Johnnie about the coming staff set-up so soon. He should have seen that Johnnie was browned off and eager to pick a quarrel. But now he had to head him off. If this had been in one of their rooms, Johnnie's tirade could have been treated as a joke. As it was, with clerks hovering somewhere behind, he had to control it.

He turned to Jim. 'All right at the ammo dump, Jim?'

'Yes, all right.' Jim caught Johnnie's eye. Johnnie turned away but jerked his head in Jim's direction, speaking to the Major.

'How's he doing, Major?'

The Major smiled. 'Bit wet. Otherwise all right.'

'Doesn't need many clues at an ammo dump.'

Johnnie winked again. Then he turned to the others. 'Well, what more about the new Air Supply racket?'

The Major said hastily, 'That's all we know. Just that there's going to be a staff. Now let's forget it.'

'Why should we? Christ, it concerns us, doesn't it?'

'Let's forget it.'

There was a silence and into it broke Scottie's slow, deliberate voice. 'You know, Johnnie, it's far better for the thing to be run on proper lines, now that it's a success.'

'Now that it's a success?' Johnnie stood up. 'Only now? What about Wingate? What about the Arakan, Imphal? The whole damn shoot? We ran it then and we can run it again. Christ! How you blokes can sit there . . .'

'Johnnie!' The Major shouted, pulling him up sharply, and there was something in the Major's tone that Johnnie had never heard before. He stared at him, his mouth still open as if to frame more words. Then he clamped it shut and sat down.

'I see.' He reached for a cigarette. Slowly and insolently he lit it and watched the Major from narrowed eyes as he did so. Then he said, 'If you want some stooge to come down from Delhi and teach you how to run things . . .' he shrugged, 'O.K., let him. I'd've thought, though, that by now we'd all have a proper pride.'

The insolence in his voice was familiar to them all. They had heard it before, in the past, but now it seemed to have a new meaning. The Major leaned back in his chair. At last he said, 'Is that all you have to say?'

Johnnie shrugged again. His bare shoulders gleamed in the light shed from the lanterns on the Major's table.

'For the moment, yes.'

'In that case, Johnnie, you can get out of this office. You seem to forget that this is a conference.'

The others made no movement, but Parrish blinked. The Major looked round at them. The expressions on their faces reminded him of that evening a fortnight back when he had said to them, over in his room, 'There's a thing called evolution.' He stared at Johnnie and repeated, 'This is a conference. In the course of time I'll explain to you why we're having them.'

'That's decent of you, Major. We used to call it having a natter.'

'What we used to do is not what we're doing now.' The Major knew it was a futile remark, but his anger when Johnnie smirked was all the sharper.

'I said you can get out.'

Johnnie stood up.

'And,' the Major pointed out, 'apart from malaria discipline, my officers are supposed to wear shirts when they parade here.'

Johnnie hesitated; involuntarily he looked down at his own nakedness. 'As you say, Major.'

The Major clenched his fists. 'There are times, as well, when a more formal address would be fitting.'

There was not a sound in the office. The Major held his breath both in anger and distress that he was pushing the scene to the limits of its absurdity. Then Johnnie stiffened up.

'Yes, sir,' he rapped out. He put on his cap, saluted, wheeled about and left them.

If the past few minutes had been bad, the next, when nobody spoke, when he felt isolated and hated, even despised, these were worse. At last he relaxed and sat back in his chair.

'I'm sorry,' he said, I'm not used to Johnnie. He's been away a month.' He paused. 'I'll go and sort him out in a minute.'

Scottie said, clearing his throat as he began, 'Johnnie didn't mean it, Major. You know what he is. Flares up for nothing.'

'It's no good anyone flaring up. No damned good at all. Christ! I don't know.' He rose. 'Let's break it up.' The others stood.

They were waiting for him to give the signal to go. He wanted to send them away and at the same time he wanted to make them stay; talk it out. He groped for the right words and they waited, patiently.

'You've all noticed that I've been clamping down a bit. Perhaps the things I've chosen seemed to you to be bloody silly. But whatever I do clamp down on is meant to be of help, later. Meant to be of help when we're really operating again, and not just by ourselves, but under someone else's direct control.' He paused. 'I don't know just how else to put it and I'm not going to try. Now let's forget it, shall we?'

They nodded, individually. He smiled and a part of his old self came back. 'I've said all that and the one bloke who needed to hear it isn't here.'

They laughed, relieved to be able to laugh and as they went out he tried to pretend to himself that they were all back on the old basis. But he knew that was not true. He knew that what he had done had killed something for ever; and even if something else came in its place, something that would knit them together and inspire them to follow him, he could not help being in his heart afraid; dismayed at what he had done and for what he could never, never bring back.

Moti Ram Sahib was waiting near the officers' basha and when Johnnie came alone from the Major's office he walked over to meet him. They met in the middle of the field.

'Hello, Sahib! How are you?'

'I am pulling on, sir.'

'Good old Sahib. You'd pull on anywhere, wouldn't you?'

The Jemadar fell into step and they walked slowly across the field.

'You had enjoyable leave, sir?'

'You bet.'

'This is not good place, sir.' Moti Ram looked carefully at Johnnie, trying to detect his mood. 'Sir,' he said, 'you will be coming to see us?'

Johnnie nodded. 'I'll come now, Sahib. Just wait while I get my jacket.'

While Johnnie was gone the Jemadar thought over what he would tell him and what he would leave unsaid. Moti Ram was angry. Not so much at Taylor Sahib as at the mad thing Taylor Sahib had done, and which had resulted in their relegation to the job at the ammunition dump. He made a gesture of dismissal. Taylor Sahib was a cold man. He was formal and correct and because this was so one obeyed his orders. But, how long could the influence of a cold man last? One obeyed Johnnie Sahib, at all times, because Johnnie Sahib spoke and acted from the heart. This he could understand, and the N.C.O.s and the sepoys understood it, too.

. Now Johnnie Sahib was coming back across the field. He thought: 'One day the time will come and I shall tell Taylor Sahib we do not understand what goes on in the mind of a man like him.'

Johnnie came up. 'Right, Sahib, lead the way', and they struck out across the damp grass, avoiding the worst of the mud, or trying to, for it was getting dark and the way could not clearly be seen.

They negotiated a wide puddle and slithered up a slight incline in the track, then down it on the other side where it turned half left and split into a fork. Moti Ram pointed off in the direction taken by the wider of the two tracks. 'Our transport is up there, sir.' Then he led the way along the narrower track which, after twenty yards, opened into a long, narrow clearing.

'At this end, sir, are the men's quarters. Down at the other end are the store bashas and a wider track leading back to the transport.'

'I see, Sahib. O.K. Let's go and look at it.'

Johnnie went into the first basha and for a moment the men who lived in it did not see him standing there in the doorway. They were grouped in the middle of the room. There were no beds, but their blankets were stretched out on the rush matting, their mosquito nets strung from ropes threaded along the central poles.

Moti Ram called them to attention and they looked round, stumbling to their feet in surprise. Then they saw Johnnie, and stood shyly, but smiling broadly. Johnnie said, 'Thik hai?'

'Thik hai, Sahib.'

Jai, the big man, waggled his head, extending a hand to show the squalor of their living quarters.

'Nai, Sahib . . . ' he began.

'Don't bloody well bind, Jai,' but Johnnie grinned as he said it and the others laughed. He stayed for a few more minutes and by the time he left the news that Johnnie Sahib was in the lines had spread through the section. Men came out of the bashas, laughing and shouting with derisive gesticulation at the tumble down huts.

'Hello, Dass. You going on leave soon?'

'Soon I am going, sir.'

There were more shouts and lewd gestures from some of the N.C.O.s and Dass turned towards them, half-angry.

Johnnie said, 'Dass wants his biwi, eh?'

'Dass biwi mangte! Dass biwi mangte!' And when the chorus had died away an unknown voice somewhere in the background pitched high and thin, called, 'Captain Sahib ki biwi abhi nahin?'

Johnnie turned to Moti Ram. 'What did he say?'

'He is saying, sir, now you have no wife here. He means, sir, that in Prulli there are no girls for you.'

'Tell him Captain Sahib will find biwi.'

The Jemadar translated and there were delighted hoots of laughter. Johnnie called out, 'Koi taklif?'

'Nai, Sahib.'

Dass put in, 'They say, no trouble, but they mean we have no trouble now you are back, sir.'

Moti Ram spoke rapidly to Dass who gave a slight shrug of his shoulders.

Then he turned to Johnnie. 'Now you have seen, sir.'

But Johnnie spoke to Dass. 'What d'you mean there's no trouble now I'm back?'

'Sir . . . ' Moti Ram interrupted, 'the Havildarji is anxious for leave. I tell him when you come back then he goes. This is all he is meaning. All who want leave will soon be going.'

But Dass was not to be thwarted. 'No, Sahib. This is not what I am meaning.' He paused and looked at Johnnie, trying as the Jemadar had done a short time before to assess how much he should say.

'Well, out with it, Dass.'

'Sir . . . '

Johnnie took him by the shoulder.

Moti Ram spoke up. 'My suggestion is, sir, that if Havildar Dass has complaint to make then he will be doing it in your office as is correct, sir.'

Johnnie removed his hand and stared at Dass; from Dass to

93

Moti Ram. Then he said to Dass, 'All right?'

There were two possibilities, Johnnie thought. Either Dass wanted to complain about Taylor, or the Major, or there was some sort of feud between him and Moti Ram that Johnnie's absence had brought to a head.

'All right, Dass?'

'Sir, interview is not necessary.'

'Captain Sahib will be saying if it is necessary, Dass.'

'All the same, Dass. Let's hear what you have to say tomorrow morning. 0930 hours in my office. Right?'

'Yes, sir.'

Johnnie moved away and the silence that had fallen was broken again by a jumble of talk and laughter. As suddenly it stopped again and Johnnie, turning round to see the cause found Jim Taylor approaching them. Taylor saluted. In his other hand he carried a lantern.

'Hello, Jim.'

'Thanks for bringing that letter. Johnnie.'

The men had fallen back and some were drifting back into their huts. Johnnie and Taylor, with the Jemadar standing a few paces away from them, were isolated now in the pool of light cast by the lantern.

'Want to see me, Jim?'

Jim hesitated. 'Not particularly. Just thought I'd come round.'

'O.K. We'll be going back in a moment. Sahib?'

'Yes, sir?'

'See that Dass comes to the office tomorrow. O.K.?'

'I will see, sir.'

'Goodnight, Sahib.'

'Goodnight, sir.'

'Come on then, Jim.' They turned away and Moti Ram smiled to himself. Now the onus was upon Dass. He would not have to say anything, for Dass would say it all for him and that would preserve his essential neutrality.

As they left the lines Johnnie said, 'Well, how's it been?'

Jim felt the reproof in his voice. It was obvious that the men had already hinted things had gone wrong; hinted if not more. Probably more. It would be easy now to say, 'Moti Ram and I haven't seen eye to eye.' Then to tell Johnnie exactly what had happened. But he said, 'All right, I suppose.'

They trudged on in silence.

Then, 'What's wrong with the Major?' asked Johnnie.

'I don't know.'

'He must be going round the bend.'

'I don't think so.'

'Don't you?'

'Well, you'd be a better judge of that. You've known him longer than I have.'

'Um. Anyway I seemed to have put my foot in it. Good old Joe Soap.'

'He didn't mean what he said, you know.'

'How d'you know?'

'He said so when you'd gone.'

'Nice of him. Perhaps he'll get round to telling me one day.'

After a while, when they had floundered together in an invisible patch of mud, Johnnie suddenly said, 'By the way, any idea what's up with Dass?'

'Dass? No. Why?'

'He wants to see me in the office tomorrow.'

'He's due for leave, isn't he?'

'It's not that. Any ideas?'

'I suppose I have.'

'Well, what are they? Don't keep 'em to yourself.'

He added, 'We've got to know what's going on in each other's minds, you know.'

'If you'd said Moti Ram wanted to see you I think I'd know why. But not Dass.'

'What about Moti Ram?'

Then Jim told him. He started from the beginning with the difference of opinion over the recce, going on to the business of the convoy, the Major's constant attendance on the strip, to the final absurdity of the landing statement. It sounded paltry and feeble. The recitation of the facts divorced from their background stripped them of importance. When he had finished he felt forced to say, 'It all sounds bloody stupid, doesn't it?'

'It might to somebody who didn't understand.'

Then Johnnie stopped walking and Jim paused.

'Look, Jim. Have you learned anything from what happened?'

'I thought I had. Now I'm not sure.'

'What makes you not sure?'

'Because talking about it makes it seem just bloody childish.'

They carried on and now they could see their own basha in the distance.

'Come into my room and have a drink, Jim.'

Jim said, 'I'm afraid we can't. The Major's put a stop to drinking in our rooms. We have an ante-room in the mess now, or what passes for an ante-room. We drink there.'

Johnnie stumbled. 'Christ! What next?'

'Don't ask me, Johnnie.'

'Look, do you want to stay in Three Section?'

They stopped again, Jim in surprise.

'That's up to you, Johnnie.'

'I know it's up to me. But do you want to stay?'

'Of course I do.'

'Right. But if you want to go that's all right by me. Just as it's all right by me if you don't.'

'Fair enough.'

'I ought to warn you that the Major and I aren't going to see eye to eye over a lot of things.'

'I guessed that.'

'And if we row about 'em you'll have to know where you stand, won't you?'

'Where d'you think that'll be?'

'That's for you to say.'

'A sort of line up between you and me against the rest? Is that what you mean?'

Johnnie did not reply.

Jim said, 'I don't think that's a very good idea, you know.'

'It could be the other way round. Them lining up against me.'

'That's not true. I'm sure it's not true.'

Johnnie blurted out, 'Balls. It's always been like that ever since I joined the company.'

'Are you sure?'

'No, I'm not sure. What's the good of talking about it; it won't get us any place.'

'You ought to talk about it. You've got a chip on your shoulder.'

'What if I have? It's my shoulder.' He hesitated. 'You're an odd sort of bloke.'

'So are you for that matter.'

'You ought to be careful about running with the hare and hunting with the hounds.'

'Is that what you think I do?'

'Well, you're sticking up for the Major.'

'Am I?'

'Sticking up for him and yet saying you want to stay with me.'

'I'm sorry you think the two are incompatible.'

'What does that mean?'

'That I can't do both and still be doing the right thing both ways.'

'I don't see how you can. We'd better forget it.'

'As you like, Johnnie.'

They went to their separate rooms without speaking. The letter from Geoff Smith was still unread, on the table. Jim picked it up, putting the lantern down and leaning over towards it so that the inked words were deep etchings in the paper. It was a long letter, telling him about Marapore, but right at the end Geoff wrote: 'Johnnie Brown says he'll bring this to you as I explained at the beginning. Poor you! He's a bit of a lineshooter, isn't he?' There was more criticism there than the bare words implied for as he read the words he could hear Geoff saying them. He knew at once that Johnnie had got on the wrong side of him.

He sat down on the edge of the bed. He was sweating abominably and the cigarette he lighted was so damp it was almost unsmokable. He was befuddled and frustrated as though invisible hands were holding him down, imprisoning his limbs and blanketing his mind. Then like pieces of machinery suddenly fitting into place came the feeling that all this had happened before. He looked down at his hand and recognised the pattern it made against the coarse grain of the wood, for the pattern was indelibly stamped upon his consciousness by the duality of this moment with other moments. It had happened before; he had left Johnnie; he had read the letter; and now he sat on the bed; and the last action had clicked the cogs that fitted, catching him unprepared, his will destroyed by the impact of the timelessness of time and the realisation that he had been moving round to this moment as surely as a wheel moves round to pass a specific point; that not only had it happened before but that it would happen again in a way dictated by whatever power ordained his life; endlessly and endlessly; emphasising the absurdity of imagining that he had power over his own actions and thoughts.

He moved; and the impact had gone. He gazed round the room and remembered he was in Prulli and that he had never been in Prulli before.

The ante-room was a small table and a few chairs placed at one end of the mess basha. They waited there. There were drinks and a few copies of *Lilliput* from England and the *Onlooker* from India. The hut was brightly lit by the lanterns they all brought with them. Johnnie came in.

'Sorry I'm late.'

The Major stood up. 'Right, we may as well eat now.'

Johnnie said, 'I'm sorry about this evening in the office, sir.'

The others were standing and for a moment nothing was said. It was unlike Johnnie; and yet it was very like him. He had apologised in front of them all; an undignified thing to have to do, but he did it with dignity and the Major cleared his throat and said, 'Forget it, Johnnie. And cut out this "sir" stuff.'

They went to the table. Jim found himself opposite Johnnie. The Major said, 'Tell us all about Marapore.'

'Looks about the same as ever, Major,' Johnnie replied.

They leaned sideways as the mess waiter placed the plates of soup in front of them. Scottie sent his back because there were thumb-marks along the grey-white edge.

'You're too finicky, Scottie,' the Major said, and Scottie's lips went in and out, as though searching for the shape of the right words to make them all laugh. 'Anyway, when you going on leave?'

'Can't afford it,' replied Scottie and, without his knowing, the right words had come. Amid the general chuckles he added, 'What about you anyway?'

'I'm going next week, Scottie.'

They all looked at him and spoons were poised over the soup. He told himself, 'They're relieved.'

He looked at Scottie again. 'You'll be acting C.O.' He grinned. 'That'll teach you not to go on leave.'

They laughed again and suddenly the Major broke in, 'It'll be good training for you, Scottie. I've recommended you for a company.'

When the news had sunk in they all turned to him and offered their congratulations. Scottie looked down at his plate and to everybody's surprise very slowly, but certainly, blushed. He muttered, 'Thank you, Major.' Then, glancing at them all swiftly he said, 'I won't get it though.'

'Why not?'

'I just feel I won't. Pass the salt somebody.' Johnnie pushed the cellar across the stained tablecloth. The Major, finishing his soup, leaned back. 'Well, if you do, Ghosh'll take over the section.'

Johnnie said, 'Good show,' and Ghosh grinned ecstatically. When the coffee came in the Major left the table and sat in one of the chairs in the ante-room. The others followed suit, or stood drinking.

Parrish and Ghosh were the first to go, and Scottie soon followed. The Major caught Johnnie's eye. He said, 'I want a word with you before you go. Mind?'

'Sure.'

Taylor put his cup on the table. He said goodnight and Johnnie called out, 'See you in a minute, Jim.' Taylor nodded and left them together.

Now that they were alone, with Johnnie watching him, the Major didn't quite know how to begin. At last Johnnie said, 'Well, Major?'

'Look. You didn't need to apologise like that in front of everybody.'

'Sorry.'

'What I mean is, it wasn't necessary.'

'I thought now that we were being regimental . . .'

'We're not being regimental. Just tightening up on ourselves.'

'I see.' But he knew Johnnie didn't really see, and somehow he didn't blame him as much as he felt he should. He fidgeted and said, 'You're not going round the bend are you, Johnnie?'

'It's not me. It's everything else looks as if it is.'

'I know what you mean. But you're wrong. We've got to move with the times.'

'In other words what we were doing before was wrong.'

'Don't be a dope.'

'Well why are we going to do it differently?'

'You're so damned irrational. You're nursing a sense of frustration and you shouldn't have one. If we're important enough to be put on proper staff-footing we ought to be damned glad.'

'You're convincing yourself, too, Major?'

The Major slumped back in his chair. Ignoring Johnnie's question he muttered, 'It's a question of wrong emphasis. When we look at it as interference we're emphasising *our* part in what's been done.'

'That's human enough.'

'It's wrong though. We shouldn't. It's the job that matters.' He knew his words lacked conviction; or if not conviction, then they were without comfort. He repeated, 'It's wrong, though. What we're doing is important, not how we do it or even that we are the people doing it. When we start operating again we'll be supplying men who are crossing the Chindwin, going back into Burma where none of them wants to be but where they've damned well got to be and where they've damned well got to be kept fed.'

'I know all that part.'

'And yet because to do that effectively we get organised, you bind and beef to the point where you're bloody well insubordinate. And that's no good to anybody.'

'I've apologised for that.'

'I know. I know you didn't mean it and I didn't mean to react in the way I did. Circumstances were too strong for both of us for a moment.' He leaned forward. 'That's what we've got to guard against.'

Johnnie opened his hands which had been clasped in front of him; with a slight gesture he indicated the 'ante-room'. 'Where does this fit in?'

'It doesn't fit in.'

'Well what's it mean?'

'It doesn't fit in because it doesn't have to. It's us who've got to fit into *it*. It's a sort of gesture, if you like. A bit of self-discipline. Not bullshit. Honestly not that.'

'O.K., Major.'

'You're not convinced, are you?'

'I don't have to be, do I? All I've got to do is toe the line.'

'That's true enough. I'd like you to enjoy toeing the line though.'

'There's something nobody can control. What a man likes or what he thinks and feels.'

The Major stared at him. Abruptly he said, 'We're talking straight, Johnnie. I want you to talk straight to those men of yours. You know they'll follow you.'

Johnnie nodded. 'What've I got to tell 'em?'

'That the happy-go-lucky days are over and if necessary that you're bloody well not God and that you've got your orders to obey. Christ, d'you realise what sort of a job poor old Taylor had with them?'

'Did he complain?'

'No. Not complain. He took me out one night and got me pissed and made me promise not to interfere on the strip.'

'Did he, by Christ?'

'I promised, too. But I was drunk. Next day something went wrong. Your bloody section sent a plane load so damned short weight it wasn't true. I tore him the biggest strip of his life I should think and stuck him up in the ammo dump. And what sort of a time d'you think he's had up there? I went along one day and your blokes were being as bolshie as hell. He had twice the amount of work to do that he ought to have had.' The Major paused. 'Young Taylor's a good type. I warned you not to spoil him and I'm warning you again.'

100

Johnnie laughed. 'The section blames Jim, and you blame me. But you're to blame, Major. You shouldn't have interfered in the first place.'

'Jesus! What sort of a company have I got if I can't interfere with the precious sections?'

'You've got a damned good company and you know it. But honestly, Major, you don't understand men. No, no, it's not your fault. It's because you're out of touch now. You don't have individual men to deal with. You don't need to know so much and you can forget how you used to look at things when you had a section yourself or whatever you did have.'

'That's a lot of cock.'

Johnnie stood up. 'It's not a lot of cock. It's honest to God truth. Why did you recommend Scottie for a command rather than Bill, or rather than me? Because Scottie's good with admin, like you, but not so good with men. He never bothers to try and understand 'em as I do or Bill does.'

The Major said nothing and Johnnie drew a deep breath. The perspiration was trickling down his forehead and he wiped it from his eyes with an abrupt movement of his hand.

'I may be a lousy administrator, Major, but I command my men. My blokes *belong* to me.'

'You're a proper softie, Johnnie.'

'Perhaps. But I'm not ashamed to admit it. I'm not upset because you haven't recommended me for a majority and a company! Know why?'

The Major nodded, 'I think so.'

'Because I'm not the type to have a company. I'm no good for anything but what I am, a bloody section commander. You know it and I know it, but I'm damned glad because it's the best thing I've ever had happen to me.'

'Getting a section?'

'Not getting a section. Making a section. Perhaps it's bloody stupid of me to say I feel like this, but I'm not ashamed of it. The section's the only thing you could take away from me that'd hurt.'

'Look, Johnnie . . . ' the Major stood up too, but Johnnie moved away, feeling his hands trembling, feeling all the hurt and the bewilderment of the day tossing in front of his mind. 'You said I've got to talk to them straight,' he said. 'I always do and I always will because we don't talk any other way.'

'I didn't mean exactly that, Johnnie. You keep them too much part of you. I can't believe that's right. Not in the end. They work

101

too much for you and too little for the war.'

Johnnie raised his voice. 'The men don't work for the war! They work for me, or for Bill, or for whoever's commanding them.'

'Look . . . '

'If I tell 'em to go down to the strip in the middle of the night to change plane loads round because some bastard's made a balls-up somewhere. I don't need to tell 'em why they have to do it. They just do it.'

'Why not try?'

'Because it's a waste of time. My way's the only way. The war for them begins and ends in what Captain Brown does, what he says and how he says it.'

The Major turned his back and pulled the cork from a bottle of gin. He poured two stiff drinks.

'Here, Johnnie.'

'Thanks.'

With the glass in his hand he turned back to face him.

'And what does the war begin and end in for you?'

Johnnie looked down at his glass and then put it to his lips and drank deeply.

'We're not important. We'll skip that part.' He looked up at the Major. 'We agree on that, don't we? You said we weren't important.'

'I did. But I don't think we mean quite the same thing.' He took a drink himself. Then he sat on the edge of the table. 'You're putting all your eggs in one basket, Johnnie. What's going to happen to you when you lose the section? After all, one day you've got to lose it. Have you thought of that?'

'We're getting off the subject.'

'We're getting very much on it. Come on, Johnnie. Answer my question.'

'It's simple. I don't think about it because I don't think about after the war.'

'I do. I think a hell of a lot. You're talking balls again! Of course you think about after the war. Christ! There isn't a man out here who doesn't.'

Johnnie said, 'Maybe. Things'll sort themselves out.'

'Don't you want to go home?'

'I suppose I do.' He drank the rest of his gin. 'I don't think about it. Before the war, Major, I didn't have much of a background.' He looked straight at him and added, 'Anyone can tell that. I don't pretend any different.'

The Major took his empty glass from him and re-filled it.

While he was doing so, Johnnie said, 'You told me you sold vacuum cleaners.'

'That was in the slump.'

'You didn't get much of a kick out of selling 'em, though. Did you?'

'In a way, yes. Looking back on it, I think I did.'

'Well, I didn't get much of a kick out of what I was doing.'

'What was that? You've never told me properly.'

'Nothing sensational. I was stuck in an office. Started as office boy when I was thirteen and I don't kid myself I'm going to go from office boy to Managing Director.' He laughed.

'What else?'

'Nothing else.'

'And now?'

'Now? Well, you know about now. I muck around in Bengal, live in a basha, sweat, drink too much, having a cushy war because I'm a backroom boy on the lines of communication.' He chained a cigarette.

'Scottie can look at a map now, Major, he can look at a map and see all sorts of things about lines of communication. He sees roads and railways, towns and villages, all connecting up, but he sees 'em as ways of lifting supplies from one place to another. I see 'em as places I've been or haven't been. I see a place and remember the things that happened there, what happened to one of the men, say. You know what I mean.'

'I do, Johnnie.'

'It's the men. What they do and what they think.' He hesitated, seemed at a loss how to go on.

'What then, Johnnie?'

'You're changing all that, changing that outlook.'

'I'm not really.'

'What are you doing then?'

'I'm not changing all that, as you put it. It changes itself, Johnnie.'

'I don't agree.' Again he hesitated. 'It couldn't change by itself.'

'Then our views are opposed.'

'My men'll always follow me. Whatever happens.'

The major picked up the bottle of gin and pushed the cork in. Then he placed the bottle in a small cupboard and closed it. He turned and said, 'It's inevitable, I suppose, that we have opposite views. Don't let's make it more than our views, Johnnie. See what I mean?'

'Yes, Major.'

'You know, if I could send you off with your section on detachment duty I would. If the opportunity arises, I will. Not because I want to get rid of you. I don't.' He rubbed his forehead and then let the hand drop limply to his side. 'I respect your attitude, but don't forget I've got one too. It's a question of finding a formula so that we can work together without losing our self-respect. I'd venture to say you'll find that more difficult than I will.'

'Why?'

'Because of what I've said, about things having a habit of not going along in a straight line. You've constantly got to be adjusting yourself, even your views, to meet certain situations. You've got to be flexible. I suppose it boils down to one fact, Johnnie. That there's only one loyalty that matters. The loyalty to yourself. And it's the most difficult of the lot, because it often means that other loyalties look as if they're going by the board.'

'I've said I don't think we're important. I mean me.'

'You may think that now. When the time comes and you're faced with losing something, or part of something, it's then you'll see what I mean.' He walked to the doorway and as he passed Johnnie he put out his hand and laid it for a moment on his shoulder. 'I hope you'll see what I mean before that.' At the door, he stopped again. 'Young Taylor, now. He's an intelligent chap. He could do well with you, if you'll let him.'

'I'm not complaining about Jim.'

'I know you're not. But as I said he's intelligent. He likes you. Did you know that?'

'I'm the best judge of that.'

'I hate to say it, Johnnie, but I don't think you are. Sometimes you're damned blind about who's a good friend to you and who isn't. Don't muck him about. Goodnight, Johnnie.'

' 'Night, Major.'

When Johnnie walked past Taylor's room he saw that a lantern was still alight by the bedside and through the net he caught a glimpse of Jim leaning on his elbow, reading. He turned back and called in at the doorway, 'Jim?'

'Yes, Johnnie?'

He came in.

'I'm going to scout round Prulli tomorrow. Coming?'

'I'll be at the dump all day.'

'I'll send Dass up there. He can handle that.'

'All right, Johnnie.'

'You're a wicked old bastard.'

'Why?'

'Getting the C.O. pissed.'

Jim laughed. 'He told you that, did he?'

'He told me why, too.' Johnnie smiled. 'Where was this anyway?'

'At Prulli station. There's a restaurant there.'

'Good. Maybe we'll get pissed ourselves.'

He turned back to the doorway. Then he said, 'Thanks anyway. Sleep tight.'

'Goodnight, Johnnie.'

Jim read for a while longer. Then he shoved the book outside the net and turned down the lamp. For a long time he watched the faint glow from the half-hidden wick. Every few minutes he drew up the towel that draped his loins and wiped the sweat from his face and chest and when he did so the pores of his skin seemed to freeze; but a slight movement would draw the perspiration again. Around him, in the darkness was the droning of mosquitoes. He closed his eyes; willing himself to sleep.

9

The following day, Johnnie discovered the brothel.

It rained for a couple of hours in the afternoon; a hard, streaming torrent from a sky so heavy it seemed to weigh down the top branches of the trees. He and Jim had spent the morning going round the section area, and Moti Ram, seeing the two officers on apparently good terms, took Dass on one side.

'What are you saying to Captain Sahib?'

'You should know this well, Jemadar Sahib.'

Moti Ram was worried and more so, when, at twenty past nine he reported to the office and found Taylor Sahib there as well.

'Shall I be bringing Havildar Dass, sir?'

'Please, Sahib.'

Moti Ram went to fetch him and Taylor got up to leave.

'Where are you off to?'

'You don't want me here, do you?'

'Dass hasn't asked for a private interview.'

He sat down again and then Dass was marched in.

'Well, Dass?'

'Sir.'

'You wanted to tell me something.'

'Is nothing sir. All is now all right.'

'Tell me what was wrong.'

Moti Ram held his breath. Outside, he had murmured to Dass, 'Think well, Dass. You and Johnnie Sahib will not be alone.' Dass swallowed and looked at Jim and then from the corners of his eyes at Moti Ram, whose face, to him, was expressionless. He swallowed again. 'Was private matter, sir.'

The Jemadar broke in, 'Private matter, Havildarji? Personal, is that what you are meaning?'

'Sahib?'

'Family matter?'

Dass looked relieved. 'Yes, sir. Family matter.'

'You know you can always tell me, Dass,' said Johnnie. 'What was the family matter?'

Dass found himself fixed by the frank stare of Johnnie Sahib. Again he swallowed and plunged into his lie, knowing that Johnnie Sahib would see right through it.

'It was my baby daughter, sir. She has been expiring. Letters daily from my wife to say she is breathing her last.'

Moti Ram murmured, 'Yih Khuda ki bat hai.'

'Yes, Sahib. It is a matter for God. But now, thanks to God, a letter this morning tells me my daughter is again living.'

'I'm glad to hear it, Dass, Now you'll wish to go on leave.'

'Sir, I am to be going next week. So tells my wife.'

'All right, Dass. By the way, why didn't you tell Lieutenant Sahib if you were worried?'

Dass was hard put to it not to smile. Johnnie Sahib was clever. Very shrewdly he had worked the subject round to the Lieutenant. Now, a few well chosen words would satisfy honour, and, in his way, he would have made his complaint.

'Sir, I did not wish to burden new officer with my troubles, for new officer always has troubles enough to pull on.'

Johnnie looked down at his desk. Dass cast a swift glance at Taylor and found himself staring into a pair of amused but quizzical eyes. Perhaps, after all, the new Sahib also had a sense of humour. A man who could smile and accept a moral defeat had, perhaps, qualities one would learn to admire.

Johnnie said, 'Well, Dass, you know very well that Taylor Sahib is here to do whatever he can for you. You won't keep such things from him again, will you?'

'No, sir. This was wrong. But I did not wish to overburden him.'

'I'm sure Lieutenant Sahib appreciates that.'

'Sir.'

'Right, Dass. Today I want you to take over at the ammo dump. Moti Ram Sahib is to stay here and Taylor Sahib and I are going to recce round Prulli.'

'Sir.'

'Right, Dass.'

Moti Ram drew himself up and shouted, 'Salute! About turn! Quick march!'

When they were alone Johnnie turned to Jim and grinned.

'If you hadn't been here he'd have said things he'd have been sorry for. As it is he'll go away completely satisfied and the boys in the section'll think he's great guns.'

'You should've been a diplomat.'

. Johnnie smiled. 'So should Dass. That lie of his now, about the daughter. It was pretty good for more or less the spur of the moment. You notice he chose his daughter rather than his son?'

'What's the difference?'

'He knew that if it'd been his son I couldn't have accepted the lie because he's a Hindu and if his son had been expiring a proper Hindu would've taken French leave rather than stay put and say nothing.' Johnnie got up. 'It's just a question of knowing how their minds work and giving 'em a chance to have their say.' He paused. 'They'll forget all that's happened now. You won't find things so difficult.'

They left the office and went round the lines.

After lunch Johnnie sent for his truck. 'Now we'll see what Prulli's really made of.'

In the daylight the restaurant at Prulli station looked even more squalid to Jim, and Johnnie paused on the threshold and said, 'Cripes!' Outside, the rain was streaming down and they had taken refuge, hoping to get some coffee.

A voice called, 'Afternoon, sir,' and looking into the far corner they saw a British staff-sergeant getting to his feet.

Johnnie went across. 'Hello, sergeant. Christ, this is a dump, isn't it?'

'I suppose it is, sir.'

'Can we get coffee?'

'Yes, sir.' The sergeant turned towards the kitchen and yelled, 'Koi hai?' Then he said. 'He'll come in a minute.'

Jim had no doubt that whoever 'he' was, would. No man,

soldier or civilian, could fail to answer that peremptory summons which had been born and bred on the parade ground. They sat down together and while the bearer ran in and out and returned quickly with coffee, Jim looked at the sergeant's uniform in astonishment. Khaki, instead of jungle-green, which in itself seemed to indicate a refusal to take a step along the road to perdition, it shone with starch; the collar was pressed and neatly folded open about the thick neck. The sleeves were rolled up and Jim swore that if he had taken a ruler and measured the width of the roll he would have found it exactly the regulation three inches. The arms which were exposed were covered with fine, golden hair; hair that on the short cropped head was shot with ginger. Obviously a regular, his whole body exuded a grim confidence in its own fitness and cleanliness. And the man, miraculously, was not sweating.

The sergeant's voice was clipped and Jim noticed he had not yet smiled, but when he asked him, 'What d'you think of Prulli?' a smile, if forbidding, came at last.

'I'm used to it, sir. Been here a year.'

Johnnie said, 'I've only been here since yesterday and I don't think much of it.'

The sergeant seemed to consider this, then he replied, 'Any place is what you make it.'

'What in hell can you make out of Prulli?'

'It depends what you want out of it, sir. Most places have got what you want if you bother to look.'

'There don't seem to be any girls, so's you'd notice.'

The sergeant was silent. Jim leaned back and said, smiling, 'if you've been here a year I expect you've got yourself organised a bit.'

'I have, sir.'

Jim looked away; probably, he thought, the dhobie's wife, brought to his billet on Saturday evenings as regular as clockwork.

'How many of you are there, sir?'

'What d'you mean, sergeant?' Johnnie was puzzled.

'How many officers in your unit?'

'Seven. Six at present because one's on leave.' He offered his cigarettes.

'I can fix up girls for you.'

'Christ!'

'When d'you want 'em, sir?'

'What a question.'

'Why not? No time like the present.'

'Ten o'clock?'

'O.K. Ten o'clock.'

'Six officers?'

'Well – we'll see.'

'As many as like to come. Not more than six, though, sir.'

'We'll be here.'

'There's one thing, sir.' The sergeant looked from one to the other. 'You'll understand I can't be held responsible?'

'What for?'

'It'll be out of bounds, sir.'

'I see. Where is it?'

'Across the river. A little place I know.'

'A brothel?'

The sergeant looked rather hurt. 'A house, sir.' Then he glanced at the doorway. 'Don't come if it's wet, sir. It's rather uncomfortable in the boat.'

Johnnie burst out laughing. 'All right, sergeant. We won't come if it's wet.'

On the way back, bouncing along in the truck, Johnnie said, 'Just you and me, Jim. And perhaps the Major. Poor old sod likes his bit of crumpet.' There had been that time long ago, in Calcutta. Johnnie felt suddenly on top of the world again; pleased with himself that he should be the one to discover the existence of girls in Prulli. He felt warm towards Jim and to the Major and the anticipation of the evening ahead drove all feelings of resentment away.

When they got back they had tea in Three Section office and then it was time for 'prayers'. And at prayers, Johnnie could not resist blurting out, as the meeting broke up, 'Christ, you blokes are slow. Here you've been in Prulli for four weeks, and I've only been here twenty-four hours.'

The Major asked, 'What does that mean?'

'I've got some women laid on for us.'

Scottie said, 'One of Johnnie's little jokes,' but Bill Parrish raised his hand. 'Johnnie never jokes about this sort of thing. Come on Johnnie, what've you found?'

'What I said. All neat and laid on by a British staff-sergeant. Backbone of the British Army.'

He explained what had happened at Prulli Station.

The Major wiped the sweat from the back of his neck.

'Are you serious?'

' 'Course I'm serious. Well . . . ' he looked round at them. 'Who's coming?'

The Major laughed. 'I imagine it's a case of who's not coming. Take less time to find out. Anyway, that's simple. Someone's got to be duty officer.' They all looked at Scottie whose lips were going in and out like pistons. He said. 'Why look at me?'

When the laughter had subsided Ghosh stood up and said, 'I will stay, Major. I am married man with six children.'

'Nobody would have thought so in Comitarla.'

'In Comitarla I was so long without leave.'

'Good old Ghoshey.'

'Good show, Ghosh.'

'I'll come some other time.'

They trooped out of the office and in half-an-hour the news that the Sahibs were going with women was all round the company; and when, at nine o'clock, they all piled into Johnnie's truck, Mohammed Din was grinning broadly.

The Major, sitting beside him, said, 'Kya bat? Bloody grinning all over your face. Kya bat?'

Din shook his head and the white teeth gleamed from the lights in the dashboard.

'Biwi, Sahib?'

'How the bloody hell do you know?'

'Sahib?'

'Thik hai, Jeldi karo.'

The truck shot off with a jerk and there were cries of consternation in the back. The Major chuckled. He looked at his watch. There would be time for a few pleasant drinks at the station before Johnnie's sergeant arrived to conduct them over the river. The truck swayed and slithered in the mud, for Din drove recklessly, entering into the spirit of the outing, and the Major suddenly laughed aloud; a truck load of officers belting down to Prulli as if all the devils in hell were after them; it was absurd; but from the shouts of laughter in the back the Major knew they were all aware of the absurdity. A spree, for such it could be called, did them as much good, he thought, as a dozen bottles of tonic; it brought them all together again, not through a relaxation of the new discipline that had put a restraining hand upon their evenings in the mess, but through a recognition of equality of behaviour. He blessed Johnnie for his discovery.

When they got out at Prulli, the Major told the driver to return at half-past eleven, and to wait for them if they had not got back by then. They trooped, then, into the restaurant and piled their caps on the end of one of the long tables. Scottie said, 'We ought not to have gin.'

'In our condition we don't need champagne and oysters.' Bill Parrish winked and they sat down and banged on the table for the waiter. 'We'll have a bottle and take it with us if we don't finish it here,' the Major suggested. A bottle was brought and one of them said, 'Why can't they get the punkah working?' The Major studied them. In the harsh glare of the naked electric bulb they looked different; their skins were, beneath the warmth of excitement, sallow and drawn and opaque. Not one of them had been in India for less than a year; he and Scottie – what was it – *two* and a half years? He drank his gin and stopped thinking, for thoughts such as these brought thoughts of home in their wake.

At ten o'clock the bearer came in and bent to whisper in Johnnie's ear. Their conversation stopped and Johnnie got up. 'Hold on here a minute.'

'Where's the sergeant?'

'Outside.'

'Don't tell me he's shy?'

Johnnie grabbed his cap from the pile and went out. His eyes still dazzled by the light inside, saw nothing in the darkness. Then a familiar voice spoke to him. 'Good evening, sir.'

'That you, sergeant?'

'Yes, sir.'

He saw now the vague outline of the sergeant's figure and went to join him. 'Won't you come and have a drink?'

'No thank you, sir. It's time to be going.'

'Right, I'll get the others.'

'How many, sir?'

'Five.'

The sergeant pointed to his left. 'I'll be waiting just there by that small hut.'

'Right. I'll bring 'em along.'

The sergeant faded into the deep shadows and Johnnie went back to the door of the restaurant. He called, 'O.K.', and the others rose, scraping back their chairs, sorting out their caps. When they were all gathered outside Johnnie said, 'Follow me,' and went off towards the hut.

The Major said, 'All aboard for the Skylark,' and Bill laughed. Low, but clear, the sergeant's voice carried to them; 'Not too much noise, please, gentlemen.'

Their chatter ceased abruptly and in silence they followed as

111

the sergeant led the way over the railway tracks and then downwards through a jumble of tackle, nets and baskets. The air was suddenly fresher with a light breeze from the open river and they could hear the soft ripple of water. Johnnie, at the front, saw the dark shapes of shallow boats and then a hand came out and clasped him round the arm; 'Steady on, sir, it's slippery.'

The lapping of the water was beneath him. There were duckboards leading on to a short, ramshackle jetty alongside which was one of the boats with a low canopy amidships. The sergeant, in front, stopped. 'In you go, sir.' Johnnie stepped off the jetty and beneath his feet was the insecurity of floating wood. He hunched himself low and made for the canopy, crouching at last beneath it. The others were coming. He stretched his hand out and whispered, 'Major?' 'Johnnie?' 'Sit down here.' The Major sat and said, 'Christ, this takes the biscuit.' The narrow boat rocked as the rest came on board. In a moment or two they were all crowded beneath the canopy. At the prow was the dark figure of the oarsman. Behind them, another man. The sergeant's khaki-drill uniform stood out clearly in the blackness. He came on board last and knelt outside the canopy, unconsciously assuming one of the traditional firing positions. Then they moved out into the stream.

It took twenty minutes to reach the other side and at one time they imagined they were being carried swiftly downstream by the current, away from their objective. The river looked immensely wide and the land on either side lay dark and silent as though sleeping. The lap of the oars came rhythmically and was the only sound in the world, until, in the distance, arose the mournful cries of jackals, hunting. The cries, though faint, came clear as bells across the water, echoing and echoing from side to side of the river, then fading away as the river wind changed direction.

The far bank loomed. In a few minutes the oarsmen shipped and let the boat drift inshore. Leading up from the water were some steps hewn roughly from stone. The oarsman at the prow leaned over and grasped the root of a tree whach was bared by the receding earth of the bank. The night seemed now intensely luminous, although there was no moon.

When they were all ashore they stood in a group until the sergeant said in his low, resonant voice. 'This way, gentlemen.' He went off along a narrow pathway which led between tall trees and out, after twenty yards or so, into a clearing where, in the shadows, they could distinguish the shape of a house built on short stilts. The sergeant went up to the house and waited for

112

them at the bottom of the steps which led up on to the verandah.

'Please be as quiet as possible, gentlemen. There are other houses close by and the ladies are afraid of the police.' They followed him up the steps. The house was in complete darkness. The Major felt on the walls and found closed wooden shutters. The sergeant stood close to the wall with his ear pressed to it. Then he tapped lightly with his fingers and uttered one word which the Major did not catch. There were still no signs of life inside, but the sergeant waited patiently; then tapped again, this time with his knuckles.

There was a short exclamation from inside. The Major frowned, puzzled. Then he realised it had been a woman's voice; a woman's laugh.

The sergeant spoke again and after a few more moments' delay a bar inside was drawn back and the door opened a few inches. The sergeant put his foot in the space and a woman spoke sharply. They talked in whispers, then, and soon the door shut and the sergeant withdrew.

'They'll be ready soon, sir. Would you all come away from the door, gentlemen?' He went to the end of the verandah where it turned at right-angles and ran down the side of the house. They gathered round.

'There are three of them, gentlemen. So you'll have to take it in turns.' The others nodded. 'You realise, gentlemen, that I can't be held responsible for the cleanliness of the girls.' They nodded again. 'It's more or less a private house,' the sergeant explained, 'and my own opinion is that there's not much risk of infection. However . . .' He reached into his pocket and pulled something out. 'I don't like the idea of risks being taken, so I've brought these with me. They're Yankee issue.'

He handed round little packets and the Major, taking his, recognised it as one containing a sheath. He was lost in admiration. Johnnie whispered, 'Everything laid on, eh?' and in the darkness Jim saw the sergeant smile, as if flattered.

'There's one last thing, gentlemen.' They stopped muttering. 'They will ask for more money than you should give. There's an average payment rising with the rank of the officer.' He turned to the Major. 'For a major, sir, fifteen rupees is enough. For a captain, twelve, and for a lieutenant, not more than ten.'

Parrish said, 'What's it for a sergeant, chum?' The others looked at him reproachfully, knowing what Bill implied. For a moment the sergeant did not reply. Then he said, 'For a sergeant, sir, the charge is seven rupees eight annas.'

Then the door creaked open.

Inside, the house was divided into three rooms. The partitions between the rooms had no doors but the lighting was very dim. Grouped in the middle room were three girls, Indians, with bright spangled sarees draped gracefully round their bodies. The gold of rings glittered in their nostrils, and in their black hair, tucked above their ears, were blooms of white flowers. A little to the right of them stood an older woman; ugly, but equally adorned.

The sergeant went up to the girls and took the hand of the one who stood in the middle. He led her away and presented her to the Major. 'Sir?'

The Major nodded and looked closely at the girl. He was disturbed by her loveliness. She smiled gently and bowed her head over hands held palm to palm in an attitude of prayer. From her hair came the cloying scent of coconut oil and from her skin a pungent odour as of burnt wood; and mixed with these was an elusive scent the Major remembered from a time before. He stood looking into her large eyes which were soft and liquid in the dim light from the oil lamps.

She held out her hand and he took it. The contact with her created the desire for her and he drew her close and let his hand slide down until it pressed against her buttocks. He was aware that the other girls had gone and that he was alone with her. She drew away from him and walked over to the darkest corner of the room, where, on rush mats, cushions were bunched. She sank gracefully on to the floor and smiled up at him.

He said, 'Nam?'

She shook her head. Then, surprisingly, she said in English, 'I have not name.' She patted the mat and he sat down by her side. She smiled, wide, and the ring in her nose sparkled above her beautiful teeth. She put out her slim hand and fingered his epaulette.

'You are Colonel.'

'No. I am only a Major.'

'This is twenty rupees.'

'Fifteen rupees and a kiss.'

'So little for such an important officer?' Her eyes widened, theatrically.

'Fifteen and more than a kiss.'

She held her hand out, palm uppermost, watching his expression as he fumbled in his pocket for his wallet. She snatched it from him and held it to her breast, laughing. He watched her.

With her head bent and her eyes upraised to his, she slowly fingered the notes. Suddenly she drew out two ten rupee notes and with a sharp little cry of victory she waved them in the air. 'See! Now you are a Colonel. I promote you for one night.'

She threw the wallet back at him and he caught it.

'You mean you promote me for ten minutes, you little devil.'

She laughed again and, rolling the notes into a little ball, she stretched down and snatched the hem of her saree, knotted the notes into it, and tied it with a flourish.

Then she leaned over and pinched his cheek; and the smell of coconut oil was overwhelming in his nostrils.

'Now you must be quick. I am afraid of the police.'

The beautiful face was suddenly hard and with a coarse motion she crumpled the bright saree into a roll over her naked belly and lay back on the cushions.

Under the canopy of the boat the heat closed round them and they were silent. They drew near to Prulli and the stench of the river rose as the boat threaded its way into the shapeless dark mass of the water-front. It brought regret and self reproach.

The sergeant spoke to the Major as he climbed on to the jetty.

'The boat is five rupees, sir. Is that all right?'

'Of course, sergeant. Here.' Again the Major held his wallet and it smelt faintly of the girl.

'Thank you, sir.' The sergeant turned away and went up to the waiting boatman. There was a short altercation between them but in the end the sergeant came back and joined them on the bank. They made their way silently up the slope and across the deserted track. The light in the station restaurant was extinguished, but a pin-point of light from a cigarette showed where the driver smoked and lounged against the truck. Before they got to the truck the sergeant stopped.

'I'll say goodnight, now, gentlemen.' They bunched round him.

'Thanks sergeant.' They stood awkwardly, wondering if they should offer him money.

'I hope everything was all right, gentlemen?'

'Of course.'

'Goodnight then.'

'Goodnight, sergeant.'

The others went but Johnnie stayed behind.

'Look, is there anything we can do for you?'

'No thank you, sir. You're already doing it.'

'What d'you mean?'

The sergeant fingered the flash on Johnnie's arm.

'I've got a young brother in Imphal. He was with Wingate too, sir.' The sergeant hesitated. 'He's a bit green but he can look after himself.'

'I'm sure he can. Smoke?'

'Thanks.'

'What about you?'

'I'm cushy here, sir. Got everything laid on.' He saw the sergeant's lips part in a wide smile. 'I'm always at the station in the afternoon, sir.'

'We'll find you there?'

'Yes, sir.'

'Look. Don't we owe you something?'

'What for?'

'Well. For the accessories, say?'

'No, sir. After all, I got a free boat ride.'

Johnnie laughed. 'I hadn't thought of that.'

'I had, sir.'

'Well, goodnight.'

The sergeant lifted a hand in farewell and Johnnie went to the truck and climbed into the back. The Major was with them.

'Did he want money?'

Johnnie looked round to see who had spoken. 'Who said that? You Bill?'

'Yes. Did he?'

'What makes you think so?'

'Such an odd sort of cuss. Perhaps he gets a commission from the girls.' The others mumbled words of agreement. Johnnie flared up, 'You were glad enough to go. Why the hell criticise the sergeant?'

'What's wrong with you?'

Scottie chipped in. 'No offence, Johnnie. It was a good party.'

In the darkness Johnnie shrugged his shoulders. 'You chaps haven't any imagination,' he said. He twisted round and thumped on the back of the cabin. The truck moved forward and he thought, 'I was a fool to bring them all.' But the temptation to reinstate himself had been too strong. In the past they had looked for things like this; parties in the mess; and girls brought back from the club at Comitarla. Now they were critical of what he had arranged. That had never been so before. They no longer looked to him. 'Things change themselves,' the Major had said. It was not their fault, nor his, if what he arranged no longer pleased them as it had done. What had been right once was wrong now.

He was glad that the drone of the engine gave them an excuse for silence because suddenly he was afraid.

10

On August the nineteenth the last units of the invading Japanese Army were thrust back across the Indo-Burmese border and the Fourteenth Army began the long march south.

From the six hundred square miles of the Imphal Plain the trek back to Mandalay began and in Prulli there were rumours of moving. The Mitchell operation ceased as suddenly as it had begun and a Yankee Dakota squadron moved in to operate a full scale air dropping commitment. The company, with Scottie in temporary command, swung into the familiar routine and when the Major returned from leave he had news for them.

'We're going south of Imphal to a place called Tamel. We'll go in a month's time and we'll be operating from there at the end of October.'

And towards the end of September, when the monsoon was dying, he stood on the strip at Prulli with Scottie, Bill and Johnnie, and a handful of men, while Jim Taylor said goodbye to them. Ghosh had left that morning by rail for Dimapur, with the main body of the company, and Johns had taken the transport of One and Two sections by road. Taylor, with Three Section transport and a dozen men from the section was to follow two days later.

The Major stood a little apart from the others because he did not feel particularly like talking. This was the end of an epoch for him and he knew that in Tamel the staff machine would take over.

It was strange to feel the warmth of an affection for a place like Prulli and he knew that to come back would be to come back to emptiness like the emptiness of Comitarla that day of the conference; but the affection was there, in his heart, and for a while he let it take possession of him. He looked across at the others and wanted suddenly to wipe out the past three months; go back to the day that he and Scottie had stood dejectedly out of the rain in the decaying basha; to start again from there, not making the same mistakes, for there had been mistakes in spite of all his care. Mistakes made here could cast their shadows forward, to Tamel and in Tamel there must be no mistakes. He made a move to go and join Scottie and Bill, but they seemed

117

deep in conversation. The aircraft in which they would fly to Imphal were close by; the crews gathered round the mobile canteen that now served the field. Johnnie and Taylor were pacing up and down, oblivious of him. He smiled. Taylor had been a good influence on Johnnie, he felt. They were getting on well together, and Johnnie was quieter. Too quiet? He took out a cigarette and smoked, alone.

Don't interfere, he told himself; let them all be. If they want me for anything, then I'm always here. He turned and looked westwards into the overcast sky; westwards in the direction of Tamel.

PART THREE

Tamel

11

Below Imphal the road to Tiddim passes through the village of Tamel; and at Tamel the fighter strip had been converted into a bomber strip. Now, in October, with the grey drift of the monsoon giving way to the bright sunshine, an army of bull-dozers, pioneer troops and local coolie labour had invaded the airfield and already changed it beyond recognition. A tarmac runway stretched for two thousand yards, eating into the fields that had been farmland before the war came. Around the runway a circular road was being cut; and on the isolated hill which commanded the aerodrome tents had grown like white mushrooms. At the southern end of the runway a wide area had been levelled to make a communal loading and parking bay for the transport planes of the Dakota Squadrons. Beyond this lay the beginning of the circuit road which itself, stony and already dusty at the onset of the dry season, led out on to the road connecting Imphal to Tiddim.

On the other side of the Tiddim road the circuit continued across a wide culvert and into the fields where the air supply company had set up its store tents in a long row. Company Headquarters, in a tent larger than the others, lay back off the road sheltered by trees. A footpath led to its open door-flaps, forking just before it disappeared into the interior, to the right, through more trees and thence out into a hedged field. In this field another large tent housed the mess; and all round the field were small, one man tents, where the officers slept.

All day long the sounds from the airfield carried across the road into the company's lines. The sun described its arc over the plain, rising and setting behind the great hills that gathered in high folds on all sides. At mid-day the heat was intense and dry. When darkness came the air cooled and touched the stars to brightness. Already a thin blanket could be used for sleeping; soon with the bitter chill of November and December a man would lie huddled for warmth but in the blessed freedom of a bed unshrouded by a mosquito net. Nothing could be further from the slog and sweat of Prulli. In Tamel, one could raise and lower two stretched fingers in an obscene gesture at its memory.

The Major had said, in Prulli, 'I'm not changing all that, as you put it. It changes itself.' It had been July then, but Johnnie still remembered the words. Every day since the Major had said the words, Johnnie had remembered them, waking sometimes on dark nights with the rain beating on the roof of the basha, walking through the mud and trodden grass talking to Moti Ram, talking to the men. The words took root and flowered, every day, every night; mostly at night like a perverse blossom that opens its petals only when the sun is gone.

The road through the company's lines in Tamel turned at one point sharply to the right and continued round to join up with the Tiddim road again. At that point the footpath to the Major's office branched off, and opposite there was another footpath, broader than the first. It rose slightly for a couple of hundred yards, bordered on its left side by a high hedge of bushes and stunted trees. At the end of this track there was a wide field and in it were pitched, in neat rows, the tents in which the men of all three sections lived. Johnnie, when the Major sited the area, had disputed this wholesale collection of sections into one domestic group.

'Why don't you like it?'

'It's wrong. Sections are separate. They should have separate domestic lines.'

The Major had smiled. But the site remained.

Leaving the office, where he had made his complaint, he trudged up the hill. He went into Moti Ram's tent and said, 'Sorry about this, Sahib. I'm trying to get us moved over into the other field.'

'This is all right, sir. We are at home anywhere. We must all pull on together, sir.'

'Getting the company spirit, eh, Sahib?'

'Sir, so many changes. This is a small matter that we shall all live together.'

'You're content to stay here?'

'Yes, sir. We do not wish to make difficulties for anybody. And perhaps we shall not be here long. War may soon be over.'

'You kicked up enough stink about the lines in Prulli.'

'Here we are all the same, sir.' He added, 'But we will be glad to go wherever you want us to go, sir.'

Back in his own tent which, in a moment of anger, he had pitched as far from the others as possible, he lay back on his bed and smoked. They had become like sheep. Anyone could lead sheep. He stubbed the cigarette and lay face downward. Looking towards the open flap of the tent he saw that the leaves of the bushes were still lifeless in the windless day. The rhythm of his breathing magnified itself and became the only living thing. He sat up.

He must not allow himself to drift, or, as the men seemed to be, become affected by the strangeness of Tamel or its promise, perhaps, of being the last lap of the course they had followed so long, together. He owed it to his men to remain stable in the midst of instability; keep himself in the image they would recognise again when they woke to their unaltered need of him; woke as they would wake; as they must wake.

He would have to close his eyes to the sight of men who seemed to be disloyal, as he had on the morning he called for twelve volunteers to go by road from Prulli to Tamel in Jim Taylor's convoy. Thirty men had volunteered. It had hurt, but he hoped he had not shown it. He must try not to show the hurt he felt now. Hurt could look like anger and anger could turn men away. All he must show was that he remained loyal to the spirit of Marapore and Comitarla. He would have none of this co-called efficient new machine. The machine was not invented that could take the place of men who worked with a will and with a common purpose; as once his section had worked; as it would work again.

He stood, and picked up his cap, clapping it on his head and jerking the brim down at one side in the old arrogant way. He went out into the glare of the sunlight and felt better than he had for many a day. He walked across the field and along the track that skirted the Major's office, and out on to the road, towards his own section's stores.

Lorries were drawn up at the side of the road and his men were off-loading tins of composite rations; tins which glinted like flashed mirrors in the sun. Inside the tent the heat filtered through the thick canvas and the dust rose from the churned earth as the sepoys went backwards and forwards from tent to lorry, stocking up against the days when operations would start. He watched them and saw his old friend Jai; Jai with the bright handkerchief tied round his forehead to catch the sweat before it fell into his eyes; Jai who, surprisingly, had been one of the thirty volunteers for the convoy. Johnnie had not let him go, he was too useful a man. In a couple of days Jim would arrive and the section would be at full strength again. The deviationists were with Taylor; but Johnnie tried not to think of them as such.

He left the store tent and went to his office. Nimu was there, supervising a squad of men who moved office furniture from corner to corner at the clerk's whim.

'Hello, Nimu. Hard at it?'

'Sir, they are being stupid.'

'Or are you changing your mind all the time? Anyway, why not have your desk at this end and your bed at the other?'

'This I have tried, sir. Now I try another way, but they are slow and lazy. We should have stayed in Prulli.'

'Maybe you're right.'

Nimu followed him into the section officer's part of the tent, screened off from Nimu's by a canvas wall.

'They think because the Japanese have been driven out of Manipur that war is soon over, sir. They do not realise that hardest work of all is now.'

'You've got something there, but they'll soon learn.'

'Sir . . . ?'

'Yes?'

'You are not leaving us, sir?'

Johnnie stared. 'Leaving? Why?'

'People are saying many officers are being promoted.'

'I'm not leaving, Nimu. Not if I can help it, anyway.'

'This is what I thought.'

'Do the men think I am going, then?'

'Not exactly, sir. It is just everyone is unsettled. We should be back in Comitarla, working as in the old days, sir.'

Johnnie sat at his desk and Nimu stood over him.

'Nimu, if you hear any of the men or N.C.O.s saying that I'm going or any bloody-fool nonsense like that you can tell 'em I'm staying.' He paused. 'You can tell 'em too that the Captain Sahib isn't just a fair weather friend, either.'

'Fair weather friend? What is the meaning of this?'

'If I tell you you'll only use it to score one over Moti Ram Sahib, won't you?'

Nimu laughed aloud. 'You should be telling me all the same.'

'Work it out for yourself.'

'Very well, sir.' Nimu went back to his own office and Johnnie leaned with his shoulders against the tent-wall, rocking gently with his toes tucked round the legs of the table. Suddenly outside, men began to shout and going to the opening he saw Dass had produced a football from somewhere and some of the men were scuffling up and down the roadway while Dass dribbled it expertly. Johnnie went out and as Dass passed him he barged against his shoulder and tapped the ball gently from Dass's feet. He stood there with his hands low on his hips, one foot placed on top of the ball, and the men lined themselves up in a semi-circle about fifteen yards from him. He watched them closely and shouted suddenly, 'Come on one of you! Win it!' Two of the N.C.Os. and Jai broke from the group and charged him. He heeled the ball backwards and ducked about just as they drew level. In a couple of seconds he was running with the ball at his feet again, back towards the other men, yelling, 'Come on Three Section! Don't let me have it all the time!' He kicked the ball high over their heads and let them run for it. Watching them scrambling he thought, 'They do it to please me.' He chivvied them on and for half-an-hour they played up and down the road and soon most of the section had joined in. The sweat streamed down Johnnie's face. He was conscious of his power and of the fact that they were black and he was white. It had never been so before and in his anger he found himself cheering derisively whenever one of them fluffed the ball. Suddenly he turned away and left them. It was no good. The spirit had gone. It wasn't the men's fault so much, nor Taylor's; nor the Major's. His own surely, was the greatest? The Major's words had come true only because he had let himself be afraid. His shadow, foreshortened by the height of the sun, was in front of him.

When he left them the game continued for a few more minutes and then they went back to the tents; back to the lorries that had been left, half-empty, with their tailboards down; back to the piles of tins in the roadway growing hot beneath the sun.

It was the last stage of the convoy and they left Dimapur before the sun rose, driving slowly up the serpentine road to the high, scarred hills of Kohima. From there the road threaded its way up and down round the shoulders of the great ridges, descending gradually to the Manipur plain. For this last day's march, Jim, with a fitter and some spare petrol on board, drove at the rear, stopping every now and then to do running repairs to the lorries which had staggered over five hundred miles from Prulli in mountainous country. It was dark when they passed through Imphal and took the road for Tiddim, and, on level road now, he drove to the front and headed for Tamel.

The journey had taken eight days, for he had been forced to spend two in Shillong, scrounging and stealing fan belts and other spare parts. Each night, as they harboured, Taylor sought out the M.T. Havildar, a thickly built Muslim called Khan, and together they would drive round searching for the local workshops, scrounging, lifting when eyes were not looking, as if it were a game. Khan, back in the harbour, would send curry and rice over to him where he sat behind his truck, his camp-bed set up in the pool of light from his hurricane lantern. Sleeping, beneath the stars, his dreams had been easy; waking in the cold mountain air and shaving in the mirror of his truck, Jim felt that life was good. And always at half-past seven, the convoy wheeled out of the harbour to face another long day's drive.

It had been a good journey. He was sorry it was over.

He saw that they were approaching an airfield and he told Mohammed Din to stop. He got out and when the leading lorry slowed down he called out to the driver to wait there until he came back to lead the convoy into the new lines. Then, back in the truck, he and Din dove forward looking for signs of the company.

A quarter moon had risen above the hills that enclosed the plain. He looked round at the alien countryside and found it strangely familiar, like a place known in dreams. Here, on the left, was the wide stretch of an airfield and on the right, rows of tents, white in the moonlight. Once again he got down from the truck and stood in the middle of the deserted road. He shivered, less from the keen wind cutting across the plain than from the feeling he had been here before. The feeling took stronger possession of him and he walked a little way down the road, stubbing his toes on the rough surface from weariness. He could see the tents more plainly. Ahead of him was a culvert and a road branching off into the fields where the tents were lined. This, he knew, was the end of the journey.

They came one by one into his tent, but Johnnie had gone into Imphal. Jim was too tired to eat, but eventually they went across to the mess tent which was divided by canvas into two sections; mess and ante-room; and in the ante-room a stove was being built for their winter comfort.

They sat in the ante-room and he answered questions about the convoy and compared notes with Johns who had brought the first one through.

'The climb up to Kohima's the worst.'

'I don't know,' said Johns; 'by the time you get there, old boy, you're thankful to be on the last lap. I think from Sylhet's bad.'

Bill said, 'Has the Major told you yet about the new set-up?'

'No, I haven't. I thought I'd let him get his wind back.'

'What's up, Major?'

'We're getting a new establishment. We're going to be called an Air Despatch Company, and sections'll be known as platoons.'

'Why all that?'

'All fits into this Ramo business.'

'Ramo?'

Scottie said, 'He doesn't know yet what Ramo means.'

'Is that the staff organisation?'

'That's it, Jim. R.A.M.O. Rear Airfield Maintenance Organisation.'

Bill leaned back in his chair, a cigarette in his mouth, his hands shoved into his trouser pockets. 'We're sitting pretty, boy. We're going to do no paper work. Ramo's going to work out everything.'

'Even our plane loads?'

'Yep. The whole shoot.'

'They'll need a pretty big staff to cope with that.'

'They'll cope.' The Major looked round and asked, 'Who's got a cigarette? I'm out.'

'Here.'

'Thanks.'

The Major sat down. He leaned forward in the familiar attitude, clasped hands held in front of him with the cigarette trailing smoke. 'Yes, they'll cope. There's a Lieutenant-Colonel commanding, Deputy Assistant Director of Supplies and Transport, and a couple of staff captains.'

'And about five hundred Havildar-clerks.'

Jim laughed. 'When do they arrive?'

The Major shrugged. 'No idea.' He nodded his head in the direction of the lines. 'They're going to be stuck up at the far end of the road. You haven't seen that side yet. The road curves right round the back on to the pukkah.'

Scottie cleared his throat. 'It's a good simple lay-out.'

'Christ, you keep on saying that, Scottie.' Bill threw his cigarette on the floor and ground it with his heel.

'There's plenty of room for Ramo anyway. They'll be fixing up a local Field Supply Depot right here in the lines. That means you'll have your reserve stores on your doorstep. Cut out all that waste of transport collecting it from dumps stuck miles away.'

Jim said, 'Who's commanding the Ramo? Do we know his name?'

There was a short silence.

'Yes, we know his name. It came in today with the rest of all this information.' The Major looked at Jim. 'You may remember him.'

'Oh?'

'Chap called Baxter. He was with me on Comitarla airstrip the day you arrived. Remember?'

'Good Lord, yes. I didn't know he was in air supply.'

'He wasn't.' Bill grimaced.

'They've been running a senior officers' course at Marapore. He passed out I suppose.' The Major turned and faced Scottie, then looked back at Jim. 'Old Scottie didn't get his company.'

'Bad luck.'

'I didn't expect to.'

'But Johns has his warning order back. Staff Captaincy for one of the Ramos. Funny if it turns out to be ours, won't it?'

Jim said to Johns, 'Congratulations.' Then he said, 'That means another new face in the company. I won't be junior any longer.' He smiled as he said it. But again there was silence, longer this time, then the Major stood up and stretched, and Jim saw the embarrassment in the awkward movement.

' 'Fraid not, Jim. I said we'd got a new establishment. It doesn't provide for second in commands.'

'What?'

'Sorry. Second in commands are going to be abolished.'

'When?'

'No idea. Any day. Any month. Perhaps not until next year. Who knows?'

'But . . . ' Jim looked round at the averted faces.

The Major touched his shoulder, momentarily. 'It's all right, Jim. I've put you up for a captaincy. Sent the recommendation in this evening.'

After a while he remembered to say, 'Thanks, Major.'

Then he asked, 'Does Johnnie know all this?'

'He does.'

Bill laughed. 'That's why he's gone to Imphal. There's a club there, we're told. He's getting pissed, I expect.'

'What did he say about Baxter?'

'What do you think?'

They talked for another half hour. The Major explained how the sections – he paused and corrected himself – the platoons were to work. Scottie would handle the regular field service rations, Bill would be responsible for ammunition and ordnance stores, fresh meat and vegetables; 'If any,' interrupted Ghosh; and Johnnie was to do petrol and composite rations.

'It's going to be an odd sort of campaign you know, Jim. We've never really supplied an army in a pukkah advance. We

126

did dropping and we did landing, separate sort of programmes. Now it's going to be different. You watch. Right in the middle of a good dropping routine they'll capture an airfield and we'll switch partly to a landing programme so's they can build supply dumps. Then back to dropping.'

'And most of the time a bit of both,' suggested Bill, and added, 'Not only both, but when the switch comes it'll be in the middle of the bloody night and you'll have to go down at three in the morning and take your dropping load off and put your landing load on instead. Glory be.'

'Too bloody true.'

'Roll on.'

Jim listened while the others talked. It meant nothing to him; this operation meant nothing at the moment when it should have meant everything. But he would not be here. He would be back in Marapore, hoping to get a platoon of his own.

The others were yawning and soon they rose one by one and went out, saying goodnight, and Jim found himself alone with the Major.

'Sorry, Jim'.

There was no need for him to ask, 'Sorry about what?' He smiled and said, 'It can't be helped.' For an instant he wondered if he should volunteer for the Ramo. But the thought had no sooner formed than it was gone; there were circumstances under which one could not stay.

'How soon d'you think it'll be?'

'Honestly, I've no idea. May be some time yet.'

Jim nodded.

'There is a chance you know,' the Major began.

'What of? Staying?'

'Yes. There's a rumour that all section transport is going to be pooled and made into a separate M.T. platoon under a subaltern.'

'Sounds pretty unlikely.'

'Yes, but it may work that way.'

The Major paused. 'If it did come to that,' he went on, 'would you take the job?'

'Ghosh is senior to me.'

'He doesn't like vehicles. You're all right like that.'

'I'd take it if he didn't want it. If I'm still here when it happens.'

'You don't sound very enthusiastic. Anyway, you'd be doing better for yourself going back to Marapore with my recommendation for your promotion.'

'If I get back to Marapore, I'll stay there.'

'Why d'you say that?'

'I just know it.'

'Marapore's all right.'

'All right if you like that sort of thing.'

'You prefer this?'

'Don't you?'

The Major smiled. It was funny, he thought, how much of himself he could see in Taylor. There was a sort of affinity between them. He said, 'Anyway, you hang on. Something might turn up. What about Ramo here?'

'Perhaps. I'll have to think about that.'

'In the meantime you've got to go on looking after Johnnie, you know.' He smiled, making light of it, but as he said it he knew he meant it. Johnnie had become more than he could cope with. Even in the last two days. Deep down inside he knew that was the truth; he had known it when they first arrived in Tamel.

Jim laughed. 'I thought he was looking after me.'

'Well let's say you're both looking after each other.'

They made their way back to their own tents and said good-night. Before he went to bed, Jim scribbled a note to Johnnie.

'In case I'm asleep when you get back, just to let you know we're here and transport's O.K.

The Major told me the bad news.

Jim.'

He went to Johnnie's tent, which Jan Mohammed had pointed out to him earlier on, and left the note on the little table. Then he returned and got undressed and into bed, where he lay on his back and smoked. When he had finished his cigarette he turned down the lantern and tried to sleep. For a long time he stared into the darkness and it seemed impossible that only the night before he had slept beneath the stars in the harbour at Dimapur. How would he return to Marapore? By plane? Or would he take that winding road once again, mounting slowly into the hills until Kohima stood sentinel in front of him? Then downwards; downwards. . . .

It was well past midnight when he heard a truck come to a halt nearby; and after a minute he heard blundering footsteps that must be Johnnie's. The footsteps went past the tent. After a while they came back through the rustling grass and he knew that Johnnie had read the note and had come to see if he were awake.

The tent flap moved and Jim waited to speak; unsure of his mood. Suddenly he sat up.

'Is that you, Johnnie?'

'Yes.' Johnnie brushed past the flap. He had no lantern and Jim turned up his own. Johnnie stood, swaying slightly, and his face was yellow.

'Hello, Jim.'

'Read my note?'

'Yes. That's why I came.'

Jim picked up his packet of cigarettes and offered one. Johnnie came and sat on the end of the bed and Jim could smell the sickly odour of rum.

'Have a good time on the convoy?'

'Yes. I enjoyed it.'

'Good. I wish I could've come by road too.'

'I stayed over in Shillong, scrounging spare parts.'

'Lucky bastard.'

'How's Tamel?'

'Piss-poor.'

Jim leaned back, supporting himself on one elbow. Johnnie smiled. 'You ought to get some shut-eye.' He stood up. He swayed and Jim thought for a moment that he was going to be sick. Then he seemed to draw himself up. 'See you in the morning, Jim.'

'Right; goodnight Johnnie.'

' 'Night.' He went to the flap and fumbled with it. Then he turned round as if he'd made up his mind about something.

'I'm sorry about – you know,' he said.

'Can't be helped.'

'Back in Mara . . .' he had difficulty with the word, 'back in Marapore you'll get section. Major's recommended it. He tell you that?'

'Yes.'

'You'll like that. You see. Getting your own section.'

'Maybe.'

'Better'n here, Jim. One way an' 'nother you've had a thin time.'

'I've had a bloody good time.'

Johnnie did not reply at once.

'D'you mean that?'

'I wouldn't say it otherwise.'

'Anyway. You'll do better in Mar'pore. If it wasn't for my old section I'd chuck in myself an' get away from all this bloody

129

balls that's going on.' He paused. 'Go back myself.' His eyes looked glassy. 'Sort old Brad out.'

'Don't be an ass.'

'Why do you want to stay anyway?'

'I'd prefer to work down here than stick around at the depot.'

'You won't work here. You see, Jim. You'll fanny around an' dress everything by the right same as our tents are and that bloke . . . that bloke Baxter . . .' Johnnie rubbed his mouth and nose with the back of his hand. He came back into the middle of the tent. 'Know who Baxter is, Jim?'

'Yes. I met him the day I came.'

'He inspected us. Down from Delhi on a cheap day return. Know what he said to the Major?'

'No.'

'Said Three Section lines were untidy. Christ! We'd been standing on our heads from April to June doing a job he didn't even know existed. That's Baxter. Now you know.'

'He probably felt he had to say something.'

'Well that type can belt up as far as I'm concerned. And I'll tell him so if I have to. You see. . . .'

'Watch your step, Johnnie.'

'What d'you mean?'

'I don't know really. But don't mess things up for yourself.'

'Is that what the Major's told you t' tell me?'

Under Johnnie's level gaze Jim felt himself flushing. He had meant it kindly and it had sounded condescending.

'Well if that's what the Major thinks, why can't he tell me himself? Is he afraid of me?'

'He didn't say that.'

'What did he say?'

'Nothing.'

'He's scared of Baxter.'

Jim laughed. 'I don't believe it.'

'You're all bloody well scared of Baxter.'

Johnnie's lips twitched and the muscles in his cheeks began to flicker. 'You're all bloody well scared of bloody Baxter and his bloody Ramo. Well I'm not.' Again, the gesture of the hand across the mouth, and then he said, 'Sorry, not you.'

'Why not me?'

'Forget it. I'm drunk. I open my big mouth too much.'

'That's what I meant by watching your step.'

'I know. I open my big mouth and I say things I don't mean. Go on. You get some shut-eye and forget it.'

'Thanks for coming in. I couldn't sleep.'

'You're an odd sort of bloke.' He paused. 'I said that before, didn't I?'

'Yes, you did. Why am I an odd sort of bloke?'

'Sometimes I think you hate my guts. Sometimes I give you reason to.' He tried to grin. 'Other times we seem to get on all right.'

'That's the same with most people.'

'How old are you, Jim? I've never asked that.'

'Twenty-five.'

'Same as me.'

They looked at each other steadily, smiling slightly. Then Johnnie said, 'Let's leave it there.'

'As good a place as any.' They said goodnight and then Jim turned the lantern down and lay back again. The flap of the tent had got twisted and he could see through it the reflection from the moon that had risen as he drove into Tamel.

12

Partly because he disliked air-travel, but chiefly because he wanted the transition from Marapore to Tamel to be more gradual than a journey by plane would allow, Lieutenant-Colonel Baxter came to Dimapur by rail. At Dimapur he found himself a place on one of the daily supply convoys which moved from the railhead down into Imphal, and as they went through Kohima he knew that psychologically he had been right to come this way.

It was not possible to detect from his expression or immobile features that the sight of Kohima moved him. He stared out at the stricken hill-side, naked now under the late October sun, and his hands which rested lightly on the despatch case on his lap jerked with a short, spasmodic movement; a movement that caught the sepoy driver's eye and was interpreted by him as a gesture of impatience, so that the poor fellow, already taut from the unexpected presence of the unknown Colonel Sahib, stiffened his own hands and for a moment the lorry swerved towards the bank which dropped sheer for five hundred feet. But Baxter hardly noticed. He was leaning forward to identify the shoulder flashes of the soldiers who were bivouaced in the hill-side. The lorry slowed, for in front of it, struggling up the steep incline, was a tank transporter. They followed it for twenty minutes and when eventually they drove past it where the road widened a little, Baxter, who had watched with interest, turned to the driver and said, 'Sharbash!' The sepoy grinned, delighted, and Baxter thought with a smile of Major Shelley, his D.A.D.S. & T. in the Ramo. Shelley was British Service and that being so failed to understand the genuine admiration he himself had for Indian troops. Shelley – in Baxter's place here – would have hugged the seat in barely-controlled panic, convinced that at any moment the Indian would drive them over the edge. Baxter was not at all sure about Shelley who had come to him with some obscure, never wholly determined experience in Normandy to back his promotion.

At two o'clock the convoy stopped at a place where the road had been built out as a staging halt. He got out of the cabin and stretched his cramped limbs, moving across to a sawn-off tree trunk where he sat down and opened his briefcase and took out the neatly packaged sandwiches he had brought. He ate slowly, observing how incongruous his highly polished brown shoes and clean khaki uniform looked in his present surroundings; incongruous but infinitely comforting, allaying in some way the little flutterings in his stomach. He looked down from the height of the roadway into the deep jungle valleys and the height gave him confidence again.

He lit a cigarette. He enjoyed smoking in the open air; the taste of the tobacco was different and always brought to him warm memories of field-days and tactical exercises without troops; standing as a young subaltern high up on a ridge, his eyes already forming into the eyes of a soldier which, studying landscape, observed only its distances, features and dead ground. Past middle age now, he saw that there was beauty in the shape of land and the pattern it made with trees and sky.

Three blasts on a whistle sent the lounging men back to the lorries and the convoy rolled forward to Imphal. When it grew dusk Baxter began to nod. There was a monotony about the journey; each corner, when turned, seemed to present the same stretch of road, bending, twisting, moving round at sharp angles until sometimes the convoy travelled in two almost parallel lines. He felt his eyes grow heavy, but with the first desire to sleep he drew himself upright with a jerk.

It was half-past seven before they were in Imphal. The last miles were easy, along a level road that stretched like a slender tongue from the hills into the plain. Along the road were draped telephone lines, and signboards in patterns Baxter knew by heart. Motor-cyclists streamed past them and at each main junction the lines looped away in the tall trees. For a while they travelled behind a lorry filled with troops; their faces all alike in the glare from the headlights; their eyes fixed on the headlights as though fascinated by them. The signboards became more numerous and momentarily there were glimpses of Military Police and wide pools of light from naked electric bulbs and grease-stained men crawling from beneath jacked lorries.

Baxter spent his first seven days making himself known and, he hoped, felt in Tamel and back in Imphal; asking, wheedling and demanding. By mid-November the area began to take shape and he felt better able to settle down to some sort of routine. Shelley was not particularly efficient and Baxter did not like him, and he saw clearly his dislike of Shelley was duplicated in the mess of the air supply company. These sort of problems were of secondary importance, though. What was important to him from the 'man' angle was the serious shortage of his own staff. Without a full complement Baxter was unable to function in the way he wanted to. The platoons were still doing all their own paper work.

When he had first arrived they were operating ninety tons of supplies a day and the total weight was going up steadily as the campaign increased its momentum. The days were marked out in routine stages; the morning drop; the afternoon drop; the receipt and break down of the demands for the following day's sorties; the collection and packing of stores to fulfil it; and the night-loading on to aircraft. A sudden demand, or change in demand in the middle of the night, had become a rule rather than the exception and Baxter grew accustomed to a sleep punctuated by the sound of revving lorries and shouting men.

He watched and his trained mind helped him to reach right down into the core of a problem. He was not a man to jump to conclusions. He took his time and waited until he felt he knew the rhythm and could detect where it quickened or slowed and broke away from an even beat. That, he told himself, was his job. That, and ensuring that what the army called 'turn-round', the flow of transport, in this case aircraft, from base to objective and back again with the minimum delay, was maintained. The solution of all problems, once one had seen into their heart, could be found by asking the question, 'How does this affect, or improve, or detract from the turn-round?'

It was because Baxter kept this one thing clear in his mind that Johnnie got into trouble.

Although no major bridge-head had been established, already in mid-November, 19 Indian Division had forced a crossing of the Chindwin and marched eastward in an attempt to link up with columns marching from the north.

It was an omen of good for the future and a heartening beginning to the campaign. With the crossing the tempo quickened and Baxter found himself employing the use of the expression 'turn-round', more and more. 'Remember your turn-round. Go out for your turn-round, all the time. All the time that's what you've got to aim for. There's a couple of lorries standing empty in front of Brown's office. Why, Major? Do you know?'

He interrupted before the Major could get out his answer; 'I'm not making an issue of it. Just saying it so you can see how my mind works, old chap. Empty lorries to me mean until I'm shown otherwise – that they are being wasted. If they're empty at this time of day they should be back in their harbour on maintenance.'

The Major smiled. He liked Baxter. There was a mutual respect between them. Baxter's complaints were never made as such. 'I'm not making an issue of it, old chap. Just telling you to show you how my mind works.'

Already Bill had christened Baxter, 'Turn-round Baxter.' 'What's old turn-round doing snooping round my tents?' Or, 'Watch out, boys, here's old turn-round coming round the bend.' The Major, with Baxter in front of him, found it difficult not to laugh at the sudden recollection of the nick-name. He was glad Baxter had been given a nick-name; it sugared the pill of his coming.

But it would not last, he knew. In time the joke would wear thin; be spoken with an acid quality in the voice. But there had to be a catch-phrase to whip up feelings a man alone could not set fire to. The worth of what he himself called 'the job' had to be reduced at the last count to one of its particular implications; turn-round. That, men would understand when 'the job' struck a false note; seemed insincere; high falutin.

Baxter had left him now and instead of 'phoning through to Johnnie he decided to go and talk to him. There were no lorries outside Johnnie's office when he arrived there, but he walked in and found Jim alone.

'Where's Johnnie?'

'I think he went down to the strip.'

The Major sat down. 'Got a cigarette?'

'Yes. Here.'

'Sorry to scrounge. I left mine in the office.'

'Any news of my posting?'

'Not yet. Don't worry. Just keep pegging away as though it wasn't going to happen.'

'That's not awfully easy.'

'I realise that. Got your figures for tomorrow yet?'

'They're nearly done. It'll be about fifteen plane loads.'

'Um. The tonnage is going up.'

'Old Turn-round was wandering about outside some time ago.'

'He said there were some empty lorries doing nothing.'

'Oh?'

'He sees everything. Don't worry.'

'Did you want me to give Johnnie a message?'

'No.' The Major got up. 'Bring your figures round as soon as you can, Jim.' He went out of the tent and down the road again, dropping in to see Bill and then Scottie. Scottie was on the point of leaving his own office for the Major's and they walked back to Headquarters together. There they studied the map he had pinned on a board. As Scottie traced the direction of the advance with his finger Johnnie's words came back.

'Scottie can look at a map and see all sorts of things about lines of communication.' But Johnnie saw only the men who were connected by the lines. 'That's wrong,' the Major said and realised he had said it aloud, because Scottie without looking round said, 'What's wrong?'

'Nothing. I was thinking.'

Men were not connected. There was no communication between them. Sometimes a duplication of action and desire would make it seem as if it existed. But it was only there superficially; emotionally. It did not go deeply to connect up the separate cores of their isolation. With Baxter's coming the others could have turned to him again; forgetting, perhaps, the things he had done in Prulli. Perhaps they *were* turning back to him; but he saw too clearly the nature of the spirit which prompted them to do so; which prompted him too; to stand together, against the day when Baxter's nick-name would lose its flavour.

Parrish came in and with him was Jim.

'Isn't Johnnie coming?'

'He's not back. But I've got our figures.'

135

'Right. Let's start.'

They called over the number of planes they each required. He called back to them the identification numbers of the planes so far allotted for the next day's drops. When he had finished he said, 'O.K.' Then he called for Prabhu. 'Send this list through to Ramo. We'll want four more planes.'

Prabhu nodded and went back to his own section of the tent.

'Any news of Ghoshy or Johns going, Major?'

'No, Bill.'

Scottie said, 'Baxter came round today and suggested that if Ghosh and Johns were going into Ramo they may as well go and spend some time with him.'

'I know, he suggested that to me.'

'What did you say?'

'He only wants them for staff work and they're doing that where they are.'

Scottie nodded. 'That's what I said, too.'

They stood up and went out to go to their own offices. The Major called them back. 'Shall we invite Baxter round to the mess again tonight?'

'If you like. But that bind Shelley'll come with him.'

'I won't then, if you'd rather not. They must get on each other's nerves eating together all the time though.'

'Do 'em good.' Bill fingered his moustache and this time when they turned away he let them go.

After supper that night the Major took Johnnie on one side. 'You're never in your office, Johnnie.'

'Why should I be?'

'Why not?'

'We've got a staff to do our paper work now.'

'You mean you've got Jim.'

'That's up to him. If he wants to do it I can't stop him.'

'You've got it all worked out, have you?'

'Yes, Major.'

'Ramo's not up to strength yet. They can't do the paper work.'

'I'm a platoon now. I don't do it either.'

'You're bloody stupid.'

'You've told me that before.'

The Major sighed. Johnnie smiled. 'You're all scared of Ramo.'

'Be your age. You're a bloody dope.'

'Maybe.'

'Watch your step. Jim won't be there to do things you refuse to do all the time, you know. What'll happen then?'

136

'Your guess is as good as mine.'

'It may be better, Johnnie.'

They left each other and the Major thought, 'I can't save him now.' He went into Jim's tent.

'Can I come in?'

'Of course.'

'Jim, is there anything you can do about Johnnie?'

'What's wrong?'

'You know what I mean. He leaves everything to you on the excuse that Ramo should do his work for him. Spends all day tearing about the strip.'

'What do you want me to do?'

'Try and make him see where his attitude's leading him.' He sat down and Jim noticed the lines of weariness in his face. The Major said, 'How do you get on in Three Section now?'

'All right.'

'You had a thin time at first. I told Johnnie about that. How you got me pissed. Remember?' He grinned, but he knew he was trying to force a mood. He was playing with his men now. Moving them about on a chess-board. Playing one against the other.

'Yes, I remember. It seems silly looking back on it.'

'It was silly at the time. This present business with Johnnie will seem silly as well, eventually.' With one hand he built, and with another destroyed; these were the actions of omnipotence. He added, 'Do what you can, anyway, Jim.'

'But what?'

The Major thought: 'I deserved that. You can't shift responsibility. You can only deny it. You can deny Johnnie. If anything happened could you command Three Section?' The question slipped out almost before he had formed it in his mind. Jim stared at him, then he said, 'Nobody but Johnnie will ever command Three Section.'

'You wouldn't do it?'

At last Jim replied, 'I'd try it if I had to, and it was for Johnnie's sake.'

The Major found his throat suddenly dry. 'That's a funny sort of answer.'

'It's what I mean. I'd try for Johnnie's sake. But it won't be necessary. Three Section'll always be his and in a day or two you'll get orders to send me back to Marapore.'

'We don't know.'

The Major got up. 'Just do what you can to make him see

sense.' Then he went out. He wondered if he should go in and see Johnnie.

Johnnie sat reading. He heard the Major's voice mumbling in Jim's tent, and Jim's faint answers; and the sound of the flap of a tent being pushed to one side. And then he waited. But the Major did not come in, and he was glad. He went back to his book, reading and turning the pages mechanically without understanding the words. His eyes grew tired and he let the book fall, neglected, on to his lap. He undressed and went to bed, keeping the lantern burning, smoking cigarettes, and expecting footsteps and the rustle of canvas of the tent flap. He fell asleep and was woken by Prabhu.

'Sir?'

Prabhu shook him gently and he sat up with a jerk. He took the piece of paper Prabhu handed to him and read what was written there over and over again. 'What is it, Prabhu?'

'These are plane numbers, sir. The top one is one loaded by Three Section. A message has come from Ramo that this one is out of order and will not fly. They want load taking off and putting on this other plane, sir.'

'That's all? O.K., Prabhu, thanks.' Prabhu hesitated.

'Ramo says for it to be done now, sir.'

'What's the time?'

'One o'clock, sir.'

'O.K., Prabhu, thanks.'

'Shall I wake one of your N.C.Os. on my way back, sir?'

'No. Leave it to me.'

'Goodnight, sir.'

Johnnie stared at the note. He shrugged his shoulders and put the note on the table. Then he turned down his lantern and settled down for sleep.

You would take a lorry load of sleep-drugged sepoys down to the strip in the small hours and seek out a plane that should have been reported out of order before night fall. If you found it perhaps the substitute plane would not be there. You would drive round the strip looking for it, the eyes still filmed with the day's weariness, the night's broken sleep. If you found it and loaded it then it might not take off until nine o'clock the following morning. You could have gone down in the first hours of daylight. If you took the chance and left the job until morning the crew would be waiting, cursing, impatient to be off and back again. Johnnie had taken the chance.

'I'm not making an issue of it, old chap. Just passing on what squadron say.' It was midday, and Baxter was strolling through the lines with the Major. 'Nevertheless let's make a rule. Let's make it quite clear.'

'Very well, sir.'

'Let's make a rule that *we* won't make mistakes. Squadron should have notified us hours before about the plane being out of order. But *we* should have made sure the substitute was loaded in time for take-off. That's what's meant by turn-round.'

'Absolutely, sir.'

'So in future, directly a message like that comes in, down we go to the strip, whatever hour of the night it is. After all, we're used to night work, aren't we?'

'Brown took a chance and lost, sir. We've taken chances like that before.'

'In rather different circumstances I suspect.'

'What sort of circumstances?'

'I mean, Major, that when the men are absolutely whacked, like say during the Imphal Flap, a thing like a plane going u.s. can be taken with a pinch of salt. The platoon commander weighs the importance of the plane against the importance of the men. At this stage in the campaign turn-round is more important than men's sleep.'

They walked on and eventually Baxter went off, back to his own office. The Major went in to Three Section. Both Jim and Johnnie were there.

'That plane last night. Squadron have kicked up a fuss.'

'Maybe it's us who should kick up the fuss.'

'In future, Johnnie, I've agreed with Baxter that when a message comes through like that, we go down to the strip straight away.'

'You mean the men go. I'm not worried about us. Christ, d'you think I care about how much time *I* spend down there? It's the men I'm thinking of, and if Squadron and Ramo between 'em can't get messages like that to us at the proper time, they can belt up.'

'Nevertheless, Johnnie, in future we go down to the strip straight away.'

'I'll use my discretion. That's what a section officer's for.' He paused. 'That sort of thing looks all right in orders on paper. I look at it different.'

As he looks at a map, the Major thought.

'Yes, Johnnie. You use your discretion. I'll be using mine as well.'

'Fair enough.'

'I'm glad you think so,' He made as if to go; the words 'don't make it so that I have to hurt you', came to his tongue, but he did not let himself say the words. He could not reach out like that to any man.

'Anything wrong, Major?'

'No.' He wheeled out of the tent and felt the silence he left behind him. Did Johnnie know that the man who sat with him was a good friend? The sort of friend who had said, 'I'll do it for Johnnie's sake.' How could he know?

The day sped on in its familiar pattern; there was little to distinguish one day from the other; the days were a date in the month written at the top of a demand for rations. But as that evening came it seemed to bring with it a sense of judgment; an odd trick of cloud, or rising dust that caught and broke the rays of the sun and spread them luminously over the whole plain, made colours change, destroyed their harmony. It was dark before all his officers were assembled at Headquarters; but Johnnie was not there; as always, Jim had come in his place. Mechanically the Major took their demands for planes and read over the numbers for loading. An extra one was needed. His brain seemed to have stopped functioning and in calling over the numbers he got them mixed up. For a moment or two there was a mild confusion.

Scottie said, 'But you gave me J.58 just then. Now you've given it to Jim.'

They were in his vision, telescoped. He stared at them and heard his own voice say, 'J.58. Yes. That's for Jim. J for Jim in any case.' And then Bill said, 'And J for Johnnie. Pipe down Scottie. Give him an S, Major.' And the laughter adjusted the focus.

When they had gone he stared at the paper. Still he had not marked off J.58 for Three Section. He scrawled his pencil across the typed words. Satisfied, he sent the list to Prabhu. 'Another plane wanted for Captain Scott's section. Send its number through to him direct when you get it from Ramo.' He picked up his lantern and made his way through the trees which rustled in the soft breeze. The breeze caught his cheek and he felt – 'Tomorrow will be different. A new era.'

They ate supper and Johnnie was silent, but for some reason the Major was not disturbed; Johnnie seemed hardly to be there. When they had finished Johnnie pushed back his chair and went out. The Major looked round. The other officers had come not to show that they noticed Johnnie's unfriendliness, or that he sat through supper most nights scowling and answering only

140

when spoken to direct. They adjourned to the ante-room. Then Scottie got up to go. 'I'm going down to the strip.' The evening passed.

At ten o'clock Jim went round for his truck and then down to the airfield to check his plane loads. Dass was still down there with a loading party, loading the last plane on the list. Jim flashed his torch on the fuselage and saw that it was J.58. He smiled, remembering how the Major had got the numbers confused.

'All right, Dass?'

'Yes, sir. All is now finished.'

'O.K. I'm going back then. I've checked the lot now.'

He returned to his truck and lit a cigarette. This was the best part of the day, he thought; the routine over and the expectation of sleep; and the hope that the sleep would not be broken; the wish that if a new demand should come it should be for Bill or Scottie. He smiled again and got into the cabin, running his hands round the smooth steering wheel with a sense of possession and familiarity. In this truck he had driven from Prulli to Manipur.

Then he remembered that any day, perhaps tomorrow, there would be an end. He pressed the starter and the engine whose sound had become almost part of him, fired. When he saw Dass's lorry move away from the doorway of the plane and glide swiftly out of the bay, he followed it.

Sleep came, and with it, dreamlessness.

To Jim it seemed as if someone had shaken his arm and he woke and saw the emptiness of the tent and the thin triangle where the half open flap let in the sounds and shapes of night. There was nobody there, but he lay listening, knowing that someone had gone by. The trees were sounds that rose and fell as the wind moved; and into the sounds came voices that were not voices but part of the wind, coming and going.

He got out of bed and went over to the flap, lifting it further. From Johnnie's tent was the pale glow of a lantern seen dimly through the thickness of canvas. The lantern moved and its light was suddenly naked, outside, and it moved forward towards him. It was Prabhu who carried it.

He said in a low voice, 'Prabhu?'

Prabhu held the lantern high. The concern Jim saw in his face made him say, 'Come inside.'

He held the flap open and Prabhu ducked under his arm and the tent was filled with light.

'Can I help, Prabhu?'

'It is another plane, sir. I am talking to Captain Brown about it.'

'Out of order, sir. See. J.58 is the number, and it should be taken out and put on H.43.'

'What did Captain Brown say?'

'That I should take the message to Moti Ram Sahib.' Prabhu hesitated, his lips moving. He cleared his throat and went on, 'But sir, Captain Brown tells for me to say to Moti Ram Sahib that there is no need to go until morning.'

'That's all right, Prabhu. Leave the note with me. You go back to bed.'

'Yes, sir.' Relieved that the responsibility was no longer his Prabhu turned to go, and as he did so Jim put up the light in his own lantern, and began to dress. The Major had said, 'Do what you can for Johnnie.' Tomorrow, or the day after, Tamel might be behind him for ever. Johnnie would misinterpret what he was doing to help him, perhaps. Motives could never be seen clearly; but it did not matter.

He crossed the field and passed Headquarters tent where Prabhu's shadow was stretched grotesquely on the canvas walls; crossing the road he walked to the lines. The stars were a canopy and the wind was cold and bitter. He huddled into himself as he walked, for warmth. In the lines he stumbled across the guy ropes of tents until he found the one in which Dass slept. He shook him awake and explained what had to be done. He stayed until he saw Dass tie his boots and stand up. Then he said, 'Pick me up at the office, Dass.'

'Sir, there is no need for you to come.'

'I want to. Pick me up at the office and don't be too long. Bring six men and a lorry.'

'Yes, sir.'

Jim left Dass and began to walk back to the office. If he had ever commanded the section Dass would have been his man. It had begun that day in Prulli when Dass lodged his disguised complaint and he had looked him straight in the eye to show that he understood and was amused. There were others, too, who would have become his men. Not many; was it perhaps not more than thirty? Enough to hearten him; and enough to disturb him for Johnnie's sake.

He stopped short.

Johnnie was coming up the road. Even in the darkness he recognised the outline of the compact little body, the way it moved, the way the feet were planted on the ground.

He had to speak first. 'Johnnie?'

'What the hell are you doing?'

'I've just got Dass up.'

'Why?'

He waited before he answered, quietly, 'You know why.'

'Did Prabhu come into your tent?'

'No. I called him in.'

'What for?'

'I was awake. I heard him.'

The light that shone upwards from the lantern made uncanny shadows on their faces. Johnnie said, 'Well?'

'It was to help.'

'Who will it help?'

There was no answer. He offered none. Johnnie pushed past him and began to walk up the hill.

'Johnnie!' Jim turned back himself and followed. 'What are you going up there for? Dass is getting the squad out of bed.'

Johnnie stopped. 'I know what I'm doing.' Then he went on again and Jim watched him until he could see him no longer.

He found Dass marshalling sepoys half-drunk with sleep.

'Send 'em back to bed, Dass.'

'Sir?'

'You heard. Send 'em back.'

'Lieutenant Taylor Sahib told . . .'

'Taylor Sahib has made a mistake.' His voice rose. 'There's no need to go down to the strip at this hour for one bloody plane load that Ramo should've told us about hours ago. Go on! Ai! Jeldi! Wapas jao!'

The sepoys remained; uncertain. He was glad that he could not see their faces, for they were faces of men who were lost to him, hearing him, not understanding him. He turned away so that he should not even see the huddled group. He was grateful for the darkness. At that other time the sun had warmed their love and their recognition. He needed the memory of that day to support him and without knowing it he put out his hand and let it rest on Dass's shoulder.

'You don't think I'm going to let my old section be messed around like this, do you? Do you?'

'Sir?'

He shook his shoulder, not in anger, but in desperation because it was as cold as ice and his own hand was heavy and lifeless. He felt Dass shiver.

'Do you? Do you think I'd let anyone mess you about?'

143

'No, sir.'

He shouted, 'Go on! Get back to bed!' From behind him he heard Moti Ram say softly, 'Sahib?' He twisted round on his heel and Dass moved away and directed the sepoys back to their tents. They cursed.

Moti Ram came near. They faced one another across the gulf of darkness and across the gulf of time and change, which they were powerless to bridge.

'Is anything the matter, sir?'

'No, Sahib. Nothing's the matter. There was a loading party got out and I've just sent 'em back, that's all.' He walked off.

'Sir . . .?'

He stopped and Moti Ram came close again.

'We do not mind the loading parties, sir. These are the orders, sir.' Moti Ram paused. He wanted to say: And we do not want you to get into trouble; but Johnnie Sahib might not understand, and to say such a thing might bring anger.

'You mean they're Ramo's orders, Sahib.'

'It is your orders we obey, sir.' The answer, without his meaning it, was phrased like a question because he was unsure of Johnnie.

'That's right, Sahib. It's my orders you obey, and my orders are to go down in the morning first thing. There's no need to wake up tired men at this time of night.'

'We are used to it, sir. It is the war.'

'Goodnight, Sahib.'

He walked away. The men don't work for the war. They work for Scottie or Bill or whoever's commanding them. The war for them begins and ends . . .

There was dull obedience left; and the husk of what had been good. He walked forward and followed the road because the road led him. The wind had freshened and he was cold, and because he was cold he began to run. He ran and his feet stumbled on the flinty stones, and when he had passed Headquarters tent he walked again and the grass of the field rustled beneath his feet. There was a light in Jim's tent. Outside it he paused. He opened the flap, but did not go in.

'Jim?'

'Yes?'

'Be on the strip in the morning and see that plane gets switched over, will you?'

'Look, Johnnie, for God's sake . . .'

He shouted, 'That's an order. Don't let's have any damned

bloody argument about it!' He turned away and went down to his own tent and as he did so he heard the Major's voice calling faintly. He stopped. The Major called again. He took no notice but went back to his tent where the light was burning.

He could hear movement in the field. He should not have shouted. Now they were all awake. He sat on the edge of his bed and waited.

The Major called, 'Johnnie?' and the voice was nearer and he could hear the Major coming across the field and Scottie asking, 'What's up?' and the Major's reply, 'I don't know.' Why did he say, 'I don't know? He knew well enough but he had said, 'I don't know', and now Scottie would come as well; and Parrish. The whole bloody lot. The whole bloody crowd.

The Major pushed his way through the flap and Johnnie grinned because under the greatcoat that was unbuttoned he could see the whiteness of the Major's legs.

'What were you shouting for?'

'Shouting in my sleep.'

'What d'you think I am, a dope?'

'Sometimes.'

The Major placed his lantern on the little table. 'Out with it, Johnnie. I'm bloody cold.'

'Go back to bed then.'

The Major half turned away, opening the flap with one hand.

'Jim!'

'What are you calling him for?'

'I heard part of what you said.'

'Then you know what's up.'

'I have an idea. But I want you to tell me.' He paused. His face flushed suddenly and he said loudly, 'Christ! Aren't you man enough?'

Johnnie got to his feet, his face reddened.

'All right, Major. I'll tell you. I got an order to unload a u.s. plane. J.58 is the number.'

'J.58?'

'And H.43 is the number of the plane that'll go instead. And it'll be done first thing in the morning.'

'And Taylor disagreed with you about that?'

'That's neither here nor there.'

'I disagree with you, too.'

'That's too bloody bad. I've already given the order.'

'Then you'll change it.' He waited. 'Won't you, Johnnie?'

'No.'

'I see.' The Major grasped the handle of his lantern. 'I've put up with a lot from you, haven't I ?' He went out and called for Jim.

Johnnie smiled. 'Go on! Call one of your blue-eyed boys. That's all you want in this company.' He reached for a cigarette and from the flap Scottie said, 'Anything wrong, Johnnie?'

As he came in Johnnie spun round.

'What the hell are you poking your nose in for, Scott? Go on back to your own bloody tent, you pen-pushing old woman! Go on! I don't need you to come an' tell me how to run my section!'

The Major came back. 'For God's sake stop shouting. Scottie, shove off will you?'

'All right, Major. Just thought . . . ' he shrugged and went and they were alone again.

'Johnnie . . .'

He put the lantern down.

'Look, I've sent Jim off again to get your men up. Are you going with him?'

'No.'

'I order you to go with him and I order you to apologise to Scottie in the morning. See! I *order* you.'

Johnnie sat down.

'Your answer's no?'

'It is, Major.'

'Very well.'

The Major clenched his hands. It was Comitarla, the day Taylor arrived. Can't you take criticism? he had said and Johnnie had replied, You pick a fine time to make it. Then he had remembered Nina, and that Nina was gone. It was Prulli, and in the mess they had drunk gin and he had said, We must find a formula. One devised formulas and catchwords, but from them, at the last, there was only emptiness and two men divided by it.

He said, 'You're disobeying my orders, then.'

'Yes, Major.'

'Well, you can disobey orders, but you've got to take the consequences.'

Johnnie moved, then bent down to pick up the cigarettes he had scattered angrily when Scottie had come in. He put one in his mouth and paused. Then he threw one to the Major. They leaned to their separate lanterns and sucked the flame up to light their cigarettes. Johnnie settled back on the edge of his bed.

'Very well, Major. What are the consequences?'

The Major passed his hand across his mouth.

Johnnie was watching him. 'A court-martial?'

'No. Not a court-martial. Unless you demand one.'

'What then?'

'I'm going to send you away.'

'You can't do that.'

'I can and I will.'

Without thinking, Johnnie replied, 'My section goes with me.' And then he remembered.

'Don't be a fool, Johnnie. How can it? You're facing this alone.'

Johnnie looked away, down at his hands which were clasped with a cigarette held in the fingers.

'You said once that losing your section would be the only thing that'd hurt you.' He licked his lips so that his words would not be mumbled. 'I know you meant it. I know it will.'

He waited for Johnnie to look up at him and because he kept silent Johnnie raised his head involuntarily and the Major saw tears beginning to form in his eyes.

'Why d'you want to hurt me?'

'I don't. You make me do it.'

Johnnie bent his head again. 'I know,' he muttered.

'I've always known we'd come to this. I expect in a way you have as well.' Standing, he was suddenly dog-tired. He wanted to sit. But one could not sit and do what he was going to do. 'We've talked about it before. I've warned you. In Prulli when we talked that night I tried to say what I'm saying now. Your section...' he hesitated, 'you kept them too much part of you. And I thought then it was wrong, because that way they work too much for *you*. I still think it's wrong, but for a different reason. It's you who's working for *them* now. You don't command them anymore, Johnnie. They command you.'

He had to wait a long time for Johnnie to speak; when he did so it was only to say, with his head still bent, 'When do I go?'

'Tomorrow.' He saw the hands tighten, and the cigarette jerk backwards and nearly fall. 'You'll get on the mail plane that goes to Calcutta tomorrow. From there you'll go by rail to Marapore.'

'On an adverse report?' The words tumbled out thickly.

'No, Johnnie. Not on an adverse.'

Johnnie looked up at last. The Major had expected to see that the tears had fallen; but his cheeks were still dry.

'Why? Why not on an adverse?'

'Because you've been a good officer.' He looked away himself and stared at the flame in the lantern. Then he looked back and

147

saw that Johnnie's eyes had followed and were fixed upon the steady flame, as though the answers to all questions were in that flame.

'You've been a binder. You haven't fitted in. But you've done your job, in your way. I don't mind a man not fitting in but his job's got to fit in, and yours doesn't anymore.'

He stopped. The sound of his voice, creating new catchphrases, hurt. At the end, there was no need for them.

'That's all there is to it, Johnnie.'

He picked up his lantern, but Johnnie did not move.

'Jim Taylor, he'll take over from you.'

This time Johnnie nodded. Then he muttered, 'He's all right. I'm glad.'

He wanted, in cowardice, to get out of the tent, but something held him. Groping for words he said, 'This isn't all cut and dried in my mind.' Johnnie looked up. 'Not all cut and dried in my mind as a solution.' He took his cigarette and stubbed it in the lid of the tobacco tin that Johnnie had on his table, and again, he saw Johnnie's eyes had followed his movement.

He said, 'There's always more than one war to fight.' Then he turned away and pushed through the tent flap and the cold wind struck round his ankles and across his forehead.

The Major had gone, and in the lid of the tobacco tin the stub of his cigarette sent a thin wisp of smoke curling from a smouldering edge.

Slowly it burnt itself out.

He bowed his head and said, 'What am I going to do?'

As if to find an answer from inanimate things he looked up again and stared at the lantern, at the makeshift ashtray with its dead stubs, at all the tokens surrounding him which were his possessions. They had been with him at the beginning and were now with him at the end. And they were nothing because the end had come.

PART FOUR

Pyongiu

13

Baxter tore off yesterday's date from the calendar and saw that it was exactly one week to Christmas Day. He grimaced and sat back in his chair. It was early and the air was crisp in the way he liked it best. He called out to Shelley, in the adjoining office, 'Did they get that petrol landing commitment to Pyongiu started last night?' Shelley called back that they had, and Baxter smiled.

He rose and went over to the map to check that Shelley had marked the captured airfield at Pyongiu with the proper coloured pin. Satisfied, he went back to his desk. It had been infinitely worthwhile pulling strings in Delhi. One had pulled strings ever since, for extra equipment, for pioneer labour priorities and recently to borrow men from various infantry units which for this or that reason had been withdrawn temporarily from forward divisions. He had a whole batch of them now bivouacked on the airfield and they had taken over ejection duties from the hard pressed men in the platoons.

He listened to the mumbling of voices in Shelley's office. One had pulled strings, too, to get Ghosh and Johns transferred to Ramo as Staff Captains. It had been a long, drawn-out process, but one had been successful. The posting orders had arrived suddenly the first week in December and the Major had handed the two officers over to him, not bothering to conceal his surprise and, perhaps, annoyance.

Now, in Ramo office, Johns and Ghosh struggled with the mountain of returns and statistics which had made their presence essential. It could not be helped that the Major's platoon officers were still doing their own staff work. The machine had grown bigger than one had anticipated. But one had to avoid discussing staff work with the Major, just as one avoided mention of Johnnie Brown.

To support the Major's summary disposal of Brown back to Marapore, one had pulled strings as never before. One had always liked the Major, indeed, had admired him in many ways, but now one felt easier in the mind, for no specific reason. Brown must always have been a thorn in the Major's flesh. One did not know and did not enquire. It had been enough that the Major had said. 'I've sacked Brown, sir. Will you back me up?' And one had shown a little surprise, had mentioned gently that an officer was entitled to some sort of hearing, had patted the Major's shoulder and then sent confidential reports to Marapore; reports that did not damn Brown but whose lines could be read between. And no more had been heard until confirmation of Taylor's promotion had set the seal of an impersonal but official approval on the Major's unconventional action. One had taken that signal round personally to the Major's office.

He looked at his desk. This morning there was yet another signal and in a few moments he would put his hat on and walk briskly along to the Major's office. He called for Ghosh who bounded in like a gazelle, still pleased as punch with his three pips and the staff pay that, when the Pay Office got down to it, would be so welcome to the wife in Bangalore. 'I want you,' said Baxter, 'to go into Imphal and see the CRE about those additional area extensions.'

'Yes, sir. I will go now, sir!

'Good.'

Ghosh jostled out and Baxter listened to Shelley and Johns talking about fishing. Baxter grinned. Shelley had not yet realised John's Indian extraction and he found it amusing to let Shelley ramble on exchanging reminiscences of England with the man who so obviously had never been there. It was a quiet, almost negative and therefore succinct way of putting one over on Shelley, who was so pompous.

As Baxter, with the signal in his hand, walked round to see the Major, he looked with approval at the bithessed road, the neat rows of stores, the white tents. Such things as this added up to something in a man's life. He sniffed the air, and the fumes of petrol from Three Section lines were, to him, pleasant. They were indicative, too, of the trend in the campaign, which looked as though it would turn at any moment into a headlong, mechanised advance.

The Major was in the clerks' section talking to Prabhu when the Colonel arrived in his tent. Baxter called to him, 'I've got a little surprise for you.' The Major came through to his office and took the signal. Baxter watched his expression; but it did not change. He thought, 'He's grown a thicker skin than even I guessed.'

'Well?'

'I've been expecting this, of course.' He read the signal through again. *All Platoon transport will be pooled forthwith to form M.T. Platoon under command subaltern Lieut. Smith, G. despatched by air ex Marapore.*

Then he handed it back to Baxter and said, 'I've had a communal M.T. park sited for some time.'

'Care to show it me?'

'Of course.' They went out together and the Major took him past Three and Two Section areas. He pointed to a level, open area on the right of the road. 'It's really a case of extending Scott's harbour to fit the whole lot. We can build a culvert over the ditch there, so that you have a wider exit. The entrance is O. K.'

Baxter nodded. 'That looks all right. I'll lay on some pioneers for you.' They turned and walked back.

'I suppose your platoon commanders'll kick up a bit of a shindy losing control of their transport?'

'I expect so.' But the Major's voice sounded strangely unconcerned. They were walking past Three Section now and Baxter said, 'Taylor's doing well, isn't he?'

'He's a good man.'

'Always difficult taking another officer's place.'

'He's all right now.' There was a slight emphasis on the 'now' and Baxter noticed it. He asked, 'The men like him, I suppose?'

'He gets the results.'

Baxter shot a sideways glance at the Major and their eyes met, but before the Colonel could see or guess at what the terse answer implied the Major had turned away again and the subject was closed. Baxter became thoughtful, and they walked the rest of the way in silence. Perhaps, through some odd quirk, the Major blamed him for Brown's dismissal; the company had been together a long time, and it must have been a wrench to discover that one of the officers was no longer up to the mark; in the circumstances one would probably blame almost anyone but the officer concerned.

'But,' Baxter told himself, 'it's no business of mine.'

When Baxter had left him the Major returned to his office and rang on the field telephone to all his platoon commanders. The lines were inter-connected and each platoon had a certain number of rings as a call-sign. By giving each call-sign successively they all came on the line together. It saved time.

'Scottie? Bill? Jim?'

They indicated they were listening.

'Round at my tent, now! O.K.?'

Without listening to their replies he hung up, letting his hand rest on the instrument, pressing it down firmly. Then he lit a cigarette and waited for them. Three of them. Smith would make a fourth; and only Scottie and Bill had been with him in Marapore.

But he did not care. He was glad, because it made it easier not to care about anything except the fact that somehow he had maintained his company as a unit; and thus maintained his pride. Pride would keep him going, too, long after Baxter had grown stale. He needed no slogan, no catch-penny phrase to stir other men; his belief in himself and his self-respect were now strong enough for his purpose. He did not wish to stir other men; he did not wish to lead, or even to have men follow. The company was still alive, and he commanded it. It was his. He had created it, and if its parts had changed its whole was indestructible.

They came in severally, and he said, when they had all settled down on stools in front of his desk, 'Anyone know a chap called Smith?' As he said it he realised how absurd a question it was, but only Scottie bothered to say, 'Probably all of us.'

The Major looked at Jim. 'Didn't Johnnie Brown say something about a chap called Smith?'

'Yes, Major.'

'Well he's coming here to take over all transport and form a separate M.T. platoon.'

'Oh, Christ!'

'What's the matter, Bill?'

'Aren't they ever going to stop mucking us about?'

'I don't see that it's mucking you about. It relieves you of some of your responsibility.'

'It relieves us of our transport as well. That's the point.'

The Major smiled. 'I don't see it.'

They shifted in their seats and for a while nobody spoke. The Major got up. 'If you come with me I'll show you where the M.T. harbour's going to be.' He went to the tent exit and he heard Bill grumbling under his breath. They followed him out on to the road and Scottie came abreast with him and said, 'My own harbour could be extended.'

'That's what I have in mind.'

When they arrived at the park they stood in the roadway and the Major pointed and explained. And then Parrish asked, 'Who's going to be senior N.C.O. in this so-called M.T. platoon?'

'What d'you mean, Bill?'

'Well, we've each got a platoon M.T. Havildar. One of 'em 'll be top dog in the new set up.'

'Does it matter?'

'There'll be friction.'

'Not if the one with the longest service is put in charge.'

'Length of service doesn't necessarily mean clues about M.T.'

'We'll let Smith worry over that little problem.' The Major turned to Jim. 'What's he like, this chap Smith?'

'A good M.T. man.'

'He's a friend of yours, isn't he?'

'We came out to India together.' Jim moved a few paces away.

'Anything else, Major?' Bill cut in.

'Nothing else. Carry on as you are until Smith gets here.'

They saluted and left him, but Jim hung back.

'Want me, Jim?'

'Would you see Moti Ram if I bring him along to your office?'

'Why?'

'I want you to tear him off a strip.'

'What's he doing?'

'Nothing.' Jim offered a cigarette. They began walking back towards Three Section. 'It needs you to show him he's for the high jump unless he co-operates more.'

'How's he not co-operating?'

'It's difficult to explain.'

'I can't go on anything vague. Isn't there anything you can pick on?'

'He's not insubordinate. He just makes difficulties.'

'What sort of difficulties?'

'If I could pick on anything special myself I wouldn't bother you.' He paused. 'All he wants is a good talking to.'

'Can't you do that?'

'I'm always doing it.'

'Always?'

'For some time now, anyway.'

'Bring him along then.'

'When?'

'This afternoon.'

'Right.'

At five minutes to three Jim reported to the Major.

'Moti Ram's on his way round.'

'O.K. What d'you really want me to say?'

'Just tell him I've reported him for non-co-operation.'

'Does it extend to the men?'

'Yes. A sort of go-slow policy.'

153

'I see. Know why?'

'My guess'll be the same as yours.'

'Johnnie?'

'With Moti Ram anyway. His favourite expression these days is "When Captain Brown Sahib was commanding the section. . . ." '

'It's quite natural, you know.'

'I've stood it for five weeks.'

'It'll take longer than five weeks.'

'Why should it? It's all bloody hypocrisy anyway.'

'What do you mean by that?'

'They didn't really give a damn about Johnnie. They used him just the same as they're trying to use me. Make me toe the line. That's why I'm bringing you into it. Make them see they're part of the company.'

The Major sat back.

'That's what I said to Johnnie the night I sacked him.'

'That they used him?'

'Yes. That they commanded him.'

'You thought that too, then?'

'I did that night. It seemed the only answer. He did what he did because he knew they expected him to stand up for them. They took advantage.'

Prabhu looked round the canvas wall that divided the tent. 'Sir, Moti Ram Sahib is here.'

'Tell him to come in, Prabhu.'

Prabhu disappeared and then the Jemadar walked in, came to attention in front of the Major's desk and saluted.

'Captain Taylor Sahib told me I must be reporting to you, sir.'

'Yes, Sahib. I want to talk to you.'

'Sir?'

'Jemadar Sahib . . . .' the Major leaned forward at his desk. 'Captain Taylor tells me that your work is unsatisfactory. What about it?'

'I do not understand, sir. I work as always I am working for nearly two years sir, under Captain Brown Sahib.'

'I don't think that can be true.'

'Sir?'

'I understand you have a habit of misinterpreting orders. By that I don't mean deliberately disobey. You're too old a soldier to do that, aren't you, Sahib?'

'Sir, I do not understand.'

'I think you understand well enough, Sahib. I don't want to

154

go into the pros and cons of what has happened. I have only two things to say to you. The first and most important is that I want you to remember that the job we are doing here has *got* to be *done*.' The Major emphasised his words by banging his fist on the table. 'Secondly, that Captain Taylor is your commanding officer in the platoon. What suited Captain Brown does not necessarily suit Captain Taylor. Both these things are worth your remembering. You wouldn't wish to spoil your good record, would you, Jemadar Sahib?'

'Sir . . . I . . .'

'Unless you have anything you wish to say, we'll leave it at that. You may go.'

'Sir . . .'

'Yes, Sahib.'

Moti Ram clenched his jaw. Then he saluted and turned on his heel, leaving the office by the front exit.

The Major sighed. 'All right?'

'Yes.'

The unpleasantness of what had happened left its mark of silence. The Major drummed lightly with his fingers, then took one of the cigarettes that Jim offered him. But there was no familiarity in the gesture.

'Right.' The Major pulled a sheaf of papers towards him.

When he left the Major's office Jim did not immediately go back to his own platoon. There were visits to make; to Ramo to see if Johns had done anything about ending the shortage of four-gallon petrol cans; to the airfield to check up on planes which had come back still loaded. One went through the actions mechanically and there was time to think; to think about Moti Ram and about Geoff Smith who was coming from Marapore. The two thoughts were connected.

His afternoon's work finished he drove swiftly back to his platoon and parked the truck outside his office. He stood in the roadway watching the men who were packing and loading petrol under the supervision of Havildar Dass. He smiled to himself. There had been a time when he had believed that of all men Dass might one day be *his* man. But Dass paid lip-service only; the hate in his eyes was veiled perhaps, veiled with puzzlement and unspoken questions; but he felt its impact no less strongly than that of Moti Ram. He went into the office. Perhaps of them all he admired Moti Ram the most. He at least was openly defiant, as openly defiant as any soldier dared to be. But he was a hypocrite along with the rest. They were all of them hypocrites. Men who had taken all that Johnnie had to give and had given nothing in return. If they had loved him they would have kept the spirit of that love alive now that he was gone. But they no longer pretended to love, for obviously there was nothing to be gained by pretence. Johnnie's star had fallen.

'Sir?'

'What is it, Nimu?'

'Jemadar Sahib wishes to see you, sir.'

'Can't he come himself and tell me that?' Jim looked up and Nimu's eyes fell.

'Well?'

'He wishes to see you on official business, sir.'

'Tell him to come in, then. Wait for these.' He finished signing the notes and shoved them across the desk. Nimu gathered them up and went back to his own office.

In a minute or two he heard Moti Ram muttering to the clerk. He called out, 'Sahib?' There was a pause and then Moti Ram marched in. In his left hand he held a folded paper.

'What is it, Sahib?'

Moti Ram put the paper on the desk and said, 'Sir, I have here my application for a transfer from this company.'

Jim picked up the note, unfolded it and read it slowly. Then, without a word, he tore it up and threw it on the floor.

The Jemadar's voice was hoarse. 'Sir! You have torn my lawful application.'

'Your lawful application is a humbug, Sahib.'

'I have no wish to serve in this company longer. Until now I always pull on to the best of my ability. Now it is no use.'

'Nevertheless, you will continue to serve.'

'You cannot keep me here against my will, sir.'

'*Cannot*, Sahib? What word is this?'

'Sir, all men are knowing that you take me in front of Major Sahib.'

'Well?'

'All men are knowing. This is indignity. I am a simple man, but also I am a proud man.'

'Well?'

Moti Ram made an abrupt movement of his hands. 'I am a Viceroy's Commissioned Officer, sir. But this you do not care about. I am marched in front of Major Sahib. All clerks, all

156

sweeper wallahs at headquarters, all throughout company hear of my disgrace.'

'What am I supposed to do about that?'

'Sir, you must be compassionate. I must go where no-one hears of this thing.'

'*Must? Cannot?*' Jim smiled and held out his empty hands.

'You take my dignity away sir. Now I cannot make the men work.'

'Will that be much of a change? Recently you haven't bothered to try and make them work. Now you cannot. I see no difference in the effect.'

'Without respect they will not follow me, sir. Or without love. Only now they follow by strict, hard discipline. And this is no good.' He paused as if to emphasise his words. 'This harsh discipline is no good.'

'Why is it no good?'

'You are not understanding us, sir. These men are far from their homes.'

'We are all far from home.'

'We are not like these man, sir. They are as children. They need love.' He paused; then in a lower voice he said, 'Like the love of Captain Brown Sahib.'

He saw Taylor Sahib clench his hands into tight fists. He went on, 'Now my heart is empty, sir. I cannot give this love, and I am no use.'

'So your heart is empty is it, Sahib?'

He said nothing. Taylor Sahib's voice was like ice.

'Your heart is empty? Well, the heart may be empty but you will have to try and carry on all the same. The heart may be empty, but there are brothers of these men in Burma. Without us they starve. They lose battles. And then all would be emptiness. You understand?'

'You understand?' Taylor Sahib repeated.

'You are poet in your mind, sir. Poet in your speech. But you are a cold man. We do not understand a cold man's poetry.' He smiled, slowly. He had kept his word. In Prulli he had known the time would come to say this thing to Taylor.

'Is that all you have to say, Sahib?'

'You will not let me go?'

'No.' Taylor got up and Moti Ram stared at the empty chair, aware that Taylor had walked slowly to the doorway of the tent. At last he looked round and found that the officer watched him.

'You are part of a machine, Sahib. So am I. If you had asked the Major Sahib for a transfer this afternoon you would have got it. It is the sort of request for which there is the right moment. But you didn't have the courage. Like that time before. Remember? That time Havildar Dass made your complaint for you?'

They watched each other and Taylor went on, 'No, you didn't have the courage. But I'm not looking for courage. I'm looking for efficiency. You can be efficient if you try. That's why I've fitted you into my scheme of things again. I'm not going to alter my programme just to suit your convenience. You will stay in the platoon. And you will make the men work.'

He walked back slowly to the desk.

'That is all I have to say.'

Moti Ram moved to go.

'No. There's one thing more.'

'Sir?'

'Respect and what you call love can't be turned on and off like a tap. If I were you I'd stop that little game.' He paused; then, 'You can go now,' he said.

The Jemadar walked out of the office and down the road and was aware of eyes watching; eyes that were mocking and yet wary. The smell of petrol was the smell of Tamel and all that had happened in Tamel had been bad and unhappy and beyond human comprehension. The smell of petrol was sickening; it was always there; even in sleep it came.

To have left Tamel would have been to find air untainted by the heavy fumes of it. But he was to stay in Tamel; there was no escaping the ghost of Johnnie Sahib that haunted and accused and stood every day behind the shoulder of Taylor Sahib; the ghost had been there just now when Taylor Sahib had said, 'You didn't have the courage. Remember? In Prulli Dass made your complaint for you.' The ghost had been there and the ghost had echoed the words too.

Was the beginning then, in Prulli? Had that been deceit?

Dass was supervising the loading of a line of lorries and as Moti Ram approached the men slackened and their voices were still and he saw Dass look at him quickly, and then away, saying to the men, 'Chalo, chalo!' They carried on, but as though his presence were a cloud that blotted the sun; for a man disgraced is a man fallen, and other men must turn their heads. He tightened his hands and forced himself to stay watching them.

Ai! But that Dass was a clever one. For was it not he who had said in Prulli, 'See! I have been to Johnnie Sahib and told him of our troubles when he was away. I, not Moti Ram Sahib!' And what a fine fellow they had thought him; and how they had loaded him with garlands about the neck when he went on leave to sleep with that wife of his and plant seeds in her belly.

And was it not Dass, too, who had said, 'See, Johnnie Sahib and Taylor Sahib are now good friends. Is it not wise that we should make this new officer our friend, too? Is this not what Johnnie Sahib has done? And have we not always followed him, and has he not always led?'

And Dass, drunken one night in the stink and heat of Prulli, drunken because his leave was over, had said, 'Johnnie Sahib is tired of us. See how he looks at us sometimes. He is going away. He will become big officer Sahib and we shall be forgotten as sands in a desert.' And if Dass, sober, regretted speaking of what was a fear, a pain in his heart, he had released the pain and the fear to spread to other men.

Yes, Dass was a clever one. Words grew on his tongue fairly like lotus on water. But in Tamel even he had been silent when he saw the great, unfathomable pain eating into the heart of Johnnie Sahib. Even he could not find words to explain what was obvious to all men; that Johnnie was outside their reach, and they outside his. Words could say that this was so; but they could not say how, or why. Neither could they say when it had begun. Perhaps it was that Johnnie had been part of destiny; and all men know that destiny is uncontrollable. When God turned His Face one could seek to propitiate by speaking words to Him; words that were heavy with doubt and because of that had the rhythm of questions in them; words that were heavy with diplomacy and had two meanings; words that no longer came from the heart because the heart was troubled; dumb.

He grew tired of watching Dass, tired of looking into but not seeing the eyes of the sepoys which flashed from time to time in his direction. He had failed. They had all failed, but his own failure was the greatest. He had had his chances; once, right at the beginning in Tamel when Johnnie Sahib had said, 'Now you have the company spirit', and he had known that it was by way of a reprimand. The other chance he had had the night that trouble came. It was then he should have said, 'Sir, you have gone away from us and without you Tamel is unbearable. You are standing here before me, and yet you are not here. Why is this? Is it perhaps something we have done? Is it because this new officer has come between us? But is he not your friend? Like Bradley Sahib? Should we not also be friends?

159

Moti Ram turned away, so that Dass should not see that he wept. He trudged behind the store and into the shadow. The tears could fall unseen as they had not fallen since the day Johnnie Sahib had gone and it had been too late to say those things, too late to breathe warmth into the cold words that *were* said when they faced each other in the darkness; faced each other for the last time, unknowingly.

On that remembered morning he had watched the sunlight pass over the trodden ground of his tent and the talk of the men outside had died as Jan Mohammed passed among them and told them that Johnnie Sahib was going. Then there had been silence; a silence so great that the mind could not think. They carried the silence with them down the dusty track and the dust had risen with the trampling of so many feet. They had stood huddled together at the junction of the track and the road, and there they had seen the truck that would take Johnnie Sahib away. An order had come from the Major Sahib's tent that they were to disperse and gradually they had done so. The sun had risen higher and a pretence was made of work. Men worked with their eyes turning to the point in the road where the truck waited.

Moti Ram shut out the memory.

Johnnie Sahib had not gone. The sense of him was everywhere. Taylor Sahib would never destroy it, however hard he tried. The Jemadar looked up, thinking he heard footsteps. But there was no-one. No-one came to him and he was glad for he knew no longer who was a friend and who was not. He was alone and it seemed sometimes that only he remembered. He had been afraid because of that and had hoped to go. But he was to stay.

One could only atone. One could never right the wrong that had been done. One could atone and pray to God and say, 'For what I have done I am sorry. For what I have failed to do I am full of regret.' One could pray, and hope that He understood, and that Johnnie himself understood; now, when it was too late.

14

Three days before Christmas a plane crashed into the fields at the end of the runway as it took off on a dropping mission. The ejection crew of four sepoys from the infantry unit Baxter had commandeered were badly burnt. The news came to Baxter and he rang through on the field telephone to the Major and explained what had happened.

The Major asked, 'Do we know the number yet?'

Baxter gave it to him. He checked his list.

'That's one of Scottie's loads. Do we get a repeat today?'

'I'll let you know. It might be too late.'

'I'll warn him anyway. One of the officers will fly with it.'

'To boost morale?'

The Major laughed. 'Well, that's the idea. Actually it's a cast iron excuse for them to go on a jaunt.' He paused. 'They need it occasionally. Too much desk work.' He smiled, picturing Baxter's face. There was a pause at the other end of the line.

'I see what you mean, Major,' Baxter said drily.

But there was no substitute plane and at the evening conference the Major asked which one of them wanted a trip the following day.

Bill said simply, 'Me.'

'But it was my load,' Scottie complained.

As they began to argue Jim said, 'I've been intending to go down with one of my petrol landings at Pyongiu to see the new strip. See how it's handled at that end.'

The Major nodded. 'That's constructive.'

He looked at the others. 'You can't all go.'

'Why not? It's a good idea. Get out of this bloody place for a bit.' Bill lit a cigarette and curled the tips of his moustache. 'Cheap trip to Burma. You ought to lay it on, Major.'

He answered, without thinking, 'Like the river?' Then he remembered it was Johnnie who had laid that on. He said, 'You go, Jim. Then we can send in a report to Ramo.'

'I hadn't counted on that.'

'You can make up something. It might give Baxter the idea to send one of us down occasionally.'

'He wouldn't do that. What'd happen to the turn-round?' Bill glanced round for approval. But the joke had worn thin, as the Major knew it would; and in Tamel there were no 'cheap trips to Burma'; there were only statistical and intelligence missions to forward areas for Ramo's benefit.

'Right, let's get on with our figures, shall we?'

They drew out their notepads.

As the Dakota lost height he felt the heat rise up from the ground. The drums of petrol were lashed in two rows, down each side of the fuselage and the smell was heady, intoxicating.

161

He stood in the open doorway and saw the long rectangle of Pyongiu airfield incongruously flat and man-made upon the natural pattern of yellow-red sandy earth which was folded into hillocks, veined with dried-up *chaungs*. Grounded planes were like children's toys set down in a military training model; but as they circled lower and lower he detected the movement of trucks by their billowing tails of dust.

They flew above a long, straight road on which lorries travelled; the road was cut through a scrub of trees, and suddenly the road and the trees tilted as the plane turned finally for its landing. Their flying shadow grew nearer, developing swift humps where the ground was uneven. He felt the impact of the wheels on earth and the sickening little jolt upwards; the second and last impact; and men and known objects came into natural eye-level as the plane slowed down the runway.

The heat was pleasant, scorching the backs of the hands, and it was a relief to smoke and stand watching from a discreet distance the unloading of the petrol drums on to the lorries which had raced up to the plane as it turned into the loading bay.

The Canadian crew had walked off, obviously familiar with Pyongiu, and he saw them disappear into a long basha built in the shelter of trees. He threw down his cigarette, heeling it into the sandy earth and walked up to a man whose skin was burnt to a deep mahogany colour. The man wore round his wrist a wide linen strap with the two chevrons of a corporal sewn on to it.

'All right, Corporal?'

'Yes, sir. You from the other end?'

'Yes. Thought I'd take a look at what happens.'

'Well, this is it.'

They watched the unloading squad.

'Whereabouts does it all go now?'

'Dump's about three miles down the road.'

'Are we sending it fast enough?'

'Too ruddy fast.' The corporal smiled and nodded at the squad. 'From their point of view, anyway.'

'How's Pyongiu?'

'Where?'

'This place.'

'Oh, all right. We call it Pongo.' He laughed.

'You're a Londoner, aren't you?'

'Yes, sir.'

They talked for some time. Then the corporal said, 'Got to go now.'

'Can I get some tea anywhere?'

The corporal pointed towards the basha. 'Over there.'

'Thanks.'

Jim walked towards it. Looking back over his shoulder he saw the loaded truck swerving away from the plane, the corporal clinging on to the side of the cabin.

He thought, 'Pongo', and laughed. Should that go in the report for Baxter?

The shade of the basha was welcome and inside it aircrews were drinking tea dished up by a British cook and a naked Burmese boy. It was obvious the boy was a mascot in Pongo. He knew only one complete sentence and a few odd words of English; mostly obscene.

Jim took his tea and as he raised the steaming mug to his lips someone said behind him, 'Hello, sir.'

The voice was familiar. He looked round and for an instant did not recognise the man who stood close to him. Then he remembered. The green cotton uniform was crumpled, stained with dust and sweat, but it was worn with a correct, soldierly air. Long, green drill trousers, with no central crease, were tucked snugly into anklets which encased boots grey with dubbin. But the boots were solid and looked dependable. And although they were not gleaming white, but faded with many washings, the stripes and insignia of a staff-sergeant were sewn on precisely the right part of the sleeve.

The staff-sergeant said, 'Prulli, sir. Remember?'

'Of course.' They shook hands. 'What brings you to Pyongiu?' One could not, Jim felt, call it Pongo to the sergenat.

'The army, sir.' And the sergeant grinned and showed his white, regular teeth.

They sat on a bench beneath a window cut out of the plaited bamboo wall.

'How long have you been gone from Prulli?'

'Just after you all went, sir.'

'Were you sorry to leave? You seemed to have got yourself pretty comfortable.'

'Sorry? No, sir. Pongo's all right, too.'

'Are you static here?'

'For a time. When we're in Mandalay I go there.'

'Seeing the world.'

'I was two years in Mandalay before the war.'

'Home from home again.'

'Yes, sir.' He paused. 'She'll look like your grandmother now.'

'What was her name?'

'I called her Supi-yaw-lat.' He hesitated. 'Kipling, sir.'

'I know, smoking a cheroot and kissing Bhudda's feet.'

The sergeant hesitated again, then in a dry, inflexible voice he quoted, as if from a training pamphlet, 'Plucky lot she cared for Idols when I kissed 'er where she stud.'

They laughed and Jim offered his cigarettes.

'Where are your lot now, sir?'

'Place called Tamel. South of Imphal.'

'I don't know it.'

'You haven't missed much.'

Suddenly he remembered something Johnnie had told him.

'You had a brother in Imphal, didn't you?'

'Yes sir.'

'Where's he now?'

The sergeant looked at the point of his cigarette.

'He bought it.'

'I'm sorry.'

Jim looked away and saw that the crew of his Dakota were taking their mugs back to the counter.

'That's my plane crew. I'll have to go.' They stood up. 'Might be down here again. I'll look you up.'

'I'm not often at the strip, sir.'

He put out his hand. 'But we'll bump into each other sooner or later, sir. Like Swan and Edgars.' He smiled and Jim shook hands and said, 'Cheerio, then.' He walked out of the basha into the glaring sunlight and shielded his eyes. He heard someone running behind him.

'Sir?'

He turned round. The staff-sergeant had followed him.

'How's Captain Brown?'

'I – I don't know, sergeant. He left us.'

'Posted, sir?'

'Yes.'

'He wouldn't like that.' The sergeant pursed his lips. Then, 'He wouldn't like that at all,' he said.

'No, I suppose he didn't.'

'I'm sorry to think he's gone.' They stared at each other and Jim felt himself forced to say, 'Why d'you say he wouldn't like it?'

'That section of his. He was always talking about 'em. To me, anyway.' The sergeant paused. 'He came a lot, sir, towards the end. Down at Prulli, sir. Not only the times he brought you. He used to come down and sometimes we'd go across the river, sometimes just sit drinking. He even came to my quarters once.'

'Yes he told me.'

'He thought a lot of you, sir. Have you got his section?'

'Yes.'

'That'll be all right, then.'

Jim moved, as if to go, and the sergeant said quickly, 'It was funny. Directly I saw you there I had a feeling he'd gone. That's why I didn't ask after him at first. But I had to in the end.'

'Why should you think he'd gone?'

'He was worried, sir. Got more and more worried. Coming back in the boat one night he told me all about it.'

'What?'

'He felt the men weren't with him any more. You know, sir, how that sort of thing gets after a time. Taking it too much to heart. I tried to make him see it was just that he imagined it.'

'It wasn't all imagination. Not all, sergeant.'

'No?'

'Did he know about your brother?'

'Yes sir. It was after I'd seen you last.'

'He didn't tell me.'

'No, he wouldn't. He took that to heart as well. More than me. I think he'd let Prulli get on his nerves. It did on mine towards the end.'

'Did you volunteer so's you could get out?'

'Yes, sir.'

'Because of your brother?'

The sergeant paused. 'I don't know. Perhaps.'

'Look, I'll have to go.'

'Goodbye sir. Sorry to've kept you. But I wanted to know.'

'I'm glad you asked.' Jim turned and ran towards the plane. The airscrews were already turning and he had to fight against the slipstream and heave himself up through the open doorway. When he stood up he looked back for the sergeant and saw him walking away towards the canteen. He sat down on a coil of rope and surveyed the empty interior that still reeked of petrol. The ropes that had lashed the drums were hanging from their hooks like so many dead snakes. The plane shuddered and he could feel the slight lift in the tail as they taxi-ed towards the runway for take-off.

In the plane, he had already left Pyongiu behind. The picture of it that moved past the doorway had no reality. Pyongiu was derelict, a place dried up by the receding tide of war which had

165

so short a time ago given it tumultuous life; and the people who moved across its hot sands and beneath its burning sun could not for all their talk of places – and people – places and people far away, establish its connection with the outside world. Pyongiu was a name on a map that a visiting plane could, for a brief moment, make recognisable as a formation of earth and tree and sky.

Now it was going. The plane rose high above it; and soon even the dust that swirled from moving trucks was frozen by distance into immobility.

And men themselves were like Pyongiu; for an hour, for less than an hour, one received an impression of them and thought one understood. The words they spoke and the things they did made a pattern whose intricacies seemed intelligible; but as one traced the pattern it began to move in subtle bewildering rhythms.

Even in Pyongiu Johnnie had reached out as if to re-demand his loyalty. But he was strangely unmoved; an exhumation cannot renew life, but a discussion about Johnnie in a place he had never been to brought him into a new perspective, and emphasised that Johnnie was part of the irretrievable past.

One had not known this Johnnie who sat drunkenly and poured out his heart to a sergeant in Prulli; and to that extent it was a new Johnnie; perhaps the real one; and if the figure were pathetic it was less pathetic than the inarticulate man one remembered.

And it was easy, once an illusion had been swept away, to re-create a man in the imagination; recreate him out of his period when the impact of his personality was lost through his absence; to turn one's judgement of him upside down; trace back from the effect to find the cause; selecting the effects to find the cause one wanted to find; to find in the end a Johnnie who had been selfish, arrogant, childish and bitter; to find, like that, a Johnnie one could resent, exorcise like an undesirable spirit from which one could not escape, even in Pyongiu.

It was cold.

And he rose from the coil of rope and stumbled forward to the pilot's cabin so that he should not be alone.

It was growing dark as he walked along the circuit road past Ramo's tents, but there had been enough light as they landed for him to see, for all its familiarity, that Tamel was no different from Pyongiu. It was a place which, for this moment, had life

166

because he lived and moved in it. When he had gone it would exist only for the men who stayed there, but not for him. It did not exist, must not exist for Johnnie, now; and because that was so, thoughts of Johnnie must not intrude and must not be allowed to intrude. There was nothing for Johnnie in Tamel. The real Johnnie was far away and what one's own mind brought back of him, allowed to come back was the Johnnie one resented. Resentment could turn to hate. One's hypocrisy would be no less then than other men's.

He raised his head a little and walked more confidently. Suddenly it seemed there was utter freedom. There was work to do; the evening conference to attend with the figures Moti Ram would have prepared for him; he hoped correctly. But first he must put on warmer clothing.

Avoiding Headquarters office he cut in through the trees to the field where they all lived. Then he stopped short.

There was a light in Johnnie's tent.

15

The tent flap was open and the light from inside it shone into the growing darkness. It was like a dream; a dream in which Johnnie had come back; or like waking from a dream; waking to find that Johnnie had never gone. He could hear voices. He moved to the tent. Someone laughed and another voice raised itself over the sound of the laughter. It was a voice from the past. Brad's voice.

He pushed his way into the tent and saw that Brad was there, stretched out on the bed, cradling his head in one arm. The tent was newly furnished; already it looked as if it had never been empty. From a chair by the side of the bed a man rose and as Brad sat up and said, 'Hello, there,' the man came forward and took his hand.

'Good to see you again, Jim. I just missed you on the strip. How was Pengu?'

'Pengu?' It was Smith. Geoff Smith.

'You've arrived then.' He turned to Brad. 'Where's Johnnie?' They were silent and looked at him oddly. He repeated, 'Where's Johnnie? I heard your voice, Brad. I thought Johnnie was with you.'

'Johnnie's in Ferozepore.'

He looked at Geoff who had spoken. 'But he was in Marapore with you. He went back to Marapore.'

'He left last week. Just before I got posted down myself.'

'He didn't know you were coming here, then?'

'No.'

Brad lay back as if waiting for the subject of the conversation to change. There was a bottle of gin open; glasses. Geoff had made himself at home. And there was no word from Johnnie. No message. He had gone into the blue. He could have written. He could have said, 'Good luck,' or 'I'm all right,' anything to prove he knew his own time had ended; that Jim's had to begin; that he relinquished. Jim went to the bed and said to Brad, 'Did you come down with Geoff?' for Brad had been in Marapore, too.

'No, I've been in Imphal some time. Thought I'd pop down to Tamel and look you all up. I met Bill Parrish on the strip and then Geoff here turns up. So we come back and make ourselves comfy. The Major's invited me to supper, too. Quite a party. The Ramo officers are coming, too.'

'You saw Johnnie in Marapore, though?'

'Not for long. I got posted soon after he arrived. Geoff here knows more about his latest movements.'

Geoff interrupted. 'Have a drink?' But Jim shook his head.

'Why's he in Ferozepore?' he asked.

'Posted. He's out of air supply.'

The edge on Geoff's voice was obvious. He had never liked Johnnie, he remembered, thinking again of the letter which Johnnie himself had carried. Geoff had written, 'He's a bit of a line-shooter. Poor you.'

He stared at Geoff, surprised to find him taller and broader than he had thought of him.

He said, 'You're taking over the transport?'

'Yes. They're not going to like it, are they?'

'They?'

'Parrish and Scott.'

'You've met them, then?'

'Yes. I've met the Major, too. He seems a decent chap.'

Jim nodded and from the bed Brad remarked, 'You look done up.'

'It's the smell of petrol. I flew with a load to Pyongiu. It gets on your stomach.'

'A gin would settle it.'

He shook his head again. 'I've got work to do. Report for Ramo. I'll see you later.'

He left them and went to his tent to put on his jacket. As he went in he found Geoff was following him.

'Can I come in a moment?'

'Of course.'

He searched for his jacket in the jumble of blankets on the bed and was aware of Geoff standing awkwardly in the entrance.

'It's good to see you again, Jim.'

He said nothing, but made a noncommittal grunt in his throat, and Geoff came further into the tent, lighting a cigarette.

'What happened to Johnnie Brown?'

Jim straightened up. He said, 'What d'you mean?'

'I mean here. What happened?'

'Didn't he say?'

'No. Not even to Brad apparently.' Geoff paused. 'Not that he seemed worried much about it. Still he was that type, wasn't he? Take all, give nothing? Hide like a rhinoceros and smug as hell.' Geoff paused again, uncomfortable because Jim looked at him in such a peculiar, searching way. 'This is a funny sort of set-up, isn't it? That chap Parrish's been on at me already.'

'What about?'

Geoff raised his shoulders, awkwardly. 'Chiefly about who I'm going to make senior Havildar. He was doing some terrific propaganda in favour of his own bloke. Mainly at the expense of yours. Something about yours drinking. Khan, isn't it?'

'Yes.'

'Is he all right?'

'Khan's all right.'

'I think he'll be the one I choose.'

He stopped, as if waiting for Jim's approval. Suddenly he said, 'Does everyone here think you worked Johnnie Brown out?'

Jim was suddenly still.

'Who said that?'

'Nobody. It's an impression I get. Not that I believe it.'

'Did Johnnie say so?'

'Good Lord, no. He said he and you were pals.' There was a moment's strained silence. Then he added, 'He must've been hell to work for. Surely everyone sees that?'

'I don't know what everyone sees.' He wanted to say, 'nor care'. Words were no good. Words were like actions; misunderstood, misinterpreted; friendship a cloak to venom and meanness.

Geoff blew out a cloud of smoke.

169

He said, 'Looks as if you and I'll have to back each other up, Jim.' Then he smiled. 'Bit of luck my coming here.'

16

The Major felt he could talk to Brad. Brad was an outsider, but he was a friend; and when it was time for Brad to go back to Imphal, the Major offered to drive him.

Sitting at the head of the full table, listening to Brad's jokes which had made Baxter laugh, even choke once over his soup, he saw how much there was of Johnnie in the Canadian; not the morose Johnnie of latter days, but the old Johnnie whose personality had made itself felt whenever a crowd of men had been together.

It was easy, he supposed, to create this effect when the effect need only last for the space of time it took them to eat their food and drink their coffee and sit talking in the ante-room. Beyond that, Brad as a leader would be no more successful in the long run than Johnnie had been. Brad, too, had moved about a bit during the past few months; Comitarla to Marapore; Marapore to Imphal. He must obviously be, like Johnnie, a man who could not be controlled or made to fit in; whose commanding officers had to find excuses for sending him somewhere else.

It was mediocrity which scored, the mediocrity of himself and all the others round the table with the one exception of Brad and perhaps the exception of Baxter whose mediocrity was too well disguised for it to matter.

As they moved into the ante-room he said to Brad, 'I'll drive you back tonight if you can wait until they've gone.'

'O.K., Major, that suits me fine.'

The rest of the evening was spent talking shop to Baxter, and because he noticed that Brad was beginning to get bored, looking frequently at his watch and trying to catch his eye, it was a relief when Baxter said, 'Well, I must be pushing off. Come on Shelley.' Ramo officers said goodnight and it was not long before his three platoon commanders followed them. He was alone with Brad and Geoff Smith.

'I expect you're pretty tired, aren't you?' he asked Smith.

'I'm all right, sir.'

'Well look, I'm going to run young Bradley here up to Imphal.

It's quite a way, so you and I can talk in the morning. You'll have to start taking over and there'll be details to iron out.'

'Right.'

'Come on then, Brad, let's go and get my truck.'

They said goodnight to Smith and as they went Brad called back, 'Thanks for the gin.'

Out of earshot the Major asked, 'What gin was that?'

'Some Geoff had. We had a tent warming earlier on.'

It was on the tip of his tongue to reply, 'We don't drink in our tents any more,' but the absurdity of it struck him. Before, it had been a gesture. It was no longer relevant and he felt angry with himself to think he had ever made such a rule. He said, 'I expect you notice the difference.'

'What difference do you mean, Major?'

'Oh . . .', he waved a hand, 'all this, in comparison with Comitarla.'

'Well, they're two different places.'

'. . . and the difference in us, too. I expect you think we've all changed a lot.'

'That's the way it goes.'

'You're just the same.'

'Oh, they'll never improve me, Major. I'll always be a one-man awkward squad.'

'You're lucky.'

'I get along.'

They found the truck and the Major said, 'You like to drive?'

'Hell, I'm liable to pile us up. I'm grounded.'

'Never mind.'

'You asked for it, then.' Brad took the wheel. He drove carefully and the Major was surprised. He kept silent until they had left the camp behind them and were heading for Imphal.

Then he said, 'I was sorry about Johnnie.' He kept his eyes on Brad's profile which was illuminated faintly by the reflected glare of the headlamps. Brad replied, 'What happened, Major?'

'Didn't he tell you?'

'No.'

'He must have said something.'

Brad turned his head quickly, then looked back at the road.

'He just said things had to come to an end.'

'Nothing else?'

The Major studied the road. He felt again as he had the night he sacked Johnnie and had wanted to get out of the tent but couldn't. Brad repeated, 'What did happen?'

'Oh . . .', he shifted his seat and groped in his pocket for some cigarettes.

'Have one of these, Major.' Brad took his packet out of a side pocket and handed it over. 'Light one for me, too.'

He lit the cigarettes.

'Thanks.'

Then, when he had waited for the Major to speak, Brad said, 'Don't you want to talk about it?'

'Yes, I do. That's why I said I'd drive you back.' He felt Brad look at him quizzically. It was like having Johnnie sitting beside him. He said, 'Stop somewhere and I'll tell you.' Brad drove slowly for a hundred yards or so, then drew up where the road widened on to a grass verge. He drove into the deep shadows and switched off the light and the engine. Ahead, the sky was pricked with stars where it could be seen between the tall trees that shook their leaves in the night wind. When they raised their cigarettes to their lips and sucked in the smoke the glow was reflected on the windscreen.

The Major began, 'I always liked Johnnie.'

It was like the beginning of a story; a story told to children. For the first time for years he felt an aching longing to have roots; roots somewhere that would sustain him. He was old enough; and after the war it would, perhaps, be too late. His only roots were here in Tamel or in Bengal. To that extent he was as immature and unformed as these youngsters he commanded, and if his fund of experience were greater, it was so only by reason of his years. It had never been canalised, never brought to fruition except perhaps with his present job; a temporary job like all the others he had had.

He said, 'I liked Johnnie from the very first moment I saw him in Marapore. He was like a man who'd come on a long journey, expecting to find nothing but finding everything.'

'Most of us find nothing, I suppose, Major.'

'I don't know.'

'What went wrong?'

'If I knew, if I really knew I shouldn't need to talk to you about it. But talking helps. And I can't talk to the others any more.' Again he felt Brad turn and look at him. But he kept his eyes on the windscreen. 'I've cut myself off and now I wish I hadn't.'

'Why did you cut yourself off?'

'Various reasons. All meant for the best. We got too close. Like a family. But a family without a head. It lacked discipline, Brad.'

'Are you sure?'

172

He had to say, 'No, I'm not sure. I'm not sure now. But at the time I *knew* it lacked discipline. I knew I had to tighten up.'

'To protect them?'

'Yes.' He was grateful that Brad understood. Had he misjudged Brad? Did Brad hide sensitivity beneath that devil-may-care exterior? Had he then misjudged the man who was so like Brad; Johnnie? Had Johnnie seen and understood how he could have saved himself; for some reason, emotional perhaps, refrained from saving himself or letting others save him?

Brad was saying, 'And then it went wrong?'

'Yes, it went wrong in one way. They resented it and I suppose they had reason to.'

'What way didn't it go wrong?'

'I kept the family intact.'

'That's something.'

He was forgetting Johnnie; many things. 'I don't really mean the family. It wasn't the men I kept together it was the company. I still command the company.'

'That's your job, Major. You can take pride in that.'

'Pride doesn't take you far. I thought it did.' He looked at Brad now. 'Men are never really in touch, but when you feel in touch the fact that you aren't doesn't worry you much.'

'And you felt in touch in the old days? In Comitarla?'

'We all did. It was something – well, something I wouldn't try to explain.'

'I know what you mean. Don't forget I was there too.'

They were silent. After a while Brad asked, 'What about Johnnie?'

'He was always different from the others. When I tightened up they resented what I did, and I think they resented me, but Johnnie didn't resent so much as resist. He resisted things changing and losing whatever it is that makes men believe in them.'

'Well things do. Johnnie fought and lost.'

'No, he won.'

'Won?'

'It's we who've lost. The whole lot of us.'

'That's double talk, Major.' Brad sent a cloud of smoke against the windscreen and the Major could feel his irritation. 'That's double talk, and if Johnnie did win it can't have been any comfort to him.'

'Winning's not always comfortable.' The Major threw his cigarette away and added, 'I'm sorry. But I wanted to talk.'

'Johnnie was my friend. You got rid of him, Major. You ought to let it rest at that.'

'Can't we be sorry for what we do?'

'I didn't mean that. I meant you should forget it.'

'And make the same mistake again?'

'Why not? You can't stop doing that.'

'We can try.'

'You take it too seriously. Look, Major . . . you've got your company and you're getting on with your job. When it's over you can go home and forget it all.'

The Major was silent. He thought; I shan't forget it. I don't want to. It's a sort of test for us.

Brad had settled back in his seat but he made no effort to start the truck. 'You've got Johnnie on your conscience,' he said at last.

'No.'

'What the hell then.'

'I've got the others on my conscience. I've made them all bitter. I'm bitter myself.'

'You thought I'd help?'

'I suppose I did.'

'Sorry.'

The Major said, 'Let me drive now.'

They changed places and when they had driven back on to the road the Major put his foot hard down on the accelerator. The truck shot forward and jolted over the uneven surface of the road. When they had gone past the airstrip at Tulihall the road was metalled. They moved swiftly into Imphal.

As they drew near the cross-roads Brad said, 'Drop me here, Major.'

'Sure?'

'Yes, drop me here.'

The Major pulled up. As Brad got out he said, 'Come round again, Brad.'

'Thanks.'

'We can always fix you up.'

'I'm not often in Tamel.'

'Whenever you are.'

'O.K. Goodnight, Major. And thanks.'

'Goodnight, Brad.'

Brad waited while the Major reversed the truck. He watched the rear light fade into the distance; then he turned round and began to walk. It was cold and he quickened his pace, stopping once to light a cigarette. When he got to the lane which led up to the club he paused again and looked at his watch. It was nearly ten o'clock. It would be easy not to go; to ignore her; to end it before it had begun. Bumping into Bill Parish like that had been in its way a warning not to let it begin, as if Johnnie from this far distance had lain a restraining hand on his arm. He stood at the end of the road, shivering in the cold, pulling hard on his cigarette, blowing the smoke out sharply from between his teeth.

He said, 'What the hell,' and threw away the cigarette. Then he walked up the lane.

Perhaps she had gone, tired of waiting for him. He imagined her sitting there, with a friend maybe. As the hands of the clock moved round she would cease to listen to what the friend said and she would be angry, or afraid; pathetically lonely, so that the fear of the things she had gone through during the past few months would claim her again.

She had said last night when they had met, 'I couldn't stand it, Brad. They sent me back. I made a fine nurse, didn't I? I couldn't stand it and I'm ashamed of myself.' Then she had asked him, 'Where's Johnnie?' and he had told her and watched her eyes darken with pain and longing. 'Then there's only you,' she had said. He saw himself replying, 'Only?' and she had laughed and put her hand round his arm.

He walked quickly up the pathway and went inside. In the long bar he could see the throng of army and air force officers through a haze of tobacco smoke. He walked down the flagged path to the lounge and when he went in he thought she had already left. There were only a few couples sitting round the basket work tables and she was not one of them.

Then behind him she said, 'Brad,' and he twisted round.

'I'm sorry, Nina, I got held up.'

'Where?' her lips were moist and trembling and he thought she was going to cry.

'In Tamel.'

'Where's that?'

'A long way away.'

She said, 'I've got to get back.'

'Not yet. Have a drink.'

'No.' She picked up her uniform cap and stood hesitantly. 'I've got to go,' she repeated.

'Come on, then.' He put his hand on her arm and she drew away. 'All right,' she said. 'Buy me a drink.' She sat down again and took out her powder compact from the bag that was slung over her shoulder. He left her because there was no bearer in the room. At the end of the room was the small service bar and there he bought two rums. When he got back she had composed herself.

'What is there in Tamel?'

'The air supply company.'

'Johnnie's?'

'Yes.'

She kept her eyes level on his, and for some time they looked at each other, waiting for the other to speak. She said, 'You wanted his sanction.'

'What do you mean?'

'For us.'

'I don't get you. He's in Ferozepore.'

'You said last night he was in Marapore.'

'I know. But they told me in Tamel he's in Ferozepore.'

She said, 'You're afraid,' and raised her glass to her lips. He gave her a cigarette and he saw that her hands were steady. He said, low, 'I want you, Nina.' She said nothing until she had drawn on the cigarette and taken another drink. 'You've got Johnnie's permission, then?'

'You're talking crooked.'

'You know what I mean. You went to Tamel and found that Johnnie's as dead as yesterday.' She smiled and then he noticed that her lips were twitching. 'All men are fools. I've learnt that.' She was silent. Then she said, 'And I've learnt about death, too. Death isn't final. It goes on.'

'Drink up.'

She did so and before they stood up he swallowed his own rum in one gulp. He took her arm and guided her out of the club. They walked without speaking down the pathway and into the lane. There were tall trees on either side and beneath one he took hold of her and pressed her close up to him. Her whole body was trembling and he gripped her hard as if to help her control herself.

He felt her hands curl into fists beneath his shoulder blades and she said, 'I'm no good, Brad. I'm no good.'

He didn't speak. He waited until the trembling had ceased. She said, 'I'm only good for one thing and that's all you want, isn't it?' She drew slightly away from him as she said it.

She watched the dim outline of his face as he came close again. She closed her eyes, then, remembering another time, and the pressure of a man's body against her own. She was glad that it was dark, for now she could pretend that Brad was someone else; that time did not exist.

176

PART FIVE

Mandalay

17

Major Shelley sat at the Colonel's desk in Ramo office with a greatcoat over his pyjamas. The fingers of his right hand drummed on the coarse-grained wood. He sat there with his left ear to the telephone and cursed because it was half-past four in the morning. He cursed the man at the other end of the telephone who had gone off somewhere to pass on his request for extra transport. In front of him was the wall map of Burma with coloured pins clustering round Mandalay; he cursed that, too. And he cursed Johns who stood at the side of the desk and who, if he had had any sense, would surely have woken the Colonel and left Shelley to sleep his sleep out in peace and come invigorated and enquiring to the office in the morning.

He said curtly, 'Give me a cigarette for God's sake.'

Johns fumbled in his pocket but found he had left his packet behind in his tent.

'Well, run and get it.' Johns went.

Shelley swore again; this time out loud. He stared through sleep-stained eyes at the calendar in front of him. He reached out and tore off yesterday's sheet. Today was March the eighteenth.

A voice at the other end barked, 'Yes?' and Shelley jumped. He shouted back, 'This is D.A.D.S. & T., Ramo at Tamel.'

'Yes?' The man seemed not to be intimidated.

Shelley smiled grimly. It was, he suspected, some mountebank little subaltern.

'I've got to have at least twelve three-ton lorries off your company. They're to report at the ammo dump in Tegenpur at 0600 hours this morning. One of my officers'll meet 'em there. Right?'

'Who did you say you were?'

Shelley paused. 'Ramo at Tamel.'

'Yes, I know. But who did you say was speaking?'

Shelley paused again. His hand gripped into a fist.

'This is a senior officer speaking. Now . . . have you got it clear what I want?'

'Is that Colonel Baxter?'

'No. It's Major Shelley.' He emphasised the word major.

'Good morning, Shelley. This is Major Hodding.'

'Hodding?' Shelley's hands twitched. 'Your fool of a clerk needn't have got *you* out of bed.'

'I was out of bed.'

'I'm sorry. We've got an urgent demand for an ammo landing commitment.'

'And you want some transport.' Hodding laughed. 'I honestly don't know what you blokes think a G.P.T. company's made of.'

'We can't spare our own and we've got to send just as many sorties as we can during the morning.'

'All right. Send your man to Tegenpur. You'll get what I can spare.'

'I desperately need twelve.'

'You can have eight at 0600.'

'Right. What else?'

'You can have twelve during the day. I mean the extra four.'

'How long can I keep 'em?'

'How long d'you want 'em?'

'As long as the programme lasts.'

'How long'll that be?'

'Until we're in Mandalay, I suspect.'

'Oh, Christ! You can have them every day from 0600 until midday. You'll have to use them to build a local dump. Your own company trucks'll have to do the airstrip loading.'

'Right. Thanks.'

'Have a nice time.'

They rang off and Shelley wrote a rapid instruction for the ammunition depot and signed it. Then he rang through to the Major's office and told the duty clerk to tell Lieutenant Smith to report to him immediately.

Johns came back with his cigarettes. 'Here you are sir.'

'Good man. Look, you've got to get off straight away to Tegenpur. I've already warned them you're coming. Get it laid on so that the G.P.T. trucks can be started loading as soon as they arrive. 5.5 shells. Get them all back here and then we'll see if we have to off load or can get the stuff straight on to aircraft. Right?'

'Yes, sir.'

'And pop round to wake up that M.T. chap, Smith. I guess those bloody wogs'll take an hour getting my message to him.'

'You want him here?'

'Yep.' Shelley coughed and spluttered as he inhaled and ex-

178

haled the smoke. His red eyes grew redder and thick veins swelled up on his bull neck. Johns felt faintly sick and was glad to get out of the tent.

When he pushed through the flap of Geoff's tent he found Prabhu had already been with the message. Geoff was sitting on the edge of his bed scratching his head.

'Hello, old boy. Prabhu's given you the gen, has he?'

'Um?'

'The gen, old boy.'

'He told me that bloody man Shelley wants me. What the hell's up?'

'Flap. Mostly a transport flap.'

'He thinks transport grows on trees.'

'Well, I'm off to Tegenpur. Cheerio.' Johns went out whistling.

'You can be off to Tipperary as far as I'm concerned,' Geoff grumbled to himself. Then he groped sleepily for his clothes. Before he left his tent he turned down the hurricane lantern and outside he saw that there was a faint reflection in the eastern sky. His feet stumbled along the trodden pathway that led across the field. When he was on the bithess his footsteps sounded hollow and unreal. The stars were still bright and there was a light shining from Ramo's office. He went in and purposely avoided saluting Shelley by removing his cap.

'Good morning, Major Shelley.'

Shelley narrowed his eyes. 'You've been a bloody long time getting here.'

'I came straight away. What's up?'

'I want four lorries off you.'

'I'm not sure I've got four lorries I can give you.'

'What d'you mean?'

'That I'm not sure.'

Shelley pursed his lips. The platoon officers had long since given up a pretence of respect for his rank. In this damned country nothing was done properly. No wonder the war had dragged on for years and years. And it would still be dragging on had it not been for the impetus given by an intake of experienced officers from the Normandy beach-heads. Shelley sighed. Ah! That was a proper war. He forced his thoughts back to the disagreeable present and stood up slowly, and he hoped, impressively.

'Four lorries have got to bloody well go pronto to Tegenpur to get loaded up with ammunition.'

'When's it being flown?'

'Tomorrow. That is today.'

'In addition to the programme already arranged?'

'Dammit, Smith! I'm not going to stand here arguing with you.'

'What I'm trying to say is if it's an additional commitment I'm not sure I've got four lorries.'

'Perhaps we'd better see your C.O.?'

Geoff pretended surprise. 'I presumed he knew.'

Shelley swallowed his anger. Suddenly he saw that he had been 'flapping'. The demand for 5.5 shells in the middle of the night had panicked him and he had got through to the G.P.T. company without bothering to check if the new demand was additional to existing demands. He had not, as Baxter was always telling him to do, reached down into the heart of the problem. And now he was going over the head of Smith's C.O.; possibly jeopardizing part of the day's commitments. This country sapped a man's brain; made him an automaton.

He said, 'Just do as I tell you, Smith, and leave the rest to me.'

'Very well, sir.'

'Four lorries to Tegenpur straight away to report to the ammo dump.' At least, he thought, have the courage of your convictions. 'Captain Johns'll be there. Right?'

'Right, sir.'

'Good man.' He smiled. Yes: he knew how to handle men. He very nearly clapped Smith on the shoulder; but Smith had gone.

Havildar Khan said, 'That bloddy Tegenpur', for Tegenpur was several miles away and the road was bad; and Geoff grinned because he enjoyed hearing Khan swear; and Khan swore every time he was woken up.

'Send Naik Hussein, and tell him to try and get our four loaded up first. Here, I'll scribble a note he can give to Captain Johns.' He took Khan's note-book from the little box by the side of the bed and held out his hand. 'Pencil?'

'That bloddy Tegenpur.' Khan handed him a chewed stub and Geoff wrote:

'Dear Johns, be a good fellow and load us up first. Or mighty quick, anyway. I can't really spare this four.'

Khan took the note and read it unashamedly with his head cocked on one side. He looked up, smiled and folded the note. 'You like a drink, sir?'

'No, thanks.'

Khan reached under his bed and drew forth a bottle of Rosa

180

rum. He pulled the cork out and wiped the rim of the bottle-neck with his hand, then tilted the bottle and poured the neat liquor down his grateful throat. He sighed luxuriously and clamped the cork on again. Then he said, 'Abhi thik hai, Sahib. Charlie?' They left Khan's tent and Khan shouted across the dark harbour, 'Ai! Hussein-a! Ai! Chalo, chalo!' The mighty voice echoed distantly and Geoff said, 'You bloody pissy-wallah.' Khan grinned. Then he moved off to shake Hussein awake.

The stars were paling and the rim of the hills that hid the rising sun was jagged against the sky. Geoff walked across the harbour and went into the little tent where he had set up his office. He lighted a lantern and looked through the day's transport demands which he had collated the night before.

As usual the platoons wanted more lorries than were available. He began arbitrarily to pare the demands down, starting with the one from Bill who, he was sure, always added two or three for luck. He reduced the demand by two, and then by another two. Scottie's demand was more reasonable. He checked again the total number of lorries at his disposal. Something had to go. He struck two lorries off Scottie's list as well. Cutting six brought the total demands down to the numbers available. He ran his pencil down Jim's figures. He needed badly to put two or three lorries on maintenance for the whole day. But Shelley had scotched that. His pencil hovered. He ought, in fairness, to cut down Jim's demands as well. The Major had said when he had first taken over the transport. 'Be fair.' He pressed his lips together and threw the pencil down. Why be fair when Parrish was not fair?

Perhaps if he had made Parrish's havildar senior of the trio Parrish would have co-operated. But he had put Khan in charge and ever since Parrish had not bothered to disguise his animosity. Sitting alone, here in the office, he could imagine Parrish saying, as he often said, 'This never happened when we commanded our own transport. It's funny, but we never seem to get any transport, Scottie and me.'

No doubt, one day, Bill would make his complaint to the Major, in all seriousness; and at that time he would add, 'We never seem to get extra transport like Jim Taylor.' He would be right, of course. Jim got anything that was going. And the only thing which rankled about helping Jim in this way was Jim's complete indifference. Surely he knew? Geoff got up from the table and turned down the light.

Sometimes he felt the only friends he had in the company

were the men of the platoon; Khan, Hussein; the drivers. They got on well together, They backed him up. And to back them up in turn he stood no nonsense from people like Parrish who still tried to run the drivers who had once belonged to him.

And Jim? He had never tried to get Jim to talk after a few fruitless attempts right at the beginning. It was easier to go on as he was, helping Jim unobtrusively, in as many ways as possible.

Why?

For the sake of old times? Geoff moved irritably. He pushed aside the tent-flap and began walking back to the lines. The four detailed trucks were already revving up.

The sake of old times. He smiled. Bill would talk of the old days and even Scottie would look pensive when they were mentioned. Time had painted the past for them so that it glowed. Men hoarded memories as a miser hoarded gold. Here, they looked back to the past for the comfort Tamel lacked. But how patently false an attitude it was. Men's memories grew dull and at that point imagination waved its wand. Tamel was no different from Marapore; and life in it was petty and stupid as that in any cantonment. The only way one could make it bearable was by looking facts in the face. With the exception of Jim Taylor these others meant nothing to him.

And Jim? Well, they had been close at one time, and that made a difference. One day Jim would snap out of it and they would have a good laugh as they had done in Marapore and in Kakul and in Belgaum; in the ship; in Cape Town; and going aboard at Liverpool. . . .

Baxter had the picture clearly in his mind. The gunners were pounding the walls of Fort Dufferin in Mandalay and the shell programme was a priority from Tamel airfield. Shelley had done the right thing, but for the wrong reasons. Baxter sighed. But the shell landings were only part of the picture. The wheels of maintenance had to keep turning; and the wheels of planning. The petrol landings ceased but preparations must be made to start them again at a moment's notice, as soon, in fact, as Mandalay fell.

It was at moments like this when one saw the parts dovetailing, when one could almost hear the faint click of two cogs connecting up, when demands on stocks, on men and on transport seemed at first glance beyond their capacity, that one could be sure just how far short one had fallen of perfection.

But Baxter was pleased; his organisation held; the results

showed clear proof of that; human endeavour and ingenuity could always overcome problems. And even when, without warning, the infantry detachment he used for ejection crews was moved away he filled the gap; filled the gap because it had to be filled, for parallel to the shell landings was a large dropping programme. He filled it by scraping the bottom of the barrel.

If there were no spare infantry then there were the aircrews themselves; always willing and able; and there were officers, and sepoys; someone could always be spared because they had to be spared. If one scraped deeply enough, ruthlessly enough, there were staff captains in Ramo and orderlies in the company.

The shell landings continued throughout the eighteenth and nineteenth of March, and on the morning of the twentieth there were still no signs of a halt being called. But by now things were going with a swing. Baxter put on his cap, shouted to Shelley that he was going to see the Major, and stepped briskly out of the tent.

It was, he felt, a morning to warm the cockles of the hardest heart. Trucks were moving up and down the road; his road; and everywhere he looked he saw squads of men at work. He nodded with satisfaction and called out to the Major as he approached the company's office. 'Good morning, to you!'

The Major was talking on the telephone. He glanced up and smiled. Then he said, into the phone, 'All right, Bill. Bring the others along.' He stood up.

'Come down to the strip with me old fellow. And we'll watch the wheels turning, eh?'

'Sorry, Colonel. I've got a conference.'

'Can't it wait?'

'No, I don't think it can. We've got a transport muddle.'

'Right, let's see what it's all about.'

'There's no need for you to bother. It's a domestic muddle. I'll soon sort it out.'

'Smith's all right, isn't he?'

'Smith's certainly all right. The trouble is our transport isn't. Don't forget how long we've had it and what it's had to do.'

'Ah, well. These things are sent to try us.' Baxter chuckled and walked over to the map where he began explaining his view of the situation. The Major only half listened, but Baxter was far too personally engrossed to realise he had no attentive audience. It was with surprise that he suddenly found the tent full of the Major's officers. He beamed at them as they saluted. They were, on the whole, good men. Knew their jobs. *Did* their jobs, and that was what mattered. Amazing what these young civilians could do once they'd had the edges knocked off. He said, 'I'll leave you chaps to it. Understand there's a bit of a transport muddle.' As he was going he felt suddenly magnanimous. 'By the way, in future, all demands from Ramo for transport'll pass through your C.O. first.' He smiled. He knew they knew he was referring to Shelley's habit of going straight to Smith. He knew he was wrong to imply Shelley had been taken to task for it; but dammit, they were coping pretty well, and Shelley was a dreadful ass. He walked back into the sunlight.

'Right, let's have it.' The Major sat on the edge of his desk. He needed the inspiration that height would give him as the others squatted on low stools. He knew what was coming and automatically his eyes met Smith's.

'Shall we hear from the M.T.O. first?'

Geoff shrugged. 'I've got nothing I want to say.'

'Right, Bill?'

Bill's face was flushed. He said, 'I can't cope any longer.'

'Why?'

'I can't cope with these shell landings when I have to go down on my bloody knees for every single lorry the Transport officer deigns to let me have. Everyone knows the G.P.T. company lorries do nothing more than deliver to my lines, but because we're using them it's made an excuse to keep me short. I can't cope any . . .'

The Major raised his hand. 'Don't let's generalise . . .'

'I'm forced to generalise. This has been cooking up for nearly three months, Major. It's got to the point where I can't ignore it as I've tried to do.'

'What's the exact complaint?'

'Smith doesn't give me my fair share.'

'Scottie?' The Major turned to him, and while Scottie opened his mouth Bill said, 'Yes, Scottie, you ought to back me up.'

Scottie shut his mouth again and looked down at the ground. He said in a low voice, 'I hate this sort of thing.' Bill grunted and Scottie clenched his hands. 'I hate this sort of thing,' he repeated, 'but I'm sure Bill's not complaining without reason.'

'Why are you sure?'

'Because it would be silly.'

'Do you feel you get your fair share?'

'There've always been transport problems. There still are.' He raised his head and the Major realised how drawn Scottie looked. He went on, 'Transport problems, stock problems, and manpower problems. That's what we cope with all the time, so let's try and sort this one out now.'

The Major thought; 'He should have had a company. He's wasted as a platoon commander.' Then he caught Jim's eye. Jim shook his head. The Major asked, 'You haven't any complaints, Jim?'

'Not any more than Scottie has.'

'Well, Bill, it looks as if you're in a minority.'

'Minority?' Bill stood up. 'The only minority I'm in is where transport's concerned. Jim Taylor always has twice as many as I ever have.'

Smith said, 'Jim Taylor usually has twice as many sorties as you.'

'Infernal bloody cheek! Twice as many sorties my bloody foot! I've been sweating and slaving my guts out . . .'

He stopped. The Major had banged his fist on the table. His face was white with anger and for a few moments he seemed unable to speak. He rose from the edge of the table and stood there in front of them; and they saw his hands were trembling.

'We've come to this, then?'

He looked at them one after the other. 'We've come to this,' he repeated. 'If someone had told me in Comitarla that we'd come to this I wouldn't have believed them.' He turned his back and went round to the chair at his desk. Slowly he sat down. 'In future your transport demands will come to me. The statement of available transport will come to me, too. I shall allot the transport personally. That means that the man who commands the company will be doing the platoon officer's work. It's a thing . . .' he hesitated, then raised his voice, 'a thing called organisation, or red tape. It wastes a bit of time. And it's a measure of your failure. A sign that you're no longer considered big enough to do the work you've always done.' He looked down at the table and said, more quietly, 'But that's how it goes.' Then he looked at them all again; in turn. He said, 'With the exception of Smith you can all go.'

They stood up and their feet scuffed the trodden earth so that little whirls of dust rose and settled again. They set the stools against the wall of the tent and saluted him. Then they went out and he saw through the open flap that they walked separately.

Smith was watching the retreating figures, too, and there was something in the tilt of his head that showed a likeness to Johnnie. Smith faced him now. There was the same frankness about the eyes, too. The same look of preparedness for what was coming and the same look of not minding.

He said, 'Well, Geoff?'

Smith did not smile. He replied, 'I asked for it, I suppose.'

Johnnie could have said that; would have said it.

'I think you did. Why?'

'You know why, sir.'

'Jim?'

'To help him.'

'Does he need help?'

'I thought he did, but perhaps I made a mistake.'

'Hasn't he told you himself you were being unfair?'

'No. I don't think he knew.'

'He must have known.'

'I thought so until just now.'

'What made you change your mind?'

'Nothing. I just knew. You can tell.'

'You've been pretty loyal.'

'Why do you say that?'

'He hasn't been particularly friendly to you, has he?'

'That's his affair. It doesn't matter.'

'You and Bill Parrish have got to learn to see each other's points of view.'

'That's not really the point, Major. Bill and I'll never see eye to eye. But I suppose from now on we'll work it out better. That's always possible.'

He held out his cigarettes and the Major took one. As he bent over the flame cupped in Smith's hands he said, 'You're a pretty forgiving sort of bloke, aren't you?'

'Am I?' He spun the match to the ground. 'So are you for that matter.'

The Major said nothing. He was tapping the edge of his cigarette needlessly on the tobacco-tin lid which served as an ashtray. Forgiving? He looked up at Smith to say something, but found he could not.

Jim was angry because he had been blind, and blindness had made a fool of him. His anger broke to the surface and he called for Dass. Dass came.

'Come with me.' He walked into the roadway and went towards the line of lorries.

'Explain what each one is doing.'

Dass explained.

'And these two?'

Dass explained again.

186

'And they are necessary at this time in the morning?'

'Sir, we must get transport whenever we can.'

'Send these two back to Lieutenant Smith.'

Dass goggled. 'Sir? But . . .'

'Send those two back.'

'We shall be wanting them this afternoon.'

'This afternoon we shall ask for them.'

'Then someone else will have them.'

'You'll have to wait until someone hasn't.'

He left Dass in the roadway and found Moti Ram standing close by. Obviously the Jemadar wanted to say something. He ignored him and when Moti Ram called, 'Sir?' he answered, 'Later, Sahib.'

He returned to his office, and hearing voices from Nimu's section he looked round the partition. Nimu sat at his desk, his finger pointing out words written on a sheet of paper to Jan Mohammed who was by his side, his head bent forward in an attitude of concentration.

'Is this the time for a reading lesson?'

They both looked up, startled, then sprang to their feet. Moti Ram came in.

'Sir,' he said, 'Jan Mohammed wants . . .'

'Jan Mohammed can go back to work, Sahib.' He looked at the little orderly who was grinning fatuously.

'Go on! Get out!'

'Chalo, Sahib bolte.' Nimu gave Jan Mohammed a little push with his hand, and then picked up and folded the paper which lay on the desk. He put it in his breast pocket and spoke rapidly to the orderly in Hindustani.

'Thik hai, Babuji.' Jan Mohammed pulled his side cap from his shoulder epaulette, placed it askew on his head and made an attempt at a smart salute. Then he dashed from the tent and Jim went back to his own office. He rang through to Bill Parrish.

'Yes?' Bill's voice was hoarse.

'Jim here. I've sent two lorries back to the park. I expect you'll be getting them.'

'Look here, old boy, I didn't mean to . . .'

Jim rang off. He pulled some papers towards him and began working out his dropping programme for the following day; the calculations had long since become automatic. Usually one could shut one's mind entirely to thoughts that could disturb. He threw down his pencil. In the adjacent office Nimu's typewriter clattered, and outside a driver was fluffing his gear change.

He had been blind; and he had been a fool. His platoon had been favoured; pampered and spoiled as they had been always, in Johnnie's day; favoured without his knowing it. 'You and me against the rest,' Geoff had implied. He had tried to fight that once before. Geoff had not given him a chance to fight it. Looking back now over the past month or two he realised the extent of his blindness; and his anger increased.

He rose and went to the open flap. He watched the squads of men who packed petrol and composite rations in the open area opposite.

Johnnie's face was suddenly close; real; as far as a man or his face could be real; but only hate was real, and hypocrisy, and the fact that men were cyphers, and so, expendable; expendable because the job they were doing fed the instruments of destruction. There was a unity in that.

The telephone rang.

He picked up the receiver and the Major's voice said, 'Jim?'

'Yes?'

'There's an emergency drop to do straight away.'

'Right.'

'One plane load. 3,000 I.T. compo rations. Balance in motor spirit.'

'Plane number, Major?'

'Ghosh has a note of that. He's on his way round to you. Baxter's told him to fly with it, but you'll have to give him another man.'

'Right.'

'Got a spare lorry for it?'

Jim hesitated. Then he said, 'I can get one.'

'O.K. Send it straight down.'

They rang off and he called for Moti Ram. When the Jemadar appeared he told him what had to be done.

'Use one of the lorries Dass is loading now.'

'We can get another, sir, from Lieutenant Sahib.'

'I said use one of the lorries Dass already has.'

'Very well, sir.'

'I want a man to fly with it.'

'Sir, already we have twelve men flying this morning.'

'Now we shall have thirteen.' He smiled, humourlessly, 'That, Sahib is my lucky number.' He went out of the tent and Moti Ram followed. About a hundred yards down the road he saw Jan Mohammed standing in the middle of a group of sepoys. Jan

Mohammed was explaining something, illustrating his speech with broad gestures.

'Tell Jan Mohammed to come here.'

'Yes, sir.'

Moti Ram shouted for the orderly. The group of sepoys scattered and Jan Mohammed was left alone, standing foolishly at the side of the store tent. Then he came running towards them.

Jim said, 'Tell him he's flying.'

'Sir, it is no use sending him. He is all the time sick.' He prodded the orderly in the ribs, then made a gesture to indicate pushing out. 'Sahib bolte tum push out karoga.' Jan Mohammed rolled his eyes and put his hands to his stomach. 'Sahib! Nai Sahib! Bahut taklif.' He put a finger in front of his face and circled it round to indicate dizziness. Jim watched him bitterly.

'Fikr nahin! Yih mera hukm hai.'

'Sahib! Sahib!'

Moti Ram said over Jan Mohammed's cry, 'Sir, in all section only one man is excused from flying. This man is Jan Mohammed, sir.'

'Who is he excused flying by?'

Moti Ram turned to Jan Mohammed and asked the same question.

'No, Sahib! *You* tell me. Don't make him say it.'

'Very well, sir. These were Captain Brown Sahib's orders.'

'I see.'

'Sir, in Marapore, Captain Sahib made all of us fly. And this man was sick, sick all the time, and begged of me to ask Captain Sahib to be excusing him. In those days, sir, I grew angry. I beat this man.' He took Jan Mohammed's arm and said something which Jim could not follow. Jan Mohammed nodded violently and doubled his fist and thumped with it on his chest. Then he grinned absurdly and rolled his head again.

Moti Ram said, 'You see, sir! I beat this man. And then I am ashamed and I am telling Captain Brown Sahib what has happened, because I am losing my temper with Jan Mohammed and this is not good. And Captain Sahib says, he says, sir, "Thik hai Jemadar Sahib. He asks and you beat him. Now we excuse him flying. Not because he is sick but because he is beaten. Nada is sick, too, but Nada has not been punished. Jan Mohammed will be my orderly."'

'In that case, Sahib, the answer is quite simple. He flies today and tonight Sepoy Nada will be my orderly. Now, tell Dass to get loaded up.' Jim turned away and went back to his office.

When Ghosh arrived Jim had finished his calculations.

'I'll drive you down in the truck,' he told Ghosh, who was looking pale; a grey tinge in the light brown skin.

'Oh, Lord, Jim! I knew Baxter would get me flying before long. I'm sure to be sick.' Jim said, 'That's going to make two of you.' They went outside together and watched the last three or four containers loaded on to the lorry. Jan Mohammed stood close to Moti Ram for protection.

'Tell him he's riding in the back of my truck, Sahib. Tell him to get in.'

'Chalo! Chalo!' The Jemadar bustled the little man towards the truck. He made no further protest but climbed meekly into the back and sat on the tool box, his hands folded on his knees, staring at the Jemadar as though not fully comprehending.

'Tell the lorry to follow on, Sahib. We'll find the plane.' Jim and Ghosh got in at the front and they drove off.

On the airfield the loading bay was almost empty. They found the plane immediately and already the crew was standing by.

'You got some chuckers out?' the pilot asked.

'Two.'

'O.K. A couple of us'll help 'em out.'

They stood around, smoking; Jan Mohammed squatted on his haunches near the fifteen hundredweight, with his back to the plane. Then the lorry arrived, and in ten minutes the load was on and roped in.

The pilot stood with his hands on his hips and surveyed the containers.

'What we carryin'?'

'Petrol and tinned rations.'

'Where's the petrol?'

'In the back.'

'O.K. Come on then, let's go.' He clambered over the containers and made for the cabin and the rest of the crew followed.

'Jan Mohammed!'

Without a word the orderly climbed into the plane and stood near the door.

Ghosh said, 'Hope it's roped in all right. Airforce is complaining about the way we lash in the shells. Have you heard?'

'No.'

'They've all got to be lashed in separately. Baxter says we Ramo officers have got to come down to the strip tonight and watch it being done.'

'Doesn't concern me.'

'You're in luck. Major said Bill Parrish is cursing blue murder.'

'How d'you lash in loose shells?'

'Don't ask me. My God! We'll be down here all night.'

Then he heaved himself up through the opening and waved back at Jim.

Jim got into his truck and drove away to the far side of the bay. He moved on to the circuit road and travelled slowly, parallel to the runway. Where the circuit curved round he pulled up. The plane was already taxi-ing to the end of the run. The sound of its revving engines came clearly across the field. He saw it shaking its flaps, like a bird preening in the wind. Then it squared up and seemed to hesitate; its engines deeper and stronger.

He got out of the truck and stood by the bonnet. As the plane began speeding up the runway he said, 'You can't touch me any more, Johnnie. You can't interfere.' The plane was carrying the last of Johnnie with it. He was sending Johnnie away.

It came, at a hundred feet, above the circuit road.

It flew low across the dried paddy fields, a bird; a steel bird; all that he had suffered was released like a bird into the clear blue air; and suddenly it hovered, as if unsure of its nest; absurdly losing the buoyancy of flight to fall, with taut, unmoving wings to earth.

And the impact was alive with fire, and shooting tongues that licked the parched sky. He began running and stumbling, feeling the heat on his face; and as he did so a moving pillar of flame detached itself from the inferno and ran across the field towards him and he heard the anguished unrecognisable cry that came grotesquely from it; saw the sudden flinging out of its arms that made it look like a burning cross before it crumpled and fell into shapelessness.

18

It was as though feeling had died, consumed by flame along with Ghosh and Jan Mohammed. A substitute plane was found and briefed for the emergency drop and Jim flew with it. As they were airborne he saw below the distorted shape of the crashed Dakota, gutted and twisted, scummed by the white froth of the extinguishers that had played too late upon it.

Below were the jungle-covered hills, purple in their shadows, their greenness warmed by the high sun; eternal and uncaring; and acres of level forest cut by a thin, red-yellow road like a weal. If men moved there, they were invisible. Invisible as the men towards whom the plane journeyed, above whom it now circled, once, twice; circled eight times ejecting its load like spawn, as if to give life to what was lifeless.

With the last containers gone Jim leaned his bare, grimed shoulder against the cold metal side; then he went forward and opened the door of the pilot's cabin. He stood behind the pilot and they flew towards the dropping zone, saw it momentarily, cluttered with the whiteness of parachutes; and then it was gone; a place like Pyongiu, without identity, meaningless; and no man had run across it from the shadow of trees.

He could not love or hate what did not exist; and there was nothing. He left the pilot's cabin and sat alone. He thought; 'If there is nothing, then there is room for love,' and he stared round the empty fuselage as if to conjure it back. But there were only the strewn gunny sacks, the coiled ropes, and the white static lines looped upon the strong point. There was the emptiness of Marapore, the emptiness of all India, the emptiness that he had sought to escape and had succeeded in recreating.

When the others had gone down to the airfield that night to supervise the lashing in of the shells he sat in the little ante-room of the mess-tent and tried to write a letter to Johnnie, but he found no words with which to tell him that Jan Mohammed was dead.

He tore up the sheet of note-paper which bore the words, 'Dear Johnnie,' and threw it into the empty stove. It was half-past eleven when Scottie returned and when Jim saw the grief on his face he remembered about Ghosh; and that Ghosh had been Scottie's second-in-command for far longer than he himself had been Johnnie's. But Scott's grief was like the man; dry, analytical; avoiding pity.

He said, 'Have you finished on the strip?'

'Yes. The others will be here soon.'

And then they waited.

Once, Scottie said, 'Are you all right, now? I mean after seeing that business?'

'Yes.'

'They said someone tried to get away. Did you see who it was?'

'No. I couldn't tell.'

Scottie nodded, and Jim looked down because he saw again the image of a man crucified; consumed by fire.

After a while the Major returned and he brought Baxter and Shelley with him. Bill Parrish came in a few minutes afterwards with Johns. They were discussing the technique of lashing in loose shells but above them hovered the shadow of what had happened. When Geoff arrived, Jim looked round and thought, with surprise, 'We're all here.' The ante-room was full. Baxter came over to him and said, 'All right, Taylor?' He said, 'Yes.' and then Baxter laid a hand on his arm and said, 'I want to see you tomorrow. I've talked to the Major.' He smiled and turned away again, and Jim heard Shelley saying loudly, 'I think I'll turn in. I've had an exhausting day.' Shelley stood there, his hands thrust into his pockets, and beneath his blotched, ugly skin there was a pallor. Baxter laughed, 'Poor Shelley. He jumped every time one of our sepoys handled those shells.' There was laughter and Shelley flushed angrily.' They're primitive, Colonel. Damned well primitive. Give me British troops every time. Those wogs look as if they've just fallen off trees.' And there was silence.

Silence so long that Shelley realised he had said something wrong; his sense of wrongness made him burst out, 'Indians are all alike!' and suddenly Scottie stood in front of him and said, 'I suppose that includes Ghosh?'

Shelley opened his mouth and stared at Scott. The Major, too, put his hand on his shoulder and contact seemed to bring him back to reality. The look of anger was quenched and he said, 'I'm sorry. It's just . . .'

He left the sentence unfinished and went out of the ante-room. The Colonel cleared his throat. 'You should be careful what you say, Shelley. You know Ghosh was Scott's second-in-command?'

'I forgot. I'm sorry.'

'In any case we chaps are rather touchy about that rather unpleasant name "wog". We just don't use it.'

'I didn't know,' Shelley replied.

Johns said, 'I made a gaff like that when I first came out, too.' He glared at Bill because Bill laughed outright, and the others moved uncomfortably, irritably.

Baxter said, 'Yes, Johns. It's easy to make a gaff like that. When you use the word "wog" in India, you can never be quite sure who it applies to.'

The Major held out the gin bottle. 'One for the road, Shelley?'
'No thanks, I'm turning in. Coming Johns?'

Johns looked at him uncomprehendingly. But gratefully. He murmured, 'Yes, sir,' and followed the retreating Shelley dutifully. 'Like a dog,' the Major thought. He said aloud, 'You will, won't you, sir?'

'I think a night-cap.' He held his glass out. 'We're a bit on edge, aren't we?'

Baxter watched the Major pour. Mentally he castigated himself for saying what he had to Johns. But Johns was so absurd, and Shelley was absurd. Poor old Scott had deserved a bit of backing up. 'We're part of a machine,' he thought. 'Men are never quite fitted for that role. They have to be held to it by discipline.' He felt a great warming to these men who stood or sat in the ante-room with him; not for what they were but for what they had made of themselves in the service.

He said, 'Thanks, Major,' and took the refilled glass. There was a need for a toast, he felt; but he would drink it silently to himself. 'To you all,' he thought, and drank deeply.

He said goodnight at last, and when he had gone the Major thought, 'We control nothing. We stand together because we fear disintegration.'

The others went and left him alone with Jim.

He said, 'Baxter wants you in Ramo. I said I thought you'd accept.'

At length Jim understood. He replied, 'And Johnnie's platoon?'

'There's Geoff Smith. We can get another subaltern for the transport.' He added, 'It might be better all round. You've tried your best.'

'It's more than our best needed,' he thought.

'Ramo might be the answer, mightn't it, Jim?'

'I don't know. Can I think about it?'

'Of course.'

Jim said goodnight, too, and alone the Major poured himself another drink and sat down, staring at the glass, and at the shape of his hand, holding it. He took out his packet of cigarettes and found it empty.

It was past midnight when the Major came into Jim's tent. Jim was awake and when the Major called softly, 'Jim?' he sat up. 'What is it?'

'The shells. They've got to come off and you've got to substitute petrol.'

Jim put his feet to the ground, and the Major, holding his lantern said:

'We're in Mandalay.'

Jim went into the dark office and woke Nimu who slept in his own section of the tent. He said, 'There is work to do,' then he lighted his own lantern. With it in his hand he stared round at the familiar tent. 'This goes, too,' he thought.

He said aloud, 'Not to Ramo. To Marapore.'

He put the lantern on his desk and in the next office Nimu was stirring. Geoff pushed open the flap of the tent and said, 'I'm getting some lorries to you straight away.'

'Thanks.'

He was alone again. Geoff had left the flap open and the road outside was white under the moon. He went out and Dass came running towards him.

He told him what to do and then continued on to the M.T. harbour to find his truck. As he drew near he heard Havildar Khan shouting. The night was alive and the moon was a sun stripped of its fire, its ability to consume and burn. He found his truck and drove swiftly to Ramo's lines where he woke up the Petrol stores Havildar and told him to be prepared. Then he drove back and the wheel in his hands was the wheel that Johnnie had grasped. The road was filled with men and they turned their startled faces into the glare of the headlamps as he came round the curve. Ahead, the lorries pointed towards him and he pulled up outside his office and shouted to Dass, 'To Ramo. Get them to Ramo.'

Tailboards swung down as the men on the road clustered around the trucks and climbed in by the light of the truck behind them. The convoy moved off; and more trucks came. Men straggled along the road.

He went amongst them, directing them into groups, bringing a measure of order out of the confusion of the night. And when he was satisfied he went down to the strip. Twin points of light hovered in the loading bay as the lorries, controlled by Smith and Parrish, backed towards the planes. One by one the lights in the planes came on, and men were illuminated in the doorways.

There was no division between night and day.

He went backwards and forwards from the lines to the airfield. The moon was lower now and had lost its brilliance. He looked anxiously towards the east, disbelieving the evidence of his watch. The men were weary and the pause between the impact of each drum on the floorboards of the lorries grew longer and on the strip it seemed that each plane took longer to load than the one before. It was like a slowing of the pulse, a growing tiredness in the heart that no drugs could quicken.

It seemed a fitting end, this slow fading away of what one had failed to comprehend; already these men were without identity. They were not Johnnie's, and they were not his. They were without roots, without ties. They belonged only to this insubstantial hour between night and morning when their eyes, turning to watch the grey sky behind the rim of the hills, gave them for that moment a look of fulfilment.

When the last lorry had gone from the field he climbed into his truck and drove it round the circuit until he reached the place where only yesterday he had watched the plane. He pulled up, and already the blackened shape was visible. It seemed to grow out of the earth; a shadow deeper than shadow; growing from shadow.

He stayed there until in the distance he heard the sound of another truck. He turned and saw it coming slowly down the hill where the aircrews lived. The whole sky had paled and he saw the truck clearly as it turned into the loading bay. Men climbed out and walked to one of the planes. After a while the engines burst into life and the sound echoed across the field. He closed his eyes and listened to the sound; listened to the change in tone as the plane came speeding up the runway. The roar of it grew louder.

Slowly, he drove back to the lines. There was still a lantern shining in the office tent for it was not light enough yet for Nimu to see. He found the clerk sitting with Dass at the table. In front of them was a piece of paper. They stood up and he said, 'Give me a lantern, Nimu,' and Nimu took a spare one from his bedside and handed it to him.

'You are going to work, sir?'

'Just a letter.' He paused. To Dass he said, 'You should be back in bed,' but Dass only smiled and shook his head a little. As he went into his own office he saw a box such as the men used to carry their personal possessions from place to place. It was on the floor and the lid was open. Inside he caught a glimpse of a child's coloured story book. He said, 'Was this his?'

Nimu came forward.

'Yes, sir. We are sorting it before sending to his home.'

'I see.'

He felt that Nimu wanted to say more, but he dare not let him. To talk of Jan Mohammed was impossible. First he must write and tell Johnnie; the words must flow unaided. But Nimu followed him to the table in his office and held out the piece of paper he and Dass had been reading.

'Sir?'

'Yes, Nimu?'

'This is Jan Mohammed's. But we are thinking you will like to see.'

'What is it?'

'It is a letter, sir.' He put the letter down on the desk. The writing was familiar and when he looked at the signature he saw that it was from Johnnie.

He asked, not clearly, 'When did this come?'

'It was yesterday, sir. It came to *him*, and I was reading it for him.'

'I see.'

He stared at the letter. He took it and began to read.

Dear Jan Mohammed,

I am writing to you because Nimuji can give you an English lesson and you can show this to Moti Ram Sahib, all the N.C.O.s and men and give them my love. I am well and happy and you will see that I am now in Ambala quite near to your home and when you come on leave come in and see me. I am not in air supply now.

I hope my old section is doing good work and 'pulling on'; tell Moti Ram Sahib that.

And when you are making Captain Taylor Sahib's bath tonight show him this and tell him to write and tell me all the news and remember me to all the other officer sahibs.

With Kind Regards,
John Brown, Capt.

He folded the note up. Then he looked at Nimu. Dass had joined them.

Nimu said, 'Sir, he is not angry.'

'No.'

Nimu hesitated, then with a little gesture that included Dass, he said, 'We were all thinking he was angry with us, sir. All thinking he had forgotten us.'

Then they were silent and after a while Jim said, 'You were all very fond of him, weren't you, Nimu?'

'He was our good friend.'

They began to move away but Jim called, 'This is yours,' and he held out the letter. Nimu shook his head. 'You should be keeping it sir.' Then they left him. He heard them speaking in undertones and there was a rustle of canvas and their footsteps on the road outside and he knew that he was alone. He unfolded the note again and spread it out on the desk. Then he reached for a sheet of paper.

He wrote:

Dear Johnnie,

Soon after you get this I shall be back in Marapore. I see I can't attempt to hold on any longer to what doesn't belong to me and never belonged to me. Ever since you went away I've felt you as a ghost at my elbow. You seemed to intrude in so many ways, trying to get back to men who appeared already to have forgotten you. But they haven't forgotten. What seemed dead I now see is still alive in them. Your letter proves you keep it living too. I'm grateful for the letter even though it comes too late. Jan Mohammed is dead. There was a plane crash and poor Ghosh died with him. I blame myself for Jan Mohammed. I made him fly because it seemed a way of beating the ghost.

So this is the end for me, and already I feel I've left Tamel far behind. What is it after all? A place where we've been; a place we've built. When we've gone there'll be nothing here. Fields. A track. Nothing to mark our time. An empty petrol tin, perhaps. An old bit of webbing. There's nothing dependable here, nothing sure, nothing that touches off in me a spark of self-confidence. Strange that I should feel I'll find that confidence back in Marapore. Not for the place but for the act of going back. Going back voluntarily. Giving up what isn't mine, without bitterness.

Yours,
Jim.

When he had finished he inserted the letter into an envelope, addressed it to Ambala, and placed it in his breast pocket. Then he lowered the wick of the lantern and sat for a while until the sound of truck engines revving close by told him a new day had begun.

✱   ✱   ✱

When the evening came the Major said that Baxter would like to see them, together.

'It's about your going to Ramo, Jim. Have you thought about it?'

Jim nodded.

In Ramo's tent they had to wait until Baxter returned from the petrol dump and Jim was filled with an overwhelming impatience to be gone, to finish. The Colonel appeared rubbing his hands. He said, 'Well, Taylor, have we decided?' Curtly he replied, 'Yes.'

He knew the Major looked at him sharply. And Baxter paused, a little put out by the tone of his voice. Then he asked, briskly, 'Well, what's it to be? Ramo? Or carry on with Three Section?'

'Neither, sir. I want to go back to Marapore.'

They did not understand.

And there was no way of making them understand. He glanced at the Major, but the Major lowered his eyes. The Colonel was saying, 'You've had a shock with that business yesterday, Taylor. Come to me tomorrow. We'll have another talk. I'm the last man in the world to keep someone in a job against their will because I know the job'll suffer. But I don't entirely discount the human element in things, y'know.' He quirked an eyebrow. 'Tomorrow you'll be thinking clearly. Come to me tomorrow.'

Baxter inclined his head to show that he could go. The Major stayed behind.

The sun was setting and the men had mostly gone for their evening meal. The road was strangely deserted and looking at it he knew a vague regret. But that was weakness.

He did not wish to go back to the mess. He must avoid at all costs an evening of answering questions, or of waiting for questions which were painfully withheld. He went to the M.T. park and got into his truck. Geoff was standing at the opening of his office tent and filled suddenly with remorse – perhaps because Geoff was of Marapore, and he was going back to Marapore – he waved to him, but drove away – before Geoff had the chance of approaching.

He drove to the airfield. It had become, now, merely a place that would be the first stage of the journey to India. Joining the Tiddim road he turned and travelled in the direction of Imphal.

He stood in the entrance to the club bar, screwing his eyes up against the bright glare and tobacco heavy air that was intoxicating. The room was immense, but it was crowded. Too crowded.

199

He saw a bearer carrying a tray. Perhaps there was another bar. He stopped the bearer.

'Dusre bar hai?'

'Han, Sahib.' The man stretched out his hand, indicating a flagged pathway to another building. He thanked the man and went towards it, sensing its quietness. Here he would sit for a while. There might be copies of the Onlooker. He smiled. Already his thoughts were coloured by Marapore.

Inside the other bar a few couples sat at tables. There was an air of intimacy. He sat down and waited to be noticed by the bearer who stood against the tiny counter with his hands folded about a tray. But the bearer was staring across at a man and woman who sat in the corner, as though expecting a summons from them at any moment. Jim looked at them. The girl was watching him. She was dark skinned and dressed in nurse's uniform. 'In Marapore,' Jim thought, 'she wouldn't be allowed in the club.' She looked a nice girl. Now she was saying something to the man, whose back was towards him. The man turned round.

It was Brad.

Brad gave a sign of greeting and called, 'Hello there,' but he turned back to the girl afterwards as though dismissing him. And Jim was glad. And yet to talk to Brad would have been a way of proving to himself that Johnnie's ghost, for him, was laid. The girl was leaning over the table, her eyes still on him, and after a while Brad turned round again, and called across, 'Join us for a drink?' He got up. As he approached Brad got to his feet and held out his hand.

'Gee, I'm sorry. But I can't remember your name.'

'Jim Taylor.'

'That's it. Sit down, Jim. This is Nina.'

Nina smiled up at him, and then he sat down between them.

'What you drinkin', Jim?'

'Whatever's going.'

'It's rum tonight.'

'That'll do fine.'

The bearer was already half-way across the room. 'They must be regulars,' Jim thought. He looked at Nina, wondering suddenly why she so obviously forced Brad to invite him.

She said, 'Are you in Tamel?'

'Yes.'

She nodded, folded her hands on her lap and leaned back in her chair. Brad caught his eye. 'Well, Jim, how's tricks?'

'All right. And you?'

'Oh, I'm doin' all right. I get a trip home next month.'

As he said it he grinned at Nina, as if, Jim thought, to reassure her; reassure her that he would be back. The bearer brought the rums and Brad began to talk about home, about friends of his who had gone home. About everything, Jim noticed, but Johnnie. Then he realised that Brad, too, would think of him as the man who had wormed Johnnie out.

He said, 'D'you ever hear from Johnnie?' and because the girl made a sudden movement he looked at her, and when he turned back to Brad he saw that his lips were compressed and his eyes unfriendly. At last Brad shook his head.

'No, 'fraid not, Jim.' He raised his glass and said, 'Here's luck.' The drank up and Brad put his glass heavily on the table; with finality. He looked Jim straight in the eye and said, deliberately, 'No, I don't know what Johnnie's doin' now.' And he turned to Nina and held her hand, dismissing the subject.

Jim thought, 'That's that.' And slowly he sipped his rum, glad to realise he did not feel hurt that Brad should think he had done this thing to Johnnie. Perhaps Johnnie himself had implied it when he and Brad were in Marapore together. It would be quite natural. Johnnie would say it, meaning it, or finding in it an excuse for his sudden return. It would be easy to prove here to Brad that Johnnie no longer thought so, or thinking so, forgave him and re-offered his friendship. The letter Johnnie had written to Jan Mohammed was in his pocket and all he needed to do was give it to Brad and let him read it.

But it did not matter what Brad thought, for in his mind Johnnie and Brad were linked, inseparable, loyal; and he himself was free of Johnnie, free because he had cut the bond; free therefore of Brad and of what Brad thought. It would have been different had he been staying on in Tamel, living in Johnnie's shadow. Brad's attitude, then, would have had the power to hurt, just as the men of the section could hurt. If he wanted proof that Johnnie's hold would not relax, that in Tamel it would be felt again in unsuspected ways, Brad's attitude was proof.

Their glasses were empty and Jim signalled to the bearer to replenish them. Nina shook her head and held her hand over the rim of her glass and as she did so she said, 'Where is Johnnie, now?'

He looked at her, surprised. 'Did you know him?'

'Yes.'

Nina? He felt Brad lean forward and saw Nina's eyes turn towards him for an instant. Nina? He said, 'I think I remember him mentioning you once.' She inclined her head and he thought: Brad and Nina: Johnnie and . . . but the name of Johnnie's girl was long since forgotten. He had mentioned it once. When was it? On the strip at Comitarla. An odd name. Chi-chi. Brad and Nina: Johnnie and a girl whose name he had forgotten. The four of them in Comitarla; long ago.

He said, 'Johnnie's in Ambala.'

She smiled. 'You've got his old section?'

'Yes.'

'Is the driver still with you? I don't remember his name. No . . . wait a moment. Din – I think.'

'Mohammed Din.'

'That's it. And there was a little orderly. Jan Mohammed. How is he?'

He looked away. Brad had gone pale. Jim thought, 'He can't know about Jan Mohammed.' To them both he explained, 'He's dead. That plane crash yesterday in Tamel.' Oddly Brad did not seem to have heard. He had kept his eyes on Nina all the time, and Nina was refusing to look back at him. There was a tenseness between them that Jim could not understand.

Nina was saying, 'Does Johnnie know? But of course, he can't know yet.'

'I've written to tell him.'

Nina hesitated. She seemed to be making up her mind about something. She asked, 'Does he write to you often?'

'No, he hasn't written me.'

'But you knew he was in Ambala.'

He felt in his pocket.

'There's a letter from him here, but not to me. To Jan Mohammed. It was with his things.' He drew the letter from his pocket and put it on the table. It lay there. Suddenly Nina put out her hand. She said, 'Can I read it?'

He said, 'Yes,' and as she picked up the letter Brad jerked back his chair and left them, saying something Jim did not catch. Enquiringly Jim turned to Nina. Her eyes were on the retreating figure but they were eyes that did not see. Her face had become expressionless. She opened the letter and held it for a long time, reading it, over and over.

With the letter in her hand she looked at him.

He knew what she was going to say.

'I was Johnnie's girl,' she said softly, and then she read the letter again.

The outlines of the chairs, the rims of the glasses became

etched; clear; far away. Brad came back and Nina pushed the letter back across the table. He picked it up as Brad said, 'You an' me'll have to go, Nina.' But Jim stood up and said, 'No, I'm going now.' When he was gone the other two would stay. The room had come back into proper focus and he smiled to see the relief on Brad's face as if Jim's going were a refuge; a reprieve.

He did not look again at Nina. He said, 'Goodnight,' and then he left them.

He walked down the gravel pathway towards his truck. Opening the door he paused with his foot on the board. He slammed the door shut again and went to the gateway where he could stand in the deep shadow of the trees. The moon was rising.

The recognition of Brad's and Nina's defection had come with the force and sting of a physical blow, for their union was a denial of the law which said that what was Johnnie's was his for always. But as the sting died he thought, 'They've broken that law, but they're being punished. They feel his judgement of them.' The law was ratified each time it was broken. There was no final escape, except in endorsement, surrender; and flight.

He must get back to Tamel and make his preparations. When he had seen the Colonel in the morning his going would be quick. He moved back to his truck; but there were footsteps on the gravel and he returned to the shadows and stayed there watching.

It was Nina.

She stood by the truck, her whole attitude one of recognition. She looked round as if she sensed his presence. He heard her call softly, 'Jim?' and after a while she went closer to the truck and rested her hand on the doorhandle. She hesitated before opening it, climbing in, pulling the door to, quietly.

In the dark cabin there was the flare of a match and a little while after the heavy fragrance of tobacco smoke drifted towards him. What did she want, he wondered? To see the letter again? Perhaps to ask him to write and tell Johnnie what she herself dare not, however much she wished to confess her sin. He thought, 'How pitiable she is'; Brad, too, was pitiable, avoiding talk of Johnnie, trying to forget his guilt.

He left the shadows of the trees and walked to the truck.

She said, as he opened the door, 'It's me. Nina.'

He said, 'I know. I saw you get in.' He slid into the driving seat and with assured little movements she offered him a cigarette and lighted it for him. He settled back and looked at her enquiringly. But she was staring straight ahead. She said, 'Tell me about Johnnie.'

He made a vague gesture. 'What? What d'you want to know?'

'Anything. Why did he leave his section?'

'Didn't Brad tell you?'

'He didn't tell Brad.'

'He just, well – he just had to leave.'

'Trouble?'

'Yes.'

'Poor Johnnie.' She drew in the smoke of her cigarette and exhaled it heavily. It curled across the windscreen. 'Tell me about it.'

He shifted uneasily. 'He and the Major had a row.'

'The Major?' He felt her smile. 'I liked him,' she said.

'If you wanted to know, you could have written to Johnnie.'

She turned to him.

'You've got it wrong, Jim. Johnnie wouldn't want to hear from me.'

'But . . .'

'He never wrote. I didn't expect him to. It was just one of those things as far as he was concerned.'

'Not to you, though?'

'Not to me. That makes it rotten for Brad.' Again she smiled. 'Funny, isn't it? I'd give my eyes for Johnnie and sometimes I think Brad would for me. But that's as far as it ever gets.' She hesitated, looking to the front. And then she said, 'I want to ask you something.'

'I thought you did.'

'Well, that makes it easier. It's just Brad doesn't want you to say anything to Johnnie if you write to him. I don't either. Say anything about Brad and me.'

'I shan't be writing to Johnnie.'

'But you said . . .'

He tapped his breast pocket. 'The letter's ready to post. I shan't add anything to it.'

'Thanks.' She lifted the cigarette to her mouth and as she sucked in the smoke he saw her hand trembling. Then she said, 'Johnnie would treat it as a joke, you see. Brad wouldn't like that.'

He did not understand what she was saying.

He repeated, 'A joke? How could it be a joke?'

She said, 'You know, Jim. A joke about me being "taken over". I think that's the expression.' She lifted the cigarette again. 'Neither of us would like that. Brad takes it seriously. He couldn't bear it to be a joke.'

He managed to say, 'And you?'

'I still love Johnnie.'

She threw the cigarette through the open window. 'I know you'll think me an awful fool, Jim. Hanging on like that to someone who's not mine and never was. I'll get over it one day and perhaps if Brad's still around things'll be all right for me.' She took Jim's hand and he felt how cold hers was. 'You've got to forgive Brad for being so rude, Jim. It was my fault. I made him invite you over because I wanted to talk about Johnnie. He can't stand that because he knows how I feel. He knows he's only a sort of substitute and I think he sees that anything I feel for him is because he's like Johnnie in so many ways.' She freed his hand but its cold impression remained. Her laugh, though soft, was bitter. 'Some kinds of love are degrading, aren't they? His for me and mine for Johnnie. And then Johnnie not caring a fig. But that's the way it goes and sometimes I wish I was like Johnnie.'

His mouth was dry and he spoke with difficulty. 'What was Johnnie like?'

She shrugged her shoulders. 'Someone who took things to heart a lot. For a time. He was in love with me while I was there. But almost before I'd gone I saw he wasn't any longer. Only for one thing. Perhaps he was lonely for a bit but then something else would have come and taken my place.'

She hesitated. 'But you don't need me to tell you that. You must've seen what he was like better than me. You took over his section.' She laughed. 'Johnnie and his section! You'd think the world was coming to an end if anyone criticised them or something. And now there he is in Ambala, happy as a sandboy. You can tell that, can't you?'

'Can you?'

Her voice dropped. 'Poor Johnnie. How did he take it at the time? Losing the section?'

'He hasn't lost it.'

She stared at him.

He went on, 'It was never mine. It always stayed his. He's been in Tamel all the time and I've felt him hanging on. You said you hang on to him, Nina. It's like that.'

She said nothing; then. 'It's not like that.'

'Why?'

'He doesn't feel me hanging on.'

'Then he's lucky. I do. And I can't fight that any more.' He tried to see her expression. 'That letter to Jan Mohammed. It's like restaking a claim.'

She had been shaking her head while he talked. Now that he had finished she said, 'You're running away.'

'No.'

'You're running away from nothing.'

'No.'

But the accusation she made brought pain and pain stifled what had been conviction; pain, and the new Johnnie she was bringing alive before his eyes; as in Pyongiu that day.

He drew away from her and leaned against the back of the seat. The truck was facing towards the club and someone came out and stood in the doorway, and even from here they could see it was Brad. In a low voice he said, 'Does he know where you are?'

'Yes.'

Brad stepped out on to the path and in the silence they heard him call her. She kept quiet still and made no answer and so he whispered, 'You'd better go.' But still she made no move and after a few moments Brad went back inside. And as she had brought a new Johnnie alive for him so were she and Brad suddenly alive for him; shadows no longer of Johnnie; shadows of themselves only if shadows at all; aware of the futility that existed between them; but facing it, finding a sort of strength in it.

Jim cleared his throat and then she said, 'Not love, jealousy.'

'What?'

'I was thinking, Jim. I said some kinds of love are degrading. Like Brad's for me. But it's not his love. Only his jealousy. And my jealousy too.'

'All love is possessive.' He could not leave Tamel believing otherwise; could not retreat from what was not defended.

'No,' she said. 'Love changes like everything else. I suppose it goes through stages.'

'How does it end?'

'It doesn't end. Not love. Johnnie's happy in Ambala. You can see that from his letter. But he still loves whatever he loved before. Love doesn't end, Jim, but it becomes unselfish, I think.'

She turned to him. 'Like mine will.' She took his hand again. 'Perhaps soon,' she went on. 'Perhaps talking about it, being able to talk about it, shows it doesn't hurt so much. You forget what was bad and remember only what was good. If you're lucky, it's like that from the beginning, I suppose. If you're not it takes time. But one day you wake up and it doesn't hurt any longer and if there's something to forgive you can forgive.'

She took her hand away and he heard the slight click of her

handbag as she opened it. Looking round at her he saw that she had taken her powder puff out and was dabbing her face with it, staring towards the club lights.

With precise movements she returned it to her bag, and pressed the clip. She pushed at the unlatched door and then got out. She held the door open and looked back at him.

'When that day comes for me I'll be able to write to Johnnie.' She paused. 'Then he'll know I'm all right, and if ever he's felt guilty about me he'll know he needn't any longer.'

She let the door fall to, and tried to press the handle down. He reached over to help her and his hand touched hers. For a time their hands remained in contact.

She said, very quietly, 'My letter will mean I'm letting go. I think *his* means that, too.' He felt her hand turn under his until they were clasped, palm to palm. 'We'll come down to Tamel, one day. Me and Brad.'

He nodded.

She was smiling in at him. Then her hand withdrew and she walked up the path and the light from the windows showed her clearly as she passed them and went in through the doorway.

When he got back to Tamel the moon was high. He switched off the headlamps and drove into the harbour past the long line of parked lorries. He left the truck at the end of the line and walked across the culvert on to the road. The lines were deserted. When he reached Three Section office he opened the flap cautiously and heard the steady rise and fall of Nimu's breathing. Quietly he went inside, leaving the flap open so that the moonlight shone brightly into the tent. He took Jan Mohammed's letter out of his pocket and placed it carefully on the clerk's table where he should find it in the morning. Then he went out and pulled the flap over.

Suddenly Nimu called, 'Is that you, sir?'

He re-opened the flap.

'I'm sorry. I didn't mean to wake you.'

Nimu was leaning up, resting on his elbow.

'Sir?'

'Yes?'

'Is it true you are going to Ramo, sir?'

'No, Nimu.'

He waited.

'You are not going to Marapore, sir?'

He could not see Nimu's face clearly.

But he said, 'No, I'm not going to Marapore.'

'They said that you were going, sir. But I am thinking you are staying in Three Section.'

'Yes, Nimu. I'm staying.'

He put the flap back into position. Then he walked away quickly.

When he came to the trees surrounding the field in which they lived he stopped, remembering the letter to Johnnie. Pulling it out of his breast pocket he stared at the envelope for a moment. Then he tore it across and scattered the pieces in the long grass. He continued along the track into the field beyond and when he saw that there was a light in the Major's tent he walked, without hesitating, towards it.